ROGER HARDY

Miracle in Carvoeiro

Roger Hardy

Published by Roger Hardy on Lulu 2009

Copyright © Roger Hardy 2009
Roger Hardy has asserted his rights under the Copyright, Designs and Patents Act of 1988 to be identified as the author of this work.

First published in 2009
Roger Hardy
Häuser Dombach 32a
51465 Bergisch Gladbach
Germany

rogerjhardy100@yahoo.co.uk
http://stores.lulu.com/carvoeiro
Copies may be obtained from Lulu (www.lulu.com), from the author or:
The Algarve Book Cellar, Edificio 'O Galeão' Loja 1, Rua dos Pescadores,
8400-512 Carvoeiro, Lagoa, Portugal.
+351 282 354 310

This book has been published privately as a marketing exercise whilst attempting to find a suitable agent and publisher. The author would be pleased to enter into correspondence with a view to achieving this objective.

ISBN 978-1-4092-5647-2

To Luis

Roger Hardy

One

Rui Fernandes paced the desolate car park, skirting the pools of lamplight, wanting to be seen and not seen. The air was sultry, humid and motionless. The only sounds came from the occasional passing car. He glanced at the face of his Tag as if the act of telling the time could magically make his dealer appear but, here in Portugal, disdain for the customer had become an art form. Now, Amsterdam; that was how to do it. A short phone call, a black seven-series BMW at the door within twenty minutes, a chic dealer and a small expensive wrap. That was first-class service. Amsterdam. A previous life.

But this was Portimão, a town that smelled of dead fish and seaweed and didn't smell of coke. It was lucky he didn't need to do this every day or even every week. He didn't need to do it at all but, when he did, he wanted it to happen like the service in First Class: 'Would you like me to cut your straw, Mr Fernandes? We have imported these finest polycarbonate straws directly from Columbia, Sir, especially contoured for European nasal insertion. We also have an interesting new variation from Afghanistan, if you would prefer. Can I arrange it in lines for you? Not at all, Sir, it's my pleasure. Have a nice day.'

He hadn't *needed* to do it since his days with Dirk. It was a treat; a well-deserved one. Was it too much to ask for the damned dealer to turn up and take his fucking money? He looked at his watch again. The guy was now twenty minutes overdue. Rui opened his mobile phone and dialed the number, knowing that there would be no reply. There was no reply. He kicked an empty can which rolled discordantly into the gutter and turned into the back street darkness, towards the glow from the quay. Change my thoughts, he reminded himself. Change my thoughts. His long shadow trailed reluctantly behind.

Rui wandered through the maze of unfamiliar streets until he realised that he was lost. Hearing the sound of distant laughter, he followed it around the next corner, and saw a brightly-lit sign a few metres away. The bar was busy. Light from the windows filled the gutters outside with gold and an open door, music and conversation beckoned him. As he walked through the warm wall of cigarette smoke, the conversation went perceptibly quiet for a second before resuming. It was a working class bar; a place that tourists would avoid. Fado plinked and moaned from a battered sound system behind the bar and an old television hung precariously from the wall silently radiated a football match. Fishing tackle, cobwebs and baskets hung dustily from the rafters. Sepia-tinted men sat smoking, talking, playing cards and a few brightly-dressed girls chatted amongst themselves. Rui ordered a beer and some slices of *chouriço* from the girl behind the bar; she served him slowly and absent-mindedly. As he sipped his beer and eyed up the talent, he sensed someone sidling up behind him.

'Haven't I seen you before somewhere?' said a voice in a smoky South African accent.

Rui had heard better chat-up lines. He turned around to see a tall, dark man. He was almost handsome but had a face lined from too many years in the sun and the broad-shouldered bearing of a man who would look right in a bush hat, wrestling a crocodile.

'You're from Jo'burg aren't you?' the stranger said.

Rui was taken aback.

'I spent some years there, yes, but I don't recognise you. Sorry,' he said but, as he spoke, a seed of recognition germinated in his mind. Yes, he had seen this man before, a long time ago, a lifetime ago. He couldn't place him; he had the strange notion of him as an object, not a person. Rui wondered whether he was gay or straight; he didn't want this stranger hitting on him; some gay men would take the simple fact that they were talking as an invitation for sex.

'I'm Ben. The name's Ben Chilcott. And you are......' The stranger paused for a moment as if struggling for recollection, '.......Rui, I think.' He offered his hand and Rui took it. His grip was strong and his palm rough.

'Yeah, Rui Fernandes,' he said, feeling naked. There was so much about South Africa that he wanted to forget. Thinking back on those years, it was like watching someone else; the ghost of that old Rui was buried in South Africa. The new one was successful in Portugal, had a business, a partner, friends and respect.

'Ah, Jo'burg, Jo'burg. What a shit hole,' said Chilcott with nostalgic distaste. He sat on a bar stool next to Rui and stared directly into his eyes. 'You were having a rough time then, if I recall right.'

7

Rui was silent as he was propelled back to that nightmare. A kaleidoscope of dark memories flashed through his mind. This was not something he wanted to talk about.

'Hello? You still there?' asked Chilcott, prodding him.

'Yeah, yeah, sorry. Yeah. Rough time. Anyway, it's all in the past. But at least I kept smiling.' He said it lightly, but his smile was forced and made his cheeks ache. God, please change the subject, he thought.

'Bro, I've found that you can never leave the past behind you. It always has a way of catching up. I mean how did you handle that car jacking? Soweto, wasn't it? That was a stupid thing to do; Soweto.' He shook his head in disbelief. 'How do you get over that? You can't forget that it happened.'

Rui froze, recalling the four drugged-up blacks who had pulled him out of the car at a set of traffic lights. He'd forgotten to drive with the doors locked. They had taken the car and everything he had, including a pair of new shoes. He remembered saying to them before he passed out; *'Please take my life but don't take my new crocodile skin shoes.......'*

He looked at Chilcott. 'Yeah, stabbed four times in the back. Anyway, how do you know about that?'

'Oh, come on, Rui. People took an interest in you. You were almost famous. Dancing on TV, your face in magazines. Quite the glamour boy.'

Rui tried to laugh it off. Did this man really know him? He had been public property in those days. People think they know celebrities, but it's a one-way relationship. Maybe this guy had been a casual one-night stand, still holding a torch while Rui had instantly forgotten his name and face as he moved on to the next one. There had been so many. Lost count at two hundred.

Chilcott laughed and slapped him on the back; the same spot where the blade had punctured his lung.

'You were lucky, my friend. Cheer up! I know lots of people who were killed in exactly the same way. At least you survived it. Car jackings, burglaries, rape, murder. South Africa has become a real shit hole. I couldn't take it any more. Had to leave, just like you. First I went to London but I wanted to live in the sun again, so I came here six months ago. Love it.'

'Me too. I run a guest house in Carvoeiro.' Rui gave him a card, relieved to change the subject.

'Carvoeiro? Isn't that a bit bucket-and-spade for you? I would have thought that Vilamoura was more your style.' Chilcott examined the card. 'Hmm...Casa Rui.....looks impressive.'

Rui was proud of his business and the painful memories dissolved. 'Oh, Carvoeiro's OK; I like it. It's kind of quaint and friendly. The business is only small but it makes good money. I've only had it two months, so I'm a bit of a stranger in my own country.' He took another sip of his beer, looking at Chilcott over the rim of his glass. 'What do you do here?'

'Oh, you know, this and that,' Chilcott replied with a shrug. 'Anything that makes a bit of money. Living in Portugal's cheap. I don't have to try too hard. So, what brings you to Portimão?'

'Thought I'd see if I could score a little pick-me-up....' said Rui, sniffing obviously.

Ben moved on his bar stool as if making himself more comfortable and lit a cigarette, offering Rui one. There was a muffled cheer from two men as Benfica scored. Chilcott lit Rui's cigarette and dragged on his own, blowing the smoke towards the ceiling, adding to the soft blue haze.

'Ah. You hoped it was going to snow. Do I detect a sense of failure in your voice?'

Rui's coded message had been understood. 'Oh, I really need a contact; I'm new here. I need someone reliable. I thought I'd found someone but the bastard never appeared.'

'Welcome to Portugal, Bro. They're nervous of new customers here. You need to be introduced.'

Bro, *Broer*. The Afrikaans word grated in Rui's ear.

'You got a contact?' asked Rui.

'In a manner of speaking,' Chilcott said with a smirk. 'You look like a man in desperate need. Well, it's your lucky day. I've had enough for tonight and I've got a few lines left. Here. Yours for thirty, Bro.' He threw a packet of cigarettes on the bar.

Rui picked up the packet which he knew contained no cigarettes, put it in his pocket, casually handed over three notes and the deal was done. He started to relax at last and began to feel a bit more adventurous; he was curious and his vanity made him want to know where their paths had crossed.

'So tell me, Ben. You've got me thinking. Where do you know me from? The cover of a magazine? A club, some sauna, where?'

'Oh, well you know the scene in Jo'burg, we were all off our heads most of the time but you must have been really out of it, Rui. Hey, don't worry about it now, Bro, you've got an appointment with a Columbian. We'll get together again soon and we can talk about the good old days.'

Discussing the good old days was the last thing that Rui wanted to do.

The cloudless sky was a pure cobalt blue, the colour reflected in the sea with a wash of viridian, wet-in-wet, peaked with white as the low waves swept to the rocks below. Seagulls slope-soared lazily along the cliff tops shrieking to each other as they had for a million years.

The white walls of Casa Rui shimmered on the hill overlooking the fishing village below. The early morning sun danced off the white tiles of the terrace and scintillated like diamonds in the puddles left by the previous night's rain. Cars were parked on the side of the road; the shiny new hire cars of visitors, the ramshackle ruins of local anglers trying their luck before going to work. The sea surged thirty metres below, fishermen connected to it by gossamer filaments.

Rui blinked through his darkest sunglasses and, visually impaired, went outside the guest house to water the plants. Nursing his hangover, he was feeling sorry for himself. He cursed the late night and for having got up so early, gagging at the taste of sun-dried seashells that no amount of mouthwash could eradicate. He'd only wanted to score the coke to give Tim a treat when he arrived from Amsterdam. Had to try it to make sure it was OK. Never again, he promised himself; well, not until the memory of his aching head had melted away like all bad things.

Tim. Stable, sensible, intelligent Tim. Rui couldn't wait to see him again, to hold him, share a bit of his life with the man that he loved, have some proper sex and know that he would still be lying next to him in the morning. After four weeks, Rui was starting to feel like a bachelor again, and bachelors do stupid things when there are no central reservations on the motorway of life.

Chilcott. He couldn't get that conversation out of his mind and wished that he could remember where they had met. A voice in his subconscious was whispering a warning. He couldn't put his finger on it. It was almost like a premonition; the shadow of his past darkening the future. Johannesburg. Jo'burg and drugs; drugs that fogged the brain and pointed to the gutter, blanking recollection, insulation from life. Memories usually become rose-tinted with the passage of time but these remained black and he found himself associating Chilcott with them as a de-personalised object, half-seen, half-remembered, as in a dream.

Whatever happens, he thought, Tim must never find out about Jo'burg.

Rui turned from the bougainvillea he had just watered. The autistic girl was making her uneven way up the hill as she did every day, arguing angrily with herself, oblivious to the world around her. Rui thought that things could be worse; at least his hangover would be gone by midday. He stood respectfully to one side.

Dressed in a shabby track suit, she looked strangely androgynous. Shouting at the air, then at her feet, she loped with clumsy steps, arms erratic. Trailing two hundred metres behind, her mother walked with an expression of resignation as she did yesterday and the day before that. They walked past the church at the top of the hill as if it were not there.

Miracle in Carvoeiro

Next door, Rui saw Thérèse Roland at her window, watching them impassively like the spectre of death at a party. Her cold glance caught Rui's and she called to him with a reedy voice. Sighing, he went to her front door. It creaked open like a scene from Hansel and Gretel. As Rui entered, Thérèse wordlessly turned her back on him and moved with difficulty to her kitchen, clutching onto furniture to help her negotiate the short distance. Short, frail and looking a decade older than her sixty years, she had uncombed silver hair and wore a light blue frock that evoked memories of carefree harvest summers in France. She looked as if she had not slept for a week. Her every step was an effort but Rui resisted the urge to help her. He had been warned.

She poured herself a coffee. An age-flecked hand placed the cup and saucer, shaking and tinkling, onto her side table; she lowered herself awkwardly into a faded armchair.

Rui was unsure whether to sit or stand. The room was full of old, mismatched furniture; the smell of cooked cabbage and damp laundry hung in the humid air. With a little trepidation he negotiated the ironing machine and drying rack, draped with towels, and wondered why she didn't use her tumble dryer. Ah, money, he thought. It cost money to run a tumble dryer. He edged past the Chinese screen set across the lounge to divide off the laundry area, noticing that the black lacquer had started to crack and flake away. The clutter in the room contrasted with the clean water-colour seascapes on her walls, loose, fresh and free in style, capturing the essence of the movement of the water and the colours of the sky with so few brush strokes that they looked as if they had been created in minutes.

'Rui, I wanted to talk to you.' She spoke slowly and wearily in a thick French accent as if every word would take a breath from her life. 'My little mandolin....'

'I'm sorry, Thérèse.....your what?' said Rui, trying to understand her francophone English as his brain throbbed inside his head.

'My mandolin. It's still hanging on your side. It wasn't part of the inventory; at least it shouldn't have been. I would like you to return it; it has sentimental meaning for me. I don't know how I forgot it.'

Rui tried to recall it, then remembered. It was an ugly little thing that looked as if it had been made by demented schoolchildren. It was still hanging on a wall upstairs.

'But, Thérèse, I thought you'd already taken everything that you said was not included in the sale of the business.'

'Rui, you know I was ill. Not thinking straight. Can't trust the damned solicitors. Have to do everything myself. I was in hospital when the sale went through. I couldn't be here to make sure things were done correctly. Please, Rui, it's special. I got it in Santiago, when I was living in Chile.'

Rui had already given her several paintings and some items of furniture as an act of goodwill, but her demands seemed to keep increasing. Rui knew that the sale of her property had been carried out properly and he had only given her the things she had asked for as an act of goodwill. He had expected to see the gesture reciprocated but there was no sign of that. This would be the last little gift.

'Well, if it's so important to you, Thérèse, you can have it. I'll bring it round later.'

'Merci, Rui. Oh, and there's one other thing I meant to tell you. You were expecting some visitors tomorrow. One of my bookings for your side. Mr and Mrs Jacobs from Canada.'

Rui interrupted her. 'Were? You used the past tense, Thérèse.'

'Yes, I know. I'm afraid they called me this morning and they've cancelled. I'm very sorry.'

Rui was more sorry than Thérèse. It was coming to the end of the season and he needed that booking; it was for two weeks in Number Ten, their best and most expensive apartment. When Rui and Tim had bought the business from Thérèse, they thought that it was a good deal all round and that they were doing her a favour, giving her enough money to pay her medical bills. However, it had soon become clear that, for Thérèse, Rui was simply another competitor.

With no choice but to accept the bad news with good grace, Rui took his leave. He had no way of contacting the people himself as Thérèse had taken the booking earlier in the year and would not divulge the contact details. Those were her rules.

Tim was arriving the next day and Rui wanted everything to be perfect. Even with the mother of all hang-overs, he was multi-tasking. This involved making a mental list, frenetically starting one job, getting diverted onto another, then another, forgetting the first, then the second, all planning becoming the victim of the most recent thought or new idea, whilst at the same time snacking on biscuits and popcorn and swigging from cans of Sumol. It was a unique and exhausting management technique but he usually achieved his targets, sometimes by luck, sometimes with sympathetic outside help, sometimes by accident. Often by accident. But now he was a man with a mission. Being new to this business, he knew that Tim had reservations about him running it on his own but he would show him that everything was under absolute control; everything would be pristine when Tim arrived, except for the lost booking and that wasn't his fault.

Must get a cleaner, he thought. His apartment was in the souterrain of the guest house. A large double bed stood at one end, an office desk with computer paraphernalia and a mess of paperwork perched against a side wall. A seating area at the other end faced a wide-screen television; a vestigial kitchen sat in a messy jumble of temporary cupboards and work surfaces under a high window. It was light and always cool, even in the summer heat. A silver pillar fan rotated soundlessly, circulating the air. Rui stood in front of it for a few moments as a wave of nausea swept over him. He waited for the perspiration on his forehead to dry before continuing with his work.

As he zoomed around with the vacuum, he made plans for the next few days with Tim, smiling when he remembered the first time he had seen him in the sauna in Amsterdam. How out of place he had looked, a man who oozed intelligence and culture, drifting like a ghost on a conveyor belt with a tide of near-naked men, each silently trying to avoid the gaze of the others like voyeurs caught in the act. Gay sauna protocol. I'm going to save that man from a death worse than fate Rui had thought. He hadn't planned anything more than a good shag. That was four years ago and two thousand five hundred kilometres away.

Over the undulating wail of his vacuum cleaner he heard a voice behind him and turned to see a face at the window looking like an angel, a sunlight halo framing her hair.

'Ursula!' exclaimed Rui, switching off the machine. 'Come on down.' The face disappeared to be replaced a few seconds later by a clatter of Armani-clad high heels coming down the wooden staircase leading to the apartment.

Ursula Hallworth was a blonde and manicured English rose, slightly on the wrong side of fifty but still with the poise of a beauty queen. She was the kind of woman who becomes the centre of attention in any room; glamorous and fragrant, soft and full-breasted; everything in excess. Her bearing was that of a young woman and she challenged the world with an elegant but puckish grin.

'Dahling!' she gushed as she flounced through the door and they clinched in a cloud of Yves St Laurent. Rui was hot and shirtless and Ursula's fingers lingered lightly on his shoulders.

'Dahling! To what do we owe this unexpected pleasure?' asked Rui formally.

'Oh, Rui, it's not fair,' Ursula said, taking one step back and ignoring his question. 'How do you stay so fit? I mean, you're no spring chicken are you? I'm always on a bloody diet; you don't have to make an effort. It's really not fair.'

'But I thought you were in England having your hair done……'

'Oh, really Rui I'm shocked that you could suggest such a thing,' she said in mock admonition. 'It was my nails as well. No one does them like Ramon, and no one looks at me like Ramon. Oh, you should see him, Rui. You'd fall in love with him as well. Wears these tight trousers that leave nothing to the imagination. Gives me hot flushes.'

'Ursula, he's probably gay.'

'Well, of course he's gay, darling. All the best looking men are. You should see his boyfriend. I spend my life falling in love with gay men. I go from one to another. I'm a serial mental polygamist.'

'You're just a gay man trapped in a woman's body,' said Rui with a laugh.

'Yes, it's a perfect disguise,' she smirked, 'and they never get jealous. It's perfect.'

'Well, if you love gay men so much, why did you marry Peter?'

'Well, darling, a girl has needs.....'

Rui nodded knowingly. 'The villa in the sun, the Porsche, the little rock on the finger.....'

'You understand me perfectly, darling.'

She looked around to find the most comfortable seat and settled into it like a hovercraft landing while Rui poured her a coffee.

'So, the lovely Tim is here tomorrow; you won't get much sleep.'

'Yeah. I want to get everything ready, but my head won't let me.'

'Self-inflicted?'

He nodded.

'No sympathy,' she said with a condescending grin.

'Yeah, I know. But I can't wait to see him again. I really miss him when he's not here.'

Ursula thought for a moment. 'What keeps you two together? I mean, you're like opposites, aren't you? You know, he's sort of....educated... and you're sort of.....'

'...not,' prompted Rui, smiling.

'And he's quite sensible really, isn't he? And you're sort of....'
'.....not.'
And you're kind of pretty, and he's kind of....'
'Not!' said Rui, laughing. 'But he's what I need. Before I met him, my life was a disaster zone. Really. Now, it's a bit like you and Peter, but without the Porsche....or the rock,' he said examining his bare third finger left-hand. 'And now......' he gestured to indicate their new business and grinned, bringing the coffee to the sofa.

'And when is the lovely Tim moving here permanently? You can't live separately can you?'

'Oh, he'll probably have to go back once or twice more to close the apartment. After that, he'll be under my feet forever,' he said, stirring four spoons of sugar into his cup.

'What's he going to do here?'

'What apart from getting in the way? He's going to run his consultancy from here. That's our agreement; I run this business and he runs his. Happiness forever.'

'Do you hear anything from the old bitch next door?' said Ursula sipping her coffee, leaving bright lipstick marks on the rim.

'Oh, I hardly see her. Occasionally she ventures out with her Zimmer frame but most of the time she stays indoors shouting at her cleaner.'

'What's her problem?'

'Apart from congenital anti-socialism? One of her friends told me that she's in remission from a brain tumour but the treatment had some nasty side effects and almost paralysed her. Now she can hardly walk. Anyway, when I first came here, I felt sorry for the old duck. I tried to be nice to her but she's completely cold. I can't work her out at all. She called me in this morning to tell me about a cancelled booking. I'm not sure if I believe her.' He looked into his cup.

'What? No profits for this month?' asked Ursula, eyebrows raised.

'Doesn't look like it,' said Rui, looking up. 'We'll have enough to cover our costs but it's the end of the season. Oh, yeah; you'll never believe this: she wants that funny little musical instrument she'd left hanging on the wall on the stairs going up to Rooms One and Two.'

'Didn't know she was musical....'

'She's not. It's like an ugly little mandolin. She got it in Chile, apparently. It has special memories for her.'

Ursula put her coffee down on the table. 'Come, let's go and have a look at it,' she said. 'Maybe it's valuable,' she said with a twinkle in her eye.

The mandolin was hanging from a dusty string high on the wall. Rui brought the step-ladder and clambered up as Ursula held it steady. He retrieved the little instrument and handed it to Ursula, who blew the dust from it and examined it with distaste. It was crudely made, consisting of a sound box that looked as if it has once been a gourd, a badly split wooden finger-board and a coarse bone-like neck with four wooden tuning pegs. The strings were slack and still dusty. Turning it over in her hands, she looked closely at the sound box and neck.

'You know I used to be a nurse?' she murmured.

'No....' There was a question in Rui's voice.

'Hm. I was very good at anatomy; in particular orthopaedics.'

'Ursula, it's a mandolin........'

Miracle in Carvoeiro

'Maybe, darling, but if I'm not mistaken, this is the top of a skull and that's a femur,' she said, pointing to the sound box and neck. The she glanced up at Rui, her expression uncharacteristically serious. 'Rui, I think it's made from bones; human bones.'

Roger Hardy

Two

Rui spotted Tim in the distance as he came out of the customs hall into the cavernous concourse of Faro airport. He watched him walking around an old Auster light aircraft hanging precariously from the ceiling as one would avoid walking under a ladder. Tim was tall and fair and walked with the confidence of a government minister. His expression changed from ministerial to chat-show host when he saw Rui and they embraced and kissed in front of a group of priests, Tim ruffling Rui's hair playfully. They hadn't seen each other for four weeks and Rui had been scared that he'd started to forget Tim's face but one glimpse had flushed away that fear.

Tim was not handsome but he was striking, with a flash of white at his temples. The kind of man who would be considered a silver fox by the more mature woman, but over the hill in a gay club. Rui felt fleetingly awkward, as if meeting a stranger, but knew that the mood would be blown away over wine, a little coke and bed.

Heading for home in the Toyota Rav 4, Rui chatted non-stop, fighting with the gears and cursing the other motorists, while Tim watched the Algarve flash past. That night, they slept like two spoons in a cutlery drawer.

Tim stretched lazily and felt the empty space next to him in the bed. The dry scrape of sweeping came from upstairs on the terrace. He slowly allowed his eyes to adjust, blinking in the blast of day, slipped out of bed and padded naked to the fridge to liberate some orange juice; fresh orange juice, made from real oranges, one of the advantages of living in the Algarve. He examined the bottle; read the label: *'Produce of Florida'*. Shrugging, he poured a glass and downed it in one, trying to wash away the lingering seashell taste.

He paused by the collage of photographs on the wall over the desk; pictures of Rui when he had been a dancer. Beautiful spangled women were draped around him like exotic birds, their breasts nuzzling him as he smiled. Set amongst them were photographs of flamboyant house parties, beautiful people with perfect teeth and expensive clothes. His eyes settled on one of Rui with his arms wrapped around a handsome man with a gentle face. He'd had the world at his feet. New Year 1995. Photographs are life the way we want to remember it; jewels set in time, unchangeable. Another picture sat on the desk next to the computer, one of Tim and Rui soon after they had met; New Year 2002. Rui's toothy smile was the same but there was a hint of sadness in his eyes, as if the intervening years had stolen something from him. Tim smiled, poured another glass of orange and took it back to bed to tuck himself up in the warm duvet.

The door opened. Rui burst in and turned on the computer.

'Come on, babycakes, I hope you're not going to stay in bed all day. Things to do............'

'Kiss,' demanded Tim sullenly, pointing to his lips, red with stubble-burn. Rui sat down at the computer to answer the emails.

Miracle in Carvoeiro

Tim groaned for sympathy but was ignored so dragged himself out of bed unnoticed and went to the bathroom. He looked at himself disapprovingly in the mirror and stepped under the hot shower to wash away the night before, feeling the warmth cascading over his body, recharging him.

'Good stuff last night wasn't it?' said Tim, coming back into the room wrapped in a white towel. 'Coffee?'

'Yeah, yes please. Yeah, it was good. Not speedy at all. I finally made a decent contact,' said Rui as he tapped away at the keyboard. 'Three emails; two enquiries and one booking for February. That's good, we're almost empty in February.' He continued to tap away, adding smilies throughout his replies, matching their grins as he did so. Tim watched as Rui worked; struggling with the keyboard, one-finger at a time, his tongue against his upper lip. As he typed, he smiled to himself, his lips moving slightly as he read what he had written before he pressed the 'send' button triumphantly.

Tim was itching to get onto the computer.

'Do you want me to organise your filing system and emails? You know, a nice methodical system. Achieve your objectives in a logical order.......know where everything is.......'

'Well, you can if you want, but I won't understand what you've done. It'll only confuse me. Don't worry, I'm managing fine.'

'But why don't you.....'

Rui swivelled to face his partner.

'Tim. You have your way of working and I have mine. Mine works for me.'

'But.......'

'No buts. If you were running this business you know that you'd turn into Basil Fawlty in two days. Me, I keep smiling, the people keep turning up and giving me money. Trust me. Besides, I am actually Portuguese. That's something of an advantage in Portugal. Don't you agree?'

'Your brain's completely fried, isn't it?' said Tim with a chuckle.

'Yeah, but at least it's sunny-side up,' beamed Rui, as he turned back to the computer.

Rui knew from experience that that his enthusiasm and optimistic nature would see him through, as if his life were punctuated by smilies. Whenever he painted himself into a corner there would always be someone who was happy to rescue him. He seemed to have a natural skill in appearing to be both in control and needing help at the same time. That partial vulnerability was a magnet to people who were flattered to be able to help. Rui had found that he could use this technique for handling most complex tasks and there was never any objection because the result was smilies all round.

Tim was enjoying the morning light on the terrace upstairs while Rui worked below. The bougainvillea on the wall shook even though there was no wind and he suspected a street dog looking for food that Rui often left by the window. As he looked over the rim of his coffee cup, a head appeared above the wall and he gagged. The face was that of a comical puppet, but full-scale, which made it seem more disconcerting; the autistic girl. Their eyes locked, then she smiled awkwardly and, with a giggle, disappeared. Tim stood up to see where she had gone, but by the time he had gone down the steps, she was on the other side of the road, jumping along the pavement that ran down the hill as if it were a game of hopscotch.

'Poor girl,' said Tim as Rui joined him, broom in hand, sat on the spare chair and took a swig of Tim's coffee.

'Every village has one. Her name's Flavia,' said Rui, watching her disappear.

'There's such a look of innocence in her eyes,' said Tim.

'Babycakes, she's autistic.'

'No, I didn't mean that. I can see that she has a problem. It's just that....' He struggled for the right words. 'The look in her eyes is like a puppy's. There's a kind of mischievous contentment there, as if her body and mind are connected to different things. I can't quite place my finger on it.' Tim took another sip of coffee. 'It's as if she's dipped her head in joy,' he said.

Tim and Rui sat on the terrace at the end of the day as the sun descended, kissed the horizon and dissolved into the sea. A cancellation. At the end of the season. For Apartment Ten. That had been bad news. Tim was thoughtful in the pink afterglow. Opening a bottle of *Vinho Verde*, he tried to think through the implications.

'Do you think they really cancelled?'

'Well, I don't know; we can't contact them to find out, Thérèse's rules, and we can't do anything about it anyway,' said Rui emptying his glass.

'Yeah, but look at it from her point of view; she made a booking for herself then sold part of the business, so the booking comes to us. Don't you think she'd try to steal the booking? She'd be losing all that money and you know what she values most in her life. It's probably all she's been thinking about for days.'

Rui was refilling his glass but hesitated, looking shocked. 'Oh, she couldn't be such a bitch, surely. Let's wait until later and see who arrives.'

'You always see the best side of people. I've got a better idea. They were due to arrive late and Thérèse goes to bed early. She can hardly walk, so she must have some way of dealing with customers who arrive late. What would you do?'

'Well, she can't leave the door open. Actually, I know what she does because I was talking to her cleaner yesterday. Lovely girl; Paula. Brazilian. Illegal. You really must meet her tomorrow. She's very unhappy working for Thérèse. I think there's a chance we could poach her.'

Tim's expression turned to perplexed. 'Sorry, I thought we were talking about the booking…..'

'Yeah, we are. I was getting round to it; Paula told me that she leaves the keys in the box outside.'

'Makes sense.'

They waited until there were two empty bottles on the table and it was dark, then crept around to Thérèse's front door like thieves, stifling their drunken laughter and trying not to breathe. They silently opened the grey box which housed the electricity meter. Inside it was a small note and a set of keys.

'Dear Mr and Mrs Jacobs,

As discussed on the phone, I'm afraid that Apartment 10 is not available so I have put you in Studio 6. Please find the key in the box.

Regards, Thérèse.'
'The scheming old bitch!' whispered Rui.
They removed the note and the keys and left their own version:
'Dear Mr and Mrs Jacobs,
Contrary to your telephone conversation with Thérèse, Apartment 10 is now available as you requested.
Regards, Rui, your new host.
Casa Rui.'

The village doesn't open its eyes before ten o'clock, but a few shopkeepers, bar-owners and restaurateurs were already busy. The sun was high in the deep blue sky, radiating benevolence. On the eastern side of the beach sat a little shop draped like a fairground, selling everything bright and colourful, everything designed to appeal to children, everything intended to put their parents under irresistible pressure to buy.

Further up the hill sat the local police station, the *Guarda Nacional Republicana,* the GNR. Policing was benign in Carvoeiro and it was a posting that the policeman felt good about in the summer when the village was full of attractive young girls. Segundo Cabo Carlos da Silva was standing by the reception desk. He looked at his watch. It was time. Carlos had dark good looks, was young, fresh, broad-shouldered and snake-hipped; a cross between a pulp-fiction hero and a Brazilian soap star. Standing by the window, he was just in time to see Paula Mendes making her way with easy steps up the hill; a daily pleasure. Paula, the simple Brazilian girl, naturally beautiful without make-up, that angel smile, those bright blue eyes. The daily sight of her made him realise that life is good, life is worth living. Simply knowing she's there, knowing that she will walk past again tomorrow.

Paula was different; she was not just any girl; she was special. She was special because she had said 'no'. Carlos watched her stop to show a friend her new top, turquoise and light blue with red and yellow here and there. It looked good; colourful and flattering, contrasting with her sun-kissed skin and glossy black hair. She twirled like a catwalk model then continued up the hill, a dance in her step, towards the GNR.

Carlos craned his head around the half-open window and decided it was time to water the flowers outside. That way he could be closer to her and she would see that he was a sensitive, caring human being and not just a hormone-fuelled man looking for another notch on his bedpost. She slowed her pace as she saw Carlos coming out of the door with a watering can. Blinking in the light, he shielded his eyes with his free hand. Paula smiled and turned away coyly, almost reluctantly. He grinned after her and she gave a bashful little wave. Carlos laughed as she danced away, raising his hand in a casual gesture, watching her perfect arse. The sight made his teeth ache.

Carlos sighed and went back into the police station. The surroundings depressed him; under-funding meant no luxuries. The telephones were relics from the fifties and they used an oil drum as a waste bin. Faded maps of the local area covered the walls along with notices in Portuguese and posters written in English for missing pets. *'Lovely nature, golden brown retriever with three legs. Answers to the name Lucky.'*

I must be losing my touch, he thought. What more does she want from me? With most women, I have to fight them off and it's

Miracle in Carvoeiro

me that decides....everything; who, when, where....everything. He looked in the brown-stained mirror hanging on the wall. 'How can she resist you?' he said under his breath. His sergeant smirked from behind the desk.

'She's too smart for you, Carlos; you're led by your dick, she's led by her head. When she's ready you won't know what's hit you.'

'But, I don't know why she's playing so hard to get. She's not even a virgin.'

'How do you know that?'

'I know, that's all.'

'Well that's probably why she's playing hard to get. Once bitten........' He absent-mindedly wiped some dust off the desktop.

'Oh, God, I could bite her all over.......' said Carlos, gazing towards the window.

'Carlos,' interrupted the sergeant. 'You're not exactly husband material are you?'

'What do you mean by that?' Carlos protested, turning back to him. 'I'm the best looking guy in the village. I'm smart, I've got a great body, I'm employed........'

'Ah, that's what women really appreciate, Carlos. Modesty. How can you fail?' the sergeant chuckled and continued to wipe away non-existent dust.

Carlos ignored the comment, deep in thought. All that time in the gym, and being a personal trainer as well.....you'd think she'd be dripping for it, but no.....'The time's not right'; 'You're still living with your parents'; 'I'm still with my aunt' ....'I'm not doing *that* on the grass'......'I'm not one of your tourist tarts, Carlos.' Her words kept repeating in his head, accusing him. The mere thought of her was enough to keep him awake at night; her modesty, her perfect breasts, her Brazilian arse, those intense blue eyes like a Mediterranean sky, her lips, the tight figure and salsa legs; the images kept revolving in his head until his dick wanted to burst. This had to stop; he had to find some way of seducing her in style.

Carlos consoled himself with the thought that he and Carmencita had planned one of their regular sessions at lunchtime. But he really only wanted Paula; Carmencita was on a plate; she was no challenge. He wanted someone whose legs didn't open quite so easily. Perhaps it was Paula's unassailability that excited him so much. Even though she'd always said 'no', she did it with a sympathetic smile that said.....'but maybe one day'. She had become, in his mind, like a goddess that could be worshipped but not touched, as if touching her might shatter the spell that she held over him. But he had a reputation to maintain. With a start he thought: maybe she's frigid; no, that would be impossible, she's Brazilian. Maybe she's a lesbian...... he checked himself at that impossible thought. No, no, the world would never be so cruel. Surely there's a God in heaven.

Carlos was outside again. He'd finished watering the plants and was about to go back into the building when he heard a voice calling from the top of the hill.

'Carlos! Carlos!'

It was Paula and she was running down the hill towards him. Things are looking up, he thought, as she stopped breathlessly in front of him. The smile had left her face and she fought for words. He held her by the arms to calm her down.

'What's up?'

'Oh, Carlos, it's Thérèse ...she's been burgled, she's hysterical.'

A crime! Fired up, Carlos grabbed his cap and strode purposefully up the hill with Paula trailing behind, taking two paces to his one. When they got to Casa Thérèse they found the crumpled and sobbing victim sitting in her lounge, her head in her hands, being consoled by several neighbours.

Carlos negotiated the clutter and knelt down in front of the old woman, who looked up at him through her tears.

'Carlos! Oh Carlos….why didn't they send the sergeant?' she wailed through her sobs, 'I've been burgled. They took my cash box. I must have dozed off and they took my cash box….they took it, my cash box. Over two thousand Euros; there was over two thousand Euros in it. Someone must have come in and taken it. I'd left it by the window.' She dissolved again and Carlos looked around for inspiration. All eyes were on him to solve the crime, to make everything right again. He stood up and turned to Paula, not sure what to do next.

'This is dreadful,' he whispered. 'I've never seen her cry before. With all her problems, I've never seen her cry.' They both looked back down to the figure, curled like an embryo, sobbing pathetically.

Carlos knew that he had to be like a swimming swan, appearing to be calm and in control on the surface but frantically paddling under the surface. He was not sure what he should do and was waiting for a good idea to come to him. All eyes were on him but his mind was blank. At that moment, there was a knock on the door and Rui appeared, beaming like the risen sun, jangling a set of keys from his index finger. Everyone in the room turned to see the new arrival. Thérèse raised her head and looked at Rui with a wet glacial stare, at once vindictive and triumphant. Carlos looked from Rui to the keys dangling from his finger, twinkling in the sunlight.

'Whose keys are those?' he asked.

'They're Thérèse's,' said Rui breezily. 'She left them for some customers arriving late last night, but they were our customers so we gave them our keys and put them in Number Ten then …….' He hesitated, looking around at the suspicious faces. 'Well, it's a long story, but basically, they're Thérèse's and I'm bringing them back. What's been happening here?'

Carlos put two and two together. The others in the room had already done so several seconds earlier. He stood up impressively, feeling in charge and proud of his authority.

'Senhor Fernandes, Senhora Roland has been robbed. You have her keys. I would be grateful if you could come to the station to help us with our enquiries.' Rui seemed perplexed and Carlos continued, 'Just to be clear; and to avoid misunderstanding, that was not a request.' He thought that sounded suitably forceful and wondered whether Paula would be impressed. Surely she would be impressed.

Tim was emerging from the bathroom when he heard the commotion next door. He tried to overhear what was going on, then walked closer to the window holding the towel to his chest. Shaking his head, he reached for his mobile, flicked it open and held it against a wet ear.

'Ursula, Ursula! Do you speak Portuguese?' yelled Tim. 'Why? Because I think Rui's been arrested.'

Ten minutes later her red Porsche Boxster squealed to a stop outside where Tim was waiting for her.

'Tell me all about it, darling,' said Ursula as they walked down the hill towards the GNR.

'I don't know much; I saw him under police escort and one of the neighbours said he'd been dragged off to the GNR. He was only trying to give Thérèse her keys back.'

'Why did he have Thérèse's keys?'

'Well, we had this booking and it got cancelled.....look, it's a long story. Can we try to get Rui out of jail before he gets shot or raped or something?'

Ursula snorted, 'I suspect they may be in more danger than him.'

In the GNR building they tried to attract the attention of the desk officer but, as they waited for him to stop scratching his balls, the door to a side room opened and Rui emerged followed by Carlos and a sergeant. Rui did a double-take when he saw them.

'Ursula, Tim, what are you doing here?'

'We've come to save you from being deported or excommunicated or executed,' explained Tim.

Rui seemed to be shaken and uncharacteristically not in the mood for joking.

'I've tried to explain it to them....oh, what's the point......'

The sergeant tucked his file under his arm and said, 'Senhor Fernandes, I want to send some officers to search your house. Do I have your permission or should I arrange for a search warrant?'

'No, come round now. I'll get the kettle on. Can I go now?' said Rui, trying to rub the fingerprint ink off the tips of his fingers.

The sergeant called Carlos and two other officers and they trooped off up the hill as if taking the accused to his execution. Thérèse watched them impassively as they walked past.

Carlos started searching Rui's apartment. He wasn't sure what the correct procedure was but he had at least identified Rui as a suspect, so he was feeling confident. As he rummaged, he listened to the conversation, feeling even more pleased with himself that he had been pretty good in English at school and had picked up a lot more from the TV, movies and pop music. He tried to remember which show he had seen where a policeman had used that trick. Play dumb and the suspects give themselves away. Was it Colombo or Miami Vice?

The Englishman was talking.

'So what's the problem with them? Surely they must understand what happened.'

'I tried to explain that I had Thérèse's keys to one room of her guest house,' said Rui in a pained voice, 'not the house she lives in, so I couldn't get into her place, even if I'd wanted to. In any case we've got the note that she left for the Jacobs.'

Ursula, mulled it over then said, 'But, doesn't she normally keep her door open during the day? Maybe whoever took the cash box didn't need the keys......'

'Oh,' said Rui in exasperation. 'She was angry at me for switching the keys last night; she was trying to steal a booking from me. Believe me, this is an act of revenge; spiteful cow. She's probably shoved the money up her arse out of spite.'

Tim showed Ursula the note. 'I think you've got a good defence,' said Ursula. 'The note, the fact that the keys weren't actually those of her house. Anyone with a brain cell can see that there's no case.'

Carlos winced slightly as he continued his search of the kitchen area.

Miracle in Carvoeiro

'It's a good job you don't have a police record here' said Tim. 'Mind you, they seemed to know you quite well at the station.'

'Oh yeah, but I haven't seen this one close-up,' he said glancing at Carlos. 'He's smokin' hot isn't he?'

'I wonder if he's married?' murmured Ursula, a lustful glint in her eye.

'I got stopped at one of their road blocks once,' Rui went on. 'One of them reminded me always to wear a seatbelt.'

'Well, that was kind of him,' said Tim and Carlos fought back a smile.

'Not really, I got an on-the-spot fine of a hundred and fifty Euros. Then there was the time when they found out that I didn't have one of those yellow jackets in the car.....'

'What? A flak jacket?'

'Yeah. I wouldn't be seen dead wearing one; have you seen the colour?'

'How much did that cost?'

'Well, the jacket was three Euros....' He hesitated.

'But?' prompted Tim.

'..... but the fine was sixty.'

'Jesus, Rui, you've only been here two months. What about parking?'

'Three.'

'Euros?'

'No. Offences,' he said remorsefully.

Carlos stopped searching, looked up at them and added in perfect English,

'Then there's the fact, Senhor Fernandes, that you have to register your car in Portugal within six months. If you don't register it here and pay the import tax it will be impounded.' He let the words sink in.

Rui, Tim and Ursula exchanged glances, trying to remember what they had said.

'Like I say, I know them quite well,' was all Rui could say.

Carlos felt smug at having disquieted them. As he continued rifling through the cupboards it occurred to him that this was the first time that he had had the chance to get involved in a real crime. The GNR's normal crime-fighting role was setting up road blocks to fine motorists for minor infringements when the office petty cash was getting low; fun, but not very satisfying. During his training they had impressed on the new recruits that they had to sweep away the old police-state attitudes from the Salazar days and serve the public. He couldn't remember Salazar and wasn't entirely sure who he was, but he knew that the policeman's job was to solve crimes and everyone was supposed to love him for it. He wondered whether maybe Paula would love him for it. Actually, love wasn't entirely necessary; sex would be a good substitute. He could settle for that. Maybe she was waiting for him to prove himself. If he was clever and smart, it could provide the key to her heart, or at least her knickers.

His mind turned back to the job in hand. This was a real crime; two thousand euros; that was more than he could earn in three months. Of course, for expats it was small change; they all had more money than they could spend.

Moving to the area under the sink, he stopped and pulled out a small piece of white paper from the refuse bin. It was not what he was searching for but it was unquestionably interesting. He opened up the small square and sniffed it, glancing at Rui. The smell was unmistakeable. It immediately transported him to Carmencita's bedroom and he felt a frisson of excitement at the thought of their rendezvous that lunchtime. He glanced behind him and put the piece of paper in his pocket, making sure that Rui had seen him. He knew that he could charge him for possession, but it was circumstantial and it was not the crime he was here to solve. In any case, that little wrap may have other uses.

'Nothing here,' he said as the other team members came in empty-handed.

'OK,' said Rui, 'now would any of you men like something to drink before you go back?'

'Coke for me,' said Carlos with a knowing smile.

Later that day, Carlos came back to Casa Rui.

'Senhora Roland has now made a formal crime report, Senhor Fernandes. We have interviewed some people but there were no witnesses to the theft, so there is only the fact that you had her key. While I was searching earlier, I should have asked to see your cash box. You do have a cash box?'

Rui nodded, got the key to the safe, removed his cash box and opened the lid nervously. Carlos peered in at the neat little pile of notes. He lifted them out and counted them without speaking. Two thousand Euros. He stared at Rui accusingly but could not wipe the smile of professional satisfaction from his face. Rui's eyes were fixed on the notes; his lips moved as if to speak but no words came out.

Roger Hardy

Three

The following Sunday, Rui and Tim had been invited to the palatial villa of Ursula and Peter Hallworth which was only a few hundred metres from Casa Rui on the cliff road leading to Algar Seco. They absorbed the opulent majesty of the interior which looked as if it had been teleported from Versailles and stood with some trepidation away from anything that appeared to be expensive or breakable. Ursula was holding court beneath a glittering crystal chandelier, bizarrely out of place against the backdrop of the sea.

Rui wandered over to Peter who was standing by a large bay window looking out over the Atlantic. Peter pointed out a framed photograph, his gold Rolex glinting in the sunlight.

'This is my daughter from my second marriage. She was a sweet child. Lovely....got married last year. Total tosser.........'

Peter was the kind or person that his friends would call a diamond geezer. He had the fortunate knack of being able to grab money out of the air and was, not for the first time, a millionaire.

'Now, this....,' he said holding up a larger picture, 'was Ursula when she won Miss Brighton.....in nineteen seventy......' he hesitated. 'When was it, my love?' Ursula broke off in full flight.

'Peter!' she admonished. 'Don't give away a girl's age! I don't suppose Rui wants to know anyway, do you, darling?' It was almost a command and Rui smiled without committing himself.

Moving between the groups of people was a short middle-aged woman, drinks tray in hand, offering champagne and taking empty glasses. She hovered between guests conspiratorially as if trying not to be seen.

'Brazilian,' whispered Ursula. 'Illegal. We saved her, poor sweet.'

Peter turned back to Rui as Tim joined them.

'What line of business are you in, Peter?' asked Tim.

'Import, mate. Champagne. Into the UK.'

'Are you going to try it here?'

'Well, I need something to pay for 'er majesty's lifestyle. Yeah, I've tried but I can't believe these people here,' Peter complained. 'You wouldn't believe the fucking bureaucracy and negative attitudes. It's no wonder that all the bleedin' supermarkets are run by French and German companies. The Portuguese have no idea at all. No bleedin' idea. Everything is too difficult, so let's do nothing. I can't do it without the cooperation of a Portuguese company and they're all in bed with the Port houses. It's all tied up. Very neat. I thought the mafia was just in Italy.'

'Oh, Peter, relax,' said Ursula. 'You don't need the money, take it easy. If you have to keep busy try something local, something small. Me, I'd prefer to sit by the pool when I'm here.' Peter turned back to Rui.

'A little bird told me you've been having a spot of bother with the boys in blue.'

'I've been framed, gov. 'Tweren't me.'

'I always used to say that, but they never believed me. Always the same. I know how you're feeling, mate. Anyway, I'm OK; I've got a perfect criminal record.'

'Perfect?'

'Yeah, five arrests and no convictions,' he said with pride.

'Well they haven't actually arrested me yet; I was helping them with their enquiries,' explained Rui with a grimace.

'Try my way.'

Rui raised his eyebrows.

'Deny everything,' Peter explained. 'Then bribe 'em on the quiet. Makes 'em go away and everyone's happy,' he said, smiling.

'Ah, but I can't really afford to bribe anyone.'

'In that case, you need to do a few favours.'

'What, for the whole GNR?'

'No. Identify one who's central and do him a favour. Come on, this is Portugal. Fix him up with a bird or something.....you know what motivates these people. You never know how grateful they're gonna be.'

Segundo Cabo Carlos da Silva was having difficulty keeping his mind on the job. He was on his knees between Carmencita's legs; she grabbed his muscular buttocks and forced him inside her. Groaning, he sank down onto her breasts, fondling, sucking, biting, thrusting. This was a good arrangement; Carmencita was low maintenance and they had been fuck-buddies for over a year.

Passion spent, he got up and went to the window, the perspiration evaporating off his body in the warm draught. The brightness outside was blinding and he half closed his eyes.

'Hey, Carlinhos,' said Carmencita, reclining on the warm bed, a cross between Goya's *Maja reclining* and a Playboy centrefold. Her skin was brown and silkily tanned, her black hair shimmered in the reflected light, her eye make-up still immaculate. 'Something on your mind?'

'Oh, it's nothing. It's the cash box theft, that's all. You remember; two weeks ago. Two thousand Euros. I found the first lead, now the sergeant wants me to take over the investigation.'

'Oh, it was such a shame. I know a lot of people don't like her but she's just a lonely old woman. Who could have done a thing?'

'Who would you guess did it?' asked Carlos, hoping for inspiration.

Carmencita raised herself from her elegant reclining position and sat on the edge of the bed, smoothing the sheets unconsciously, running her fingers over where Carlos had been.

'Well, sounds like there's only one possibility. I don't know that Fernandes but he sounds a bit suspicious to me. South African, isn't he? Maybe he's from Moçambique; they always think they're better than the Portuguese and they all have too much money.'

'So why would he steal?'

Carlos remembered the wrap that he had found in Rui's apartment. A coke habit is God's way of telling you that you have too much money, he thought. It was good that Carmencita could afford it occasionally; it was way outside his pay scale. He sniffed unconsciously. Money for drugs; it wouldn't be the first time that had happened. Fernandes had only recently bought the business; it was the end of the season. With all the start-up costs, money would be tight; temptation strong.

'How do you think he got his money in the first place?' Carmencita mused.

'Oh, God knows,' said Carlos, gazing out of the window. 'I don't know where these expats get their money from. They have so much of it. They've got nothing else to do except sit around and drink.' He turned back to Carmencita. 'I've got a friend in the Spanish police and he says they're all at it.'

'At what?'

'Crime. One way or another. He says that's why they come here. They can't stay in their own countries; they'd get arrested. So they come here. Portugal is the new Spain.' Carmencita shrugged in agreement.

'You know,' continued Carlos, 'I have a strange feeling about that Fernandes. I think he may be gay as well. He thinks I'm cute; he said so. I heard him. He was speaking English and thought that I didn't understand. I don't know what they take us for. Sometimes I wonder whether the expats think we're all peasants.'

'Well, be flattered, Carlinhos,' she said, getting off the bed and joining him by the window. 'At least he has good taste.' She rested her hand on his shoulder.

As he looked out of the window, the thought occurred to him that he could keep Fernandes under surveillance, unseen. If he was in charge of the investigation, he had to think of something. He thought about the Coastguard office next to the church. Casa Rui could be seen from there.

'I'm going to spy on him, that's what I'm going to do,' he said with enthusiasm. 'I'm going to have a stake-out.'

Carmencita went back to the bed and laid back, her head on the dishevelled pillows, her breasts almost falling to each side of her chest. Carlos watched her and wondered whether he had the energy and enough in the tank for a second session. He loved her breasts; they were even better than last year. This year they were a bit bigger and a bit firmer; he had asked her to do it but later felt guilty as if he was treating her like a blow-up doll. He'd been surprised when she had agreed; he assumed that her motivation was more to do with her career as an exotic dancer and that pleasing him was a bonus. He thought that her lips seemed a bit fuller than last year as well but wasn't sure. When he was confronted by her breasts, he could think of nothing else; it was if his dick was switched on by them. She forgave him his indiscretions with other girls and he almost forgave hers. It was a comfortable arrangement. The coke was a bonus.

'Do you want another line, baby?' she said, checking to see how much was left from the dusty little pile sitting on the corner of her bedside cabinet.

'No, thanks, I have to be on duty this afternoon. Can't be too wired. You have it.'

He looked in the mirror on the wall, hoped that he wasn't too wide-eyed and came and lay beside her in post-coital *tristesse*.

'Sure you can't stay?' she purred, turning to him.

'No, really. I have to go in ten minutes. Patrol.' At least I'll be wide awake, he thought.

Carlos wondered how long these meetings would go on for. He had fallen into a routine with Carmencita and whilst he was relaxed with it, he didn't want routine in his private life; he had enough of that in the force. He wanted excitement. He was younger than she was and he knew that they would never be more than fuck buddies. Somewhere out there was Senhora Right, and he already thought he knew who it was. He remembered his plan; professionalism. Impress her with professionalism. The stake-out.

Carlos got off the bed, energised by his new idea and put his uniform back on. Breathing in, he tightened his belt and adjusted his tie in the mirror as she watched. Not bad, he thought as he saw himself smiling back. He threw a grin of tarnished purity at her and it was not until he was halfway down the road that he realised he had forgotten to kiss her.

Rui was cleaning the windows at the front of the guest house when he heard raised voices from Casa Thérèse coming from the first floor. Tim put his head out of the window.

'What's up?'

'Dunno. It's Thérèse. I think she's screaming at Paula again.'

Rui inched himself as close as he could to but couldn't hear what was being said. He ran upstairs to eavesdrop from the first floor balcony, his curiosity overcoming a nagging feeling of guilt. Tim followed and hovered behind, not wanting to seem as interested as Rui but desperate to hear what was going on.

'It's like Eastenders,' he whispered.

'Shhh,'

The voices were now clearly audible.

'You stupid girl!' shouted Thérèse sharply. 'That was valuable. Look what you've done to it. That'll come out of your wages, my girl. This week and next. I've never met anyone as lazy or clumsy as you! You take advantage of me. You think I'm sick and won't notice these things, but believe me, there's nothing I miss.'

Paula was crying. 'It wasn't my fault, Thérèse. The string broke. It's old and ugly..........'

'I will decide what's old and ugly around here, my girl, not you. You wouldn't know what's valuable and what isn't. And you're illegal. I've a good mind to report you to the police. Send you back where you came from. See how much damage you can cause there. It wouldn't surprise me if you didn't steal my two thousand Euros....you or one of your criminal friends. Brazilians! Huh. You're all criminals. You just come here to steal from honest hard-working people.'

Sobbing, Paula burst out of the room to cry on the balcony, her face in her hands. Rui watched, speechless. She looked over and saw him and he stepped back.

'Rui.....'

Thérèse emerged as she said his name and glowered at him.

'Well, what are you listening to? Go away and mind your own business,' she spat. 'Hmph. Surrounded by thieves.' She was about to turn and go back into the house but Rui felt his temper boiling.

'Thérèse, I don't know what this is about, but you can't talk to people like that. How can you say those things to Paula? She's only doing her best. God, I've only known you for a few weeks and you are probably the nastiest person I have ever met, and I've met some nasty people in my time, believe me.' His hands twitched as he clenched and unclenched his fists.

'Doing her best? Huh,' she retorted. 'Mind your own business. Your time will come. If you think she's so great, you employ her. I don't want her here any more. Take her.' Her face was contorted with fury.

Paula interjected, 'But Thérèse, how will you cope....? You can hardly walk.....'

Miracle in Carvoeiro

'Huh!' said Thérèse. 'Starting to feel sorry now, are we? Cleaners like you are everywhere. Go if you want. I can soon replace you. You're nothing.'

'Paula,' said Rui, trying to keep calm. 'Come over to my side. I need a cleaner. I'll give you a job.' Paula's red, wet eyes thanked him. She turned and disappeared into the house, leaving Thérèse on the balcony.

'Good riddance, you little thief. And don't think you'll get any money this week,' she shouted after her. She turned to Rui, gave him a withering look and was gone.

Carlos had been to inspect the Coastguard lookout and was walking back to the GNR past Casa Rui when he glanced into the window of Rui's apartment. He did a double-take. He could have sworn that he saw Paula sitting there. Going to the window, he peered in. Yes, it was her. Absolutely perfect, he thought. He tapped on the window and Rui and Paula turned around in surprise. Rui didn't seem pleased to see him, so he tried to smile encouragingly and was invited down.

Lean and hungry, Carlos strode into the apartment, removing his hat with Hollywood nonchalance. He was torn between smiling at Paula and scowling at Rui and realised that he couldn't do both at the same time.

'Come in, why don't you,' said Rui sardonically. 'Please, have a seat.'

Once Carlos had sat down he realised that he needed some motive for the visit. He couldn't say that it was to see Paula's beautiful face. She had to see him being professional, fair, thorough and intelligent. I can do that, he thought.

'Paula.......what are you doing here?' He looked at her, noticing that her eyes were watery and bloodshot.

'I don't work for Thérèse any more; I left this morning. We had an argument. She's such a bitch. Now I work with Rui....Mr Fernandes. If you're looking for a thief go and see Thérèse.' She took out a handkerchief and wiped her nose.

Carlos was delighted. He wanted to take her in his arms and make everything better, then take her to bed and make things better still. It had been almost impossible to see Paula when she had worked for Thérèse, but now she was working for Fernandes and he needed to talk to him a lot, so that his world brightened considerably. He was concerned about how he could be a serious, threatening, heavy police officer with Fernandes but still be a sweet, charming, handsome, desirable, intelligent man with Paula. And all at the same time. There didn't seem to be much commonality, but he decided that Paula was the priority and the investigation came second. In a flash of inspiration, it occurred to him that he could combine them. Paula would know all about Thérèse's business. He should interview her. That way he could be professional and fair and hear her sweet voice all at the same time.

Pulling up a chair, Carlos set it down backwards and sat on it, western-bar style, his arms draped over the back, fingers pointing towards Paula. He cleared his throat and started to ask her questions about Thérèse's daily routine.

As she spoke, his eyes never left hers and he realised that he was not really listening and had to ask her to repeat herself. Look for the dilation of the pupils, he told himself. It's a sure sign of lust. He thought he had detected it but wasn't sure, so kept looking. She was glancing at him, then away, then to him again, as if nervous. He loved her eyes, framed by her perfect olive face and silky hair shining in the sunlight. Reluctantly, he drew the interview to a close having learned nothing new about the case.

'If there's nothing else, Carlos, I have to start cleaning,' Paula said sweetly, glancing at Rui. 'I don't want to upset my new employer.' Carlos watched her go through the door and listened to her footsteps becoming fainter.

He was silent for a while. There was the stake-out, of course; he would do that to see whether he could uncover anything but, until then, he wondered whether it was really necessary to make an enemy of Fernandes, especially in view of his new employee. He glanced at Rui and felt a frisson of pleasure at having power over him. Looking around, he sniffed. The shadow of coke and the memory of the sting in his nose flashed through his mind as it wandered away from the case and back to Carmencita. No, it was too risky; too stupid. But, the police did it all the time, surely. He had seen it on TV. They had the law on their side and that gave them power and invulnerability. Fernandes would jump at the chance to make the pressure go away. There were no witnesses to what he was about to say and he could always deny it.

Carlos realised that Rui was waiting for him to speak. Instead, he took a deep breath, slowly removed the small square of paper from his pocket, smoothed it out and set it on the coffee table. They both looked at it.

'Oh, come on....' protested Rui. 'You can't get me for the theft so you're going to pin something else on me? No.'

The silence was thick. They both started speaking at the same time.

'No, *Cabo*, you first,' said Rui with forced politeness.

'Well, Senhor Fernandes……….' Carlos sniffed and hesitated before continuing. 'It's funny the things that visitors want on holiday isn't it? For some people sun and sea isn't enough. You probably get your guests asking you all sorts of strange questions; where can I get this, where can I get that……'

'All the time.'

'Some questions can be quite difficult to answer, I guess.'

'Sometimes impossible.'

'Nothing's impossible, just difficult sometimes.'

'I suppose it depends on who you know…..' said Rui.

Carlos realised that Rui was getting the gist of what he was not saying. He was silent for a moment as if working out how to move forward. A trickle of perspiration ran down his side under his shirt.

'Senhor Fernandes, you'll get a call from a girl tonight. She'll give you a phone number. Simply call that number. I don't think you'll be sorry.' Rui looked surprised at what he was hearing and Carlos continued, 'Of course, you know that policemen's wages are shit and I couldn't afford to make a phone call like that………..but I guess that's not a problem for you.'

Carlos could see that Rui understood as they smiled knowingly at each other. The tension had been defused and Carlos felt proud of the way he had handled the situation. Then he turned serious again.

'But, Senhor Fernandes……….'

'Yes?'

'This doesn't change anything. I'll still be watching you.'

As the sun was setting, Carlos unlocked the door to the coastguard observation room built onto the side of the chapel at the top of Rampa da Nossa Senhora da Encarnação. Coastguards. Huh, he thought, there was as much chance of seeing a coastguard here as seeing the Archangel Gabriel cleaning the floors next door. Still, he was pleased that GNR had access to the place because it was a perfect lookout position. The entrance to Casa Rui could be clearly seen from the window.

Carlos was very familiar with it because he had also turned it into the best knocking shop in Carvoeiro; the sofa could be turned into a bed and there was wine in the fridge. Kids shrieked in the little playground outside the window and he watched as a dog took its elderly owners for a walk.

He was beginning to have second thoughts about the conversation with Fernandes. It had been so unprofessional. On the other hand, once Carmencita had called him with the number of her dealer and made the personal introductions, Fernandes would have a reliable source of good stuff. Carlos would then not be so dependent on Carmencita. OK, he would be a bit in the power of Fernandes, but there would be no evidence, no witnesses and if things got nasty he could always prosecute him for possession; all he'd need was a forensic swipe and a denial of everything else. No, he was worrying needlessly. It would work. Everything would be OK. He flipped open his mobile phone and called Carmencita.

In a claustrophobic and sombre apartment in the back streets of Carvoeiro, Senhora Ramalho and Flavia sat in silence. The furniture was old and worn and the place smelled of garlic and onions. Flavia became agitated, groaned and started to move convulsively. Senhora

Ramalho sighed as she dozed. It had been a difficult day and she was tired. Flavia was her daughter and it was her duty to keep her safe from a world that didn't understand her. People would cross to the other side of the street when they saw them approaching. She was sweet and loving but people never saw past the outward signs of her mental turmoil; never saw the gentle soul within. Senhora Ramalho felt completely isolated. This was the cross she had to bear and she did it gladly but she had no choice; no relief. No money, no possibility of work. A life of dependent poverty in an impoverished state. She roused herself, looked at her old wristwatch and eased out of her armchair.

'Come on, Flavia. It's bed time.'

Flavia was sitting at the table in her grey tracksuit, moving her arms in excitement. She ignored her mother and was fixed on her work. She loved the colours and shapes that she had made; they were so beautiful; then she moved them and made them neat again and they were even more beautiful. Everything was so beautiful.

She had arranged neat little piles of what appeared to her mother's unfocussed eyes to be playing cards. As Senhora Ramalho put on her glasses, the room came into focus; the clarity rooted her to the spot and she froze.

'Flavia! What have you been doing? What have you got there?'

She went to the table and put her hands over her mouth in disbelief. '*Oh meu Deus*!' she exclaimed as she saw the neat piles of Euro notes. Hundreds of Euros; thousands of Euros. She had never seen so much money. Flavia was in rapture and awkwardly reached for one of the notes and put it to her mouth. Her mother was in shock. Could there be so much money in the world? Where in the name of God could she have got it? What should she do? It was so much money and, goodness knows, they needed money but where did it come from? Was it a gift? A thought insinuated its way in her mind; an embryonic thought that might have been there all the time, all her life perhaps. It grew in power: could it have been a gift from God? Perhaps a gift in reward for a lifetime of suffering? Perhaps it was Our Lady of Fátima…..Yes, a miracle, that was it. Perhaps Flavia had seen her, seen Our Lady.

There were so many thoughts in her head, so many unanswered questions; Senhora Ramalho was confused. She clutched her crucifix and knew that she needed to talk to someone. The crucifix burnt in her hand and she released it in shock. Then she knew. She sunk to her knees and beseeched Santa Maria while Flavia made excited noises to herself. As she prayed, she felt as if a burden had been lifted from her, it was as if light had replaced the darkness and she thought that she understood. Now she was calm.

Yes, the Lord is merciful; for all bad things there is a greater good. Flavia had never uttered a word that anyone could understand………..Touched by God………..that was what the Arabs said about mad people; they had been touched by the hand of God.

Roger Hardy

Four

Carlos made himself a coffee and sat down by the window of the coastguard lookout nursing the warm mug. The room was military in its austerity; faded magnolia and nicotine brown. The furniture was utilitarian and cheap. He picked up the powerful binoculars and trained them out to sea where yachts drifted languidly; butterflies poised on a sparkling ocean. The children whooping and screaming in the playground outside were a strange backdrop for a surveillance activity.

Carlos had not covered this in GNR College but he had seen enough American movies to know that the stake-out was standard practise in New York and LA. Fernandes would have visitors; other expats with nothing on their minds – perhaps there was a network. He could take car numbers and check them out. Paula would be proud to see him using his initiative and he would be proud to seduce her right here in this room. A few cars came and parked, but they were hire cars with tourists heading for the beach; no one entered or left Casa Rui.

After a while, the door of the guest house opened and he saw Rui come out, jump into his Rav and drive off. Instead of his great stake-out plan, he was now looking at nothing. He felt at a loss and wondered what the New York cops would be doing in the same situation. They would have had the advantage of monitoring the house, listening to Fernandes's phone calls and internet, maybe having a bugging device so that they could hear what was being said behind those walls, gathering evidence of criminal activities. He guessed that they would, by now, have been galvanised into action to trail the suspect, jumping into their police cars to follow him, sirens wailing, but that was not a realistic option for Carlos; he didn't even have a bike.

He decided that he needed to discuss the whole idea of stake-outs with his sergeant. It was mid-Autumn but the sun was shining as if it were summer; the coastguard office was stuffy and Carlos liked to be outside; he could always do a check up on the church next door; maybe sit in the sun for a bit and wait for Fernandes to return.

The breeze was cool on his face and he meandered around the building, the remains of the old fort with its ancient engraved portal, then went to the front door of the church. Neatly placed against the door was a grey metallic box, carefully positioned, like an offering. Picking it up, he opened it; it was a cash box containing a single hundred Euro note and a small silver crucifix. He closed the lid and examined the outside; as he was doing so, he had a sudden flash of anguish. Shit. A cash box; maybe it was Thérèse's! Fingerprints! It would have fingerprints on it; the fingerprints of the thief.......and his own, he abruptly realised. Taking out his handkerchief, he carefully wrapped it around the box to minimise the contamination.

After waiting outside Casa Thérèse for two minutes, Carlos finally saw the old lady making her slow progress, aided by the

Zimmer frame. She opened the door and peered at him like a mole, eyes blinded by the light.

'Senhora Roland, I found this by the church a few moments ago,' he said holding out the box. 'Is it the one that was stolen?' She snatched it from him and examined it in the handkerchief, opening the lid. 'Careful, Senhora. Fingerprints. It might be covered in fingerprints.'

'Yes, Carlos, I recognise it; this mark on the side. The money must be mine. Oh, only a hundred.'

'....and the crucifix?'

'No. I don't have anything like that. I'm not religious.'

'I'm afraid that I'll have to keep it all for the time being. We have to do some tests. You understand.'

'Can't I keep the money?'

'No. You'll get it back but it may also have prints on it. Better to be safe than sorry.' Thérèse looked disappointed.

When the tests for the fingerprints came back a few days later, they confirmed that Thérèse's and Carlos's finger prints were all over the box and there were others for which there was no match on their database. What was confirmed, however, was that Rui's prints were not amongst them. Carlos was discouraged; his first suspect in his first case was turning into a dead-end, but he saw no reason to tell Fernandes just yet, if at all. He might have been wearing gloves. It felt good to have him in his power, even if the pretext was now probably false.

The following Sunday, Senhora Ramalho and her daughter Flavia made their way up the hill, separated by their usual distance.

Flavia was wearing her grey tracksuit decorated with a damp mark where a yogurt stain had been removed. Senhora Ramalho was dressed conservatively for church although they would not go in; the last time had been an embarrassing episode that she preferred to forget. Still, she needed to talk to Father Afonso and wanted her dress to be appropriate for speaking to God's representative. She would wait at the playground and listen to the service from outside the church.

Flavia arrived at the church first and sat on one of the children's swings looking at her feet as her mother caught up. Moments later, a shiny red Mazda MX-5 sports car arrived noisily. It screeched to a halt in the church car park and Father Afonso Gonçalves Mendonça got out, slamming the door behind him. He ran to the church fumbling for his keys, and opened the door as if he was being chased by demons.

'Father! Father Afonso!' shouted Senhora Ramalho, walking towards him, waving, trying to attract his attention. He stopped in mid-action and glanced towards heaven for some salvation before turning to see who it was.

'Senhora Ramalho! How nice to see you! How is Flavia?' The young priest had a keen and expressive face, thick eyebrows and soft eyes.

'Father, it's about Flavia that I wanted to talk to you,' she said with a tone of resolve. He watched Flavia swinging lazily, counting her fingers, lost in a world of her own.

'She's one of God's children, as we all are,' said Afonso. 'But, I'm afraid that I'm very busy this morning, Senhora; I have a service to organise and I'm rather late, you see.'

'Father,' she said, grabbing him by the arm. She was hesitant, trawling her soul for the right words. 'Could she be more than that? Could she be……..special?'

He thought before answering. 'We are all made in the image of God, Senhora.'

Senhora Ramalho wavered before continuing. 'But, she has no sin, Father.'

There was no element of doubt in her words. He seemed to be stunned by the bluntness of the statement.

'Well, Senhora, you may have a point,' he said thoughtfully. 'Yes, someone in their own world, who cannot interact with the outside world, probably has no sin. Sin comes from the world but, in Flavia's case………. it's a fascinating philosophical subject.' He hesitated. 'But can we discuss it some other time. I really am very late, you see.'

'Did you find my gift, Father? I left it by the door.'

Afonso spun around towards the open door but there was nothing there. He shook his head.

'Senhora, I know you have a generous heart but I also know that I'd give it back to you. I know that you need it more than the Church. The love you give to Flavia is all the gift that God needs.'

A look of disappointment came over her face like a cloud. 'Father…….Oh, I don't know how to put this………' she glanced away, struggling to find the right words. Then she fixed him with a piercing, almost saintly, look in her eyes. 'Father, do you think that it's possible that she could have been touched by God?'

Afonso was taken aback; the hairs on the back of his neck bristled and he gathered his thoughts.

'Oh, Senhora. That's an Islamic concept. I know of it, of course, and I have always found the idea appealing. Yes, those who have seen God can never be the same as those who have not. But, really, people saw God only in biblical days; it doesn't happen in modern times. We have Jesus in our lives. He is real and we don't need to see Him.'

'But, Fátima.......'

'Ah, yes, *Nossa Senhora*. A vision....but the children who saw Her......were not like Flavia.' At that moment, the first cars started to spill into the car park for the service. 'I'm sorry, Senhora, but I have to prepare for the service. Perhaps later? Can we talk about it later?'

Thérèse opened her front door and manoeuvred the Zimmer frame so that it could support her. She liked to get out of the house occasionally and breathe the clean morning air. Most of the people who knew her would be in church; she could hear them singing. Her shambling progress up the hill was painfully slow and she had only managed to shuffle fifty metres or so when the church doors opened and people started to emerge; she had wanted to avoid them and had timed it badly. Cursing to herself, she tried to manoeuvre the Zimmer frame so that she could retreat but her foot got caught in one of its legs and she fell heavily on the road. A car appeared round the corner and screeched to a halt. The door opened and the driver got out and ran to her assistance. She cursed him and he hesitated nervously, not sure what to do. She tried to get up, but had fallen awkwardly and found that she could not. Some of the churchgoers ran towards her to help; Flavia saw them and joined in excitedly.

Being younger than them, she moved with surprising speed and reached Thérèse ahead of the others. The girl looked at Thérèse then knelt down next to her, her arms moving in excitement as if she had found a lost puppy. As the others joined to help, one of her clenched hands, in a random movement, hit Thérèse hard in the face and she fell back. The others were horrified; Flavia was strong and the blow sounded painful. Senhora Ramalho pulled her daughter away and the others attended to the collapsed form on the road, clustering around her, trying to help to get her up again.

As Senhora Ramalho watched from outside the group with Flavia, she saw them go silent and start to pull back from the prone figure, widening their circle like a ripple in a pond. As the gaps opened between them, she could see Thérèse standing in the centre like a resurrected goddess. The Zimmer frame was still on its side on the road. Thérèse looked confused; a red bruise growing near one eye. Then she smiled. One of the congregation crossed herself and clutched her rosary to her heart.

Roger Hardy

Five

The following day, Rui was outside the guest house cleaning the shutters when he noticed a middle-aged woman dressed in black standing on the opposite side of the road. He had seen her earlier and wondered why she was still there. Finishing off, he padded back down to the apartment where Tim was packing.

'Have you seen the old girl on the other side of the road?'

Tim stopped folding a shirt and went to the window. 'Perhaps she ran out of volts after climbing up the hill. She's probably got solar cells on her back and is waiting for a recharge.'

'She's been there for ages. Just stands there. I think she's watching Thérèse's house.'

Tim returned to his shirt. 'She's probably the style police. Studying Thérèse's collage of scallop shells. Why did she do that? It's so tacky.'

'Well, she may be French but she needs a few lessons in good taste.' Rui chuckled but then frowned. 'You know what she reminds me of?'

'No? What?'

'One of those poor lost souls that you see going to Lourdes.......'

'Perhaps she's casing the joint. Maybe she wants to steal Thérèse's cash box. Oh, no, I forgot; you stole that didn't you?'
Rui scowled.

A taxi approached around the bend at the top of the hill, slowed and stopped outside Thérèse's house. Rui went back to the window, assuming it was one of her guests arriving. The rear door opened and a woman got out. Rui was about to go upstairs to tell her that Thérèse was out when he realised that the woman getting out of the car was Thérèse herself. As he watched in amazement, she walked steadily to the driver's side, took out her purse and paid him, then strode towards her front door.

'No, it's not possible....' said Rui.
'What's that?'
'It's Thérèse. She's walking. I don't believe it.'
Tim joined him at the window. 'Christ. What's happened to her? Yesterday she was a cripple and now she's not even walking wounded. She caused enough trouble when she was driving the Zimmer frame. Now what can we expect? Quick. Go up and find out what's happened.'

Rui was already halfway to the door and clattered up the stairs to get to Thérèse before she had a chance to let herself in.

'Thérèse,' he called, in his sunniest voice, trying to appear honest and appealing.
She looked around and almost smiled. 'What can I do for you, Rui?'
'Er.....Oh, I only wanted to apologise for shouting at you,' he said, not wanting to approach the main subject directly.

'Oh, it's forgotten, Rui. Regrets are only the past crippling us in the present,' she said. Her face was bright. The weariness had left her voice and her whole tone was light, almost jovial. 'Was there something else?'

'Well, yes....... Thérèse; you're walking......'

'Yes, of course. It's marvellous,' she said. 'I've been to see Dr. Müller and he says it's spontaneous remission..... *Spontanheilung* he called it. Oh, he's so German, but he's sweet. Actually, he doesn't know the reason. It could be the medication finally taking effect. He said he wouldn't have believed it if he hadn't seen it with his own eyes.'

'Well, I'm very pleased for you, Thérèse,' said Rui as she walked towards her front door. The woman on the other side of the road crossed herself and moved slowly on in a cloud of contentment.

'Thank you, Rui.' She was about to put her key in the lock when she paused and turned back. 'Oh, you won't forget about that two thousand Euros you owe me, will you?'

The following day, Tim returned to Amsterdam. Ursula and Peter had gone back to the UK to see relatives leaving Rui feeling lonely and a little depressed. He didn't feel like sitting in a Carvoeiro bar getting drunk; he had seen too many expats going down that road, with their beer guts and red noses. In any case, he knew that he would be bad company.

It was the end of the season. He was used to being active but his work was done, he had no arrivals the next day and his lover was two thousand five hundred kilometres away. He had money in his pocket but nothing to spend it on. It was Saturday and the prospect of watching BBC Prime was deeply unappealing.

Perhaps a little something up the nose and some porn on the TV might be a good substitute, he thought. He flipped open his phone.

Two hours later, Rui was sitting in the kitchen of the Portimão flat of his new suppliers, Chico and Maria. They sat enjoying a cold Sagres beer from the can, watching Chico working. He was a large man in jeans and a singlet; large but not fat. His arms were muscular but his eyes showed no aggression; the set of his face was like that of a lion at rest. He could as easily have been a prize fighter as a man of the cloth. Two small bags of white powder were open in front of him and he was meticulously mixing quantities from each, weighing them on brass scales before placing small quantities onto squares of paper which he then folded into tiny envelopes.

'What's that?' asked Rui pointing to the two bags.

'One's pure, the other's speed and bicarb,' Chico said like a chemist at a dispensary.

'And mine?'

'Pure; no speed,' he said. 'So where did you get my number?'

'It was an anonymous phone call from a woman. Don't know who it was, but I'm glad I called.'

'It's OK. I know. She called me as well to introduce you. Can't be too careful. How many is it?'

'Two please.'

Chico gave him two small wraps then placed the others in a box and hid it under the sink before sitting down for a cigarette. Rui took out some notes and handed them over.

The flat was neat and tidy. Rui walked over to the only window and glanced out; all he could see were the backs of other

Miracle in Carvoeiro

houses. If he craned his neck, he could just see the moon and a few stars; white and powdery. There was the sound of crying from upstairs and Maria got up from the table and left the room.

'So, where are you from, Chico? Brazil?' asked Rui, sucking on his beer.

'Now, you see?' said Chico with an expression of mild annoyance. 'That's what everyone thinks. Simply because we're black. We're Portuguese. As Portuguese as you.'

'Well, I'm from South Africa really, but I've got a Portuguese passport. Portuguese parents,' explained Rui.

'In that case, we're probably more Portuguese than you, but everyone assumes we're Brazilian. No, we're from Cabo Verde. Portuguese.'

'So what brought you here?'

'A new start. We've got a little girl and we wanted a good education for her. Wages are shit in Cabo Verde, but they're not much better here if you're black. The Brazilians will work for nothing and they expected me to do the same. It wasn't what I had in mind, but we're here now.'

'What did you do back there?'

'Tourism. I had an education, Rui, but here they want me to pick up rubbish. That's why I do this. That's the crazy thing. The Portuguese think we're all doing crime or drugs but I found I had to do it just to survive.' He sneered. 'It's a business. Never touch the stuff myself.'

Maria re-appeared. Her husband grabbed at her hand and kissed it.

'What's the crisis?'

'Oh, she had a bad dream, that's all. She only needed a little hug. She's asleep again now.'

Chico looked at his wife from the corner of his eye; she was petite with short hair, a tight little figure and sexy legs and Rui could see a glint of lust or love in his eye; he suspected that it was probably the latter.

'Been together since we were at school,' said Chico proudly. 'How many Brazilians can say that?'

The mobile phone rang and she answered it.

'OK, reservation for two people in ten minutes. OK.' She put the phone down. 'It's Pedro again. He must be having quite a party.'

Chico went to the sink and took a couple of bags from his stash, put them in his pocket, kissed Maria on the forehead, and let himself out, Rui following.

As Rui was in town he thought he might as well see what was happening. He had his stash for later so maybe another beer and then home. The smell of the Portimão quayside blended with the humid evening air; a mixture of fish, stagnant water and decay. The town's only gay bar was in a poorly-lit and run-down area of the old town where the streets were cobbled and shabby houses backed directly onto the road. Some sheltered a ghost of former glory, with chipped *Azulejos* encrusting the walls, saints watching over the sinners. The road was narrow, barely a car's width, and split by a bridge between the houses that carried the elevated road to the old bridge across the River Arade a few metres from a cluster of popular fish restaurants, now closed, cold and quiet.

Miracle in Carvoeiro

The gay club hid behind a large but anonymous doorway; Rui rang the bell and it creaked open as if it had its own enchanted life. The first person he saw inside was the last person he wanted to see. Chilcott, Ben Chilcott the Boer with the good memory and the ability to remember things that Rui would have preferred to stay forgotten. It was too late to pretend that he hadn't seen him so he wandered over and accepted a drink. Chilcott was drunk and swaying.

'Howzit?' asked Rui, although between South Africans, it was not a question, more a greeting.

'Hey, Rui. Howzit. How's the world of high finance and glossy tourism?'

'Oh, it's one continuous whirl of cocktail parties, caviar and champagne.'

'So you're empty?'

'Yeah. Not much happening out of season. The tourists are all in hibernation, living on acorns.....'

'While you live on air?'

'Oh, well, we did OK during the season so I'm not exactly suffering.'

'Quite a change from South Africa, hey?'

Rui tensed. He really didn't want to go there.

'Ben, no offence but I came to town to wind down. I made a few wrong decisions....no, that's not really true. I was unlucky.......anyway, it's all in the past. There are some things better left behind, Ben, believe me. Leave it behind and move on.'

'I've found that it always has a way of catching up with you, Bro.'

It occurred to Rui that Chilcott must have an amazing memory. One incident out of so many after so long. The car jacking had made the papers but only on page three. He was relieved when Chilcott changed the subject.

'How did you find that coke I gave you?'

'Good, thanks.'

'Thought you would have become a regular customer. You know; twice-nightly and matinees ……'

Chilcott had some kind of inside track on Rui's life in South Africa but Rui still couldn't work out the connection. 'Oh come on, Ben, that was in the past. It's just an occasional treat these days.'

Chilcott did not sound convinced. 'Got another supplier? I'm always interested in new suppliers, if the stuff's kosher. Sometimes it's difficult getting good shit.'

'Well, yeah. Haven't tried it yet but I'm told it's good.' Rui got out his mobile phone and scrolled through his phone book. 'Try this guy. The name's Chico.'

'Hmm….Chico; don't know him.' Ben wrote down the number and gave the phone back. 'Thanks, I'll pay him a call.'

'By the way, Ben,' said Rui keen to resolve a matter that had been troubling him since their last meeting. 'Last time, you didn't say where we'd met before; you seemed to know me pretty well, or was that only a-friend-of-a-friend stuff?'

Chilcott turned to him in disbelief. 'I thought you were covering up, Bro. Christ, Rui, you must have been really out of it. Yeah I knew you and you knew me. Oh Rui, come on…….'

'Really, I can't remember.'

'Well, I guess I was one of many but I never forgot it. I guess I didn't make much of an impression……'

'You're talking in riddles,' Rui said, like a last-ditch defence; he thought he knew what was coming next.

'Bro, for Christ's sake! Do I have to spell it out? Jo'burg? Connaught Mansions? Rui, I was one of your fucking customers.'

An hour later, Rui was standing on the old bridge gazing out over the estuary towards the sea; he had been drifting around the town, deep in thought. A cool breeze blew in from the west and ruffled the surface of the river but his mind was in the southern hemisphere. A door of a quayside bar opened and music flowed out, dissolving in the air. The tune floated in his head; he could still remember the steps and the girls, Sun City, Paris or had it been Monte Carlo? He had only ever wanted to dance through life. As he remembered, the melody in his head faltered and became darker, slower, more threatening.

Fuck. Who the fuck was Ben? How did he know so much? Where did he fit in? He struck a disconnected chord, like a face on TV or someone seen regularly in a crowd but never met. A customer. A drugged up customer in the fucked-up scrapyard of his life. Yeah, drugs affect memory, but it's probably the memory protecting itself with a fog of omission; a seething miasma from the centre of which emerged Satan, leering and beckoning. His mind drifted, confused, searching. Dirk.

If Satan ever appeared on earth he would appear as Dirk. What would he be doing now? Probably long dead. The best looking man in South Africa. Stunningly handsome, witty, funny, amoral, now dried bones. Dirk and his trail of lovers. There were no limits to his life, nothing that would ever frighten him in his pursuit of pleasure or vice. Drugs were his fuel; excess in everything and no morality except what snaked in his own mind. Dirk twisted those in his immediate circle and left them like roadkill in the gutter. Rui was one of those picked up and dragged along by a swiftly passing car and left to die.

As the memories surfaced again, he could smell the sting of ammonia in his nostrils as Dirk made the crack; the first energising hit, the endless but impossible quest for a repeat as the drug filled his body but with less effect. Then sleep. Eventually. A restless wide-open sleep with only one dream and a million thoughts and regrets. Then a repeat of the whole routine the next day.

He remembered the day that Dirk had got the phone call. The offer from an older man; an offer that he couldn't refuse. He followed the trail of money, leaving Rui alone with nothing but the fuel of his own addictions. After that came the search for drugs. Then the supplying. Then the stabbing. Then rehab. Never to dance again.

After months of unemployment, Rui had been offered a job as receptionist at a gay massage den. He'd been perfect for the job; handsome, charming, fun, efficient. The trouble was that customers had starting asking more of him. He had no experience as a masseur but that was not a problem. A massage was not what they were there for. He started to earn good money and his reputation spread. Then he decided to start out on his own.

Then the drugs started again. It had been an accident; he'd been offered something which was stronger that he'd expected but it switched on the whole nightmare again, as if it had been on standby. Except, this time it was good for business. The clients loved it. Some came just for it. Working from his apartment, Rui could earn more in an hour than in a full day of normal work. Drugs were good for this business; they meant money, they meant that addictive rush which took primacy over the sex, they meant the possibility of sex without attraction. The customers came and went; home to misery; back to their wives or boyfriends or dogs or empty spaces, leaving Rui in a pall of forgetfulness to mask the great cavern in his life.

Some of his clients only came to talk to someone who knew what it was to be on top of the pile and what it was to be in the gutter. Chilcott's face flitted through his mind, the merest suggestion of a ghost, maybe real, maybe a customer. He tried to think back to his punters; there had been so many but, no matter how hard he tried, he couldn't recall one face. Not one.

Roger Hardy

Miracle in Carvoeiro

Six

Two weeks later, Tim was back in the warmth of Carvoeiro; Amsterdam a cold memory. He was acclimatising on the terrace having a morning coffee when he saw Flavia coming up the hill. This time it was different. Gone was the grey shabby tracksuit; in its place a red Nike. Following behind was, not only her mother, but four other women as well. That's nice, thought Tim. She must have been quite isolated, she was always on her own before. Now she has some friends.

Father Afonso was sweating in anticipation. He had been summoned to see the Bishop of Faro who had heard rumours emanating out of Carvoeiro. He drove to the Largo de Sé, the main square of Faro, with the understated Cathedral ahead of him, the red ochre stone tower contrasting with the white of the main building. To the left of the square sat the Bishop's palace, broad and low with a roof like a mountain range. He parked his sports car, incongruous next to the Bishop's black limousine, smoothed his hair flat again and went with eager steps to the main entrance.

The white-haired Bishop welcomed him with a hand shake and a smile. He was younger than the colour of his hair or his rank suggested, and was dressed in a black suit and purple clerical shirt with a pectoral cross emblazoned on it. His every gliding footstep oozed authority, but his face was tempered with gentle grey eyes that seemed to deal compassion and forgiveness with every glance. The Bishop's wood-panelled office was large and opulent; books lining the walls and gold ornaments placed here and there to contrast with the warm darkness of the wood; there was a rich brown leather suite in one corner, its surface shimmering in the reflected light from the Georgian windows which looked out onto the bright quadrangle behind. A chandelier glinted above his desk, augmented by a Tiffany-style desk lamp. The Bishop sat down behind his desk and bade Afonso to make himself comfortable. Tea arrived as if summoned by a prayer.

'So, Father, tell me what you know.'

Afonso took a deep breath before replying.

'Eminence, I'm not even sure what has been going on in Carvoeiro. I'm ashamed to say it, but that is the truth. People stand gazing at the church, and sometimes they crawl to it on their hands and knees.'

The Bishop was silent as he listened, his elbows on his desk, hands raised and fingertips touching like the steeple of a cathedral.

'We call them pilgrims, Father,' said the Bishop, his voice verging on the sarcastic. He continued, 'What I have heard is that one of your flock has had an encounter and there is talk of a miracle.'

'Yes, Eminence,' said Afonso, not sure how to respond.

'Father Afonso, we have to be very careful of things like this.'

'Eminence?'

'I know that Carvoeiro is small, but so was Fátima, once. At Fátima there wasn't even a miracle, only a vision.'
'Repeated over three years, Eminence.'
'But never witnessed by anyone except the children.'
'Two were beatified, Eminence.'
'Please don't instruct me, Father,' the Bishop snapped. 'The church was cajoled into it by external forces; we had lost control. To this day, no one knows whether those children really did see the Blessed Virgin. The idea was enough. The government couldn't ignore it and nor could the church. The fact is, we had lost control. It was the people who wanted it.'

Afonso shrugged in confusion.

'But Eminence, the Holy See was in full agreement.'

'When there is a mass movement like that, even the Pope has to acquiesce,' said the Bishop with a dismissive flick of his hand. 'Poor people find consolation in their misery; that's where they find God; in the dirt, in the dust of desolation. You and I know that our congregations need guidance. Without it, they could revert to superstitious paganism. The temptation to believe in something greater than themselves but something that is not condoned by the church is the sort of thing we must always be aware of.'

'But no one in Carvoeiro has talked to me about it, Eminence. It's almost as if there is a conspiracy of silence.'

'That is the most sinister kind of conspiracy, Father Afonso. Perhaps they have discovered some comfort and are afraid that you will deprive them of it. But when it comes to the religious lives of your flock, you should be in control. The church determines doctrine; you apply and they accept it. That way lies salvation for their souls and happiness. Everything else leads to chaos.'

Afonso shook his head. 'I'm sorry, Eminence. I have no experience of matters like this. I am a modern man, a rational man who accepts that the Church holds the light in a secular world. Believe me, in my church superstition has no role to play.'

'I believe you Father. But, there are some who would say that superstition has always had a role in the Church. I hope we can be tolerant whilst still pushing the party line, so to speak.'

'Eminence, I don't entirely understand.'

The Bishop sat back on his chair and surveyed the younger man.

'Think for a moment. Suppose there *has* been a miracle or a vision or the like. It hasn't happened since Fátima, but this is a new century. Father, consider this: you may actually have a miracle on your hands. Miracles start from ordinary people experiencing extraordinary things. When it happens, of course no one believes it. It's like your next door neighbour claiming to have seen the Archangel Gabriel; naturally you're sceptical. That's how miracles start. They start with doubt and disbelief.'

Afonso groaned, still more confused.

'Eminence, I don't understand. At one moment you talk of control, and the next you talk of miracles.'

'I think the truth is that we do not know yet how to deal with this. In fact we don't yet know whether we have anything to deal with at all. But I think that it is essential to find out what has been going on; why people are crawling up your hill, then we can work out how best to handle it.'

'I understand, Eminence.'

'We must not lose control over this situation, Father. Let's talk again in one week.'

'*Allez! Allez-vous en*!' Thérèse stood outside her guesthouse waving a broom at two pilgrims who had been standing outside for more than an hour, praying with their rosaries. They scuttled off towards the church, shocked.

'Senhora Roland!'

Thérèse turned round to see Father Afonso coming up the hill.

'Senhora Roland,' he continued as he got closer, 'I'm so glad I caught you. Do you have a moment?'

'Not really, Father. Can you make it quick? I'm not coming back to church if that's what it's about.'

'No, nothing like that, Senhora Roland. Your soul is safe for the time being.'

Thérèse relaxed and gestured to the priest to come inside.

'I'm so pleased to see that you're walking again. There's talk in the village about it, you know. Some are talking of a miracle.'

'Miracle, *pfui*, Father. I'm in remission. Spontaneous remission. According to the Herr Doktor.'

'I'm so pleased. Do you have any idea what caused it?'

'I really don't know. Dr Dieter says the same. He says that it might have been the fall or maybe the medication taking effect. Or it could have happened on its own. He can't explain it.' She told him about when she had fallen in the street. How she had suddenly been able to walk again.

'That's amazing. And you say she touched you?' said Afonso.

'Touched me? The deranged idiot hit me. I've still got the bruise here...look.' She pointed to a small grey patch near her eye.

'And you don't connect the two events?'

'Father if I still believed in all that *merde* I'd have gone to Lourdes years ago. Then you'd have had a bloody miracle. The only miracle now is how I haven't pushed one of those damned pilgrims off the cliff. Why do they keep hanging around outside?'

'Senhora Roland. I hope you don't think I approve. I'm simply trying to find out what's going on. The Bishop is quite insistent.'

It was clear to Afonso that Thérèse was in no mood for a philosophical debate and was the person least likely to be the recipient of God's good grace. He made a hasty retreat.

As he closed the front gate behind him, he saw another pilgrim coming up the hill. He watched as she stopped and, looking behind her, went down on her knees. A few seconds later Flavia appeared round the corner in her new track suit. Behind her trailed ten other women with her mother. None were talking but their lips were moving. Flavia stopped and picked a flower. It was beautiful, so beautiful. She examined it curiously from all sides as if she had created it. Her followers caught up and stood near her. She gave the flower to one of them who went down on her knees as Flavia continued her processional.

Afonso went to the woman, still prostrate in a kind of ecstasy.

'The flower. Look at the flower,' she said breathlessly. Afonso was not sure what to do but admired the flower and helped her to her feet.

'I'll keep it forever,' said the woman. Afonso could see a tear in her eye. 'Forever.'

'Senhora, why do you follow her?'

The woman looked at him, focussed with a squint and recognised the priest.

'Oh, Father, she's one with you. You know her; she's like you. Her face. Don't you see the light?' She said no more, turned around and walked slowly and blissfully down the hill.

As Afonso made his way pensively up the hill, Rui came out of his guest house shaking a floor mat. The priest went up to him and introduced himself.

'Sorry, Father,' said Rui, 'I see them, of course, but I don't know what it's all about. I thought you would know. It's a bit disconcerting for my customers.'

Afonso looked rueful.

'Well, we all want to know. You won't believe this, but it's nothing to do with me. Have you heard nothing?

'All I've heard is that it's something to do with money.'

'Money? No talk of miracles?'

'Not that I've heard of.'

Afonso was more confused than ever as he wandered back to the church. A miracle here, money there. A gift. What was it the mother had said? He fought for recollection, then it came to him: she has no sin. He thought of the Bishop's reaction. Oh, please God, let it not be true, he muttered.

It was Christmas in Carvoeiro. The village was like a tomb.

'But what are all the Portuguese doing?' asked Tim, waiting for Rui to get ready. 'I couldn't believe the lack of Christmas decorations when I came in last night. You know, Amsterdam is like a garden of lights, Christmas trees everywhere, bands in the streets, carol singers.'

'Yeah. It's more of a religious thing here,' said Rui, appearing from the bathroom dressed only in a towel and plastering gel in his hair, spiking it in the centre.

'Religious?'

'Yes, you know, apparently it's in celebration of the birth of baby Jesus, sent to redeem the world,' he said with a rising intonation at the end like a question. He dropped the towel and Tim watched him lecherously as he squirted himself with Paco Rabanne and went to select his clothes for the party.

'Oh, not that Mr. B tee-shirt again,' said Tim. 'Try the long-sleeved blue one. Anyway I know all that, dummy, but it's really a midwinter festival; you know, the Roman Saturnalia; merry-making, the giving and receiving of gifts, all that stuff. The Christians knew that they couldn't stop it being celebrated so they hijacked it.'

'Well, here it's more baby Jesus and less Roman orgy.' Rui examined himself in the mirror and nodded. 'I guess it's because they never needed a midwinter festival here. I'm sure you northerners will do your best to turn it back into a Roman orgy, but it's a bit like farting against thunder.'

The windows at Scamps cocktail bar glowed orange with life and warmth. As Rui and Tim made their way up the road on the far side of the cliff, the noise of music and laughter grew. It had become chilly outside; a northerly wind had proclaimed the arrival of winter. Rui opened the door and cigarette smoke wafted out. Inside, the atmosphere was colourful and humid. Peter and Ursula, the couple from the beach shop and some other friends were sitting at two tables, pushed together. Candles flickered from green and red table

Miracle in Carvoeiro

decorations and the tables were covered with half-full glasses and two open bottles of champagne in silver ice buckets, dripping with condensation. Ursula, wearing festive bright red lipstick and with flashing antennae on her head, waved at Rui and Tim and carried on with her joke.

'So the Frenchman says: When I make lurve, I coveur my wife wiz cream and zen lick it off; she 'oveurs ten centimetres above ze bed.'

Rui came over and gave her a big sloppy kiss. 'Not now....later you sexy devil....oooh mother.... put me down until I've finished telling this joke.....so the Italian says 'When I make-a da love, I massage 'er weez olive oil and rub eet into 'er body; she rises a metre above ze bed.' Then the Englishman says 'Oh, that's nowt. When we've finished shagging, I wipe me cock on the curtains and she goes through the fookin' roof!'

While the laughter subsided she made space for Rui and Tim and more cocktails arrived, red, green and yellow, each with an absurd little umbrella, a memory of summer on the beach. Peter poured out more bubbly.

'Imported it meself,' he said, with pride.

Tim raised a glass in toast. 'So you managed to set up the business?'

'Yes,' he said with satisfaction. 'In the end it was easy. I simply had to persuade the right person.'

'Persuade?' asked Tim.

'Yeah. Well, first I tried having meetings; that didn't work. Then I tried filling in forms; they're all in Portuguese and even the Portuguese don't understand them, then I tried persuasion. That's how it's done here. I persuaded them by forcing large wads of Euro notes into their pockets. When you've stuffed enough in, it's amazing how the wheels start to turn. Got to find something to keep me busy and pay for 'er 'ighness.' Ursula raised her glass in acknowledgment.

'So persuasion works,' said Rui.

'Every time, mate. Did you take my advice?'

'Yeah, but it's bloody bankrupting me,' said Rui, looking into his glass.

'Have you heard of Peter's *new* idea?' interjected Ursula, a puckish smile on her face, conscious that she knew and no one else did. The crowd waited for her to divulge the secret but she coyly allowed her gaze to nonchalantly float around the room.

'Stop milking it, Ursula,' said Peter. 'Go on, tell 'em.'

Her eyes twinkled with mischief. 'It's wicked. It's a sex shop. We're going to open a sex shop. We're going to call it Cockatoo. Cockatoo! D'ya geddit?'

'A sex shop? Here in Carvoeiro? Here in conservative and Catholic Portuguese Carvoeiro?' asked Tim, astonished.

'Market forces, mate,' said Peter with confidence. 'Give the punters what they want. No competition, see? There's two empty shops up restaurant hill. I've got me eye on one of 'em.'

'Do you think they'll allow it?'

'What's not to allow? If I stuff enough Euros into their pockets, I'd be fairly confident,' he said with a self-satisfied smile. Tim raised his eyebrows and looked at Rui whose expression said that this was a long shot. 'It'll work, mark my words,' said Peter, seeing their doubtful expressions. 'I know how to get things done around 'ere. I've got this tame solicitor, friend of the Mayor. Name of António Amores. Says he can fix everything. Good man.'

'I wish you luck,' said Rui.

'I'll need more than luck, mate. Ursula wants to run it,' he said with a grimace.

'Can't wait to get my hands on the merchandise,' she said. They chatted a bit more, joking about Ursula's new role before she changed the subject.

'Now what about the miracle, chaps?' asked Ursula. 'You've seen those people hanging about up the hill. It's your much-loved next door neighbour; she's walking again. It's a miracle.'

'I was talking to Maria at the newsagents,' said Tim. 'She said she'd heard that Thérèse was cured by that autistic girl. That's why they're following her.'

'No, it was spontaneous remission. Everyone knows that,' said Rui.

'I'm only telling you what she said. Anyway, she heard something else,' said Tim. 'You know Santiago de Compostela?'

'Not personally,' said Ursula. 'Who is he? Spanish? Is he married?'

'Not who, where. It's a shrine in northern Spain. Anyway, Maria says that they've organised a coach trip for the faithful. From Santiago de Compostela to Carvoeiro. Carvoeiro of all places. Apparently there's some connection with Saint James.'

'Coach trip? I thought they were meant to crawl here.....'

'Well, it's probably a thousand kilometres. Might be a bit hard on the knees.'

'What are they going to do? Visit Thérèse? She's going to love that.'

Tim shrugged.

'No,' said the blonde woman next to Peter. 'It's about money; that's what I heard. You pray to Thérèse and you get money; something like that.'

Her partner shook his head. 'I heard that the Virgin Mary appeared before a young girl.'

'No, that was at Fátima,' said Peter.

'What about this connection with Saint James?' said Tim.

'What?' said Rui. 'We've already got Nossa Senhora da Encarnação; we don't need another patron saint. How many virgins does a village need? Besides, I spoke to Father Afonso the other day and he told me that he didn't know what was going on either.'

'It sounds like a publicity stunt to me,' said Peter. They all nodded and he poured more champagne.

'Senhora Ramalho, did you have a good Christmas?' asked Father Afonso as he stood at the door of her tiny flat. He could hear Flavia inside.

Senhora Ramalho didn't want visitors; not in her flat. Not Father Afonso. Yes, she had had a wonderful Christmas, thank you. For the first time in years she had been able to afford a dinner to fit the occasion but she was feeling guilty because she had had to use some of God's gift. She was sure that the Lord wouldn't have minded; why send the money otherwise? But she felt that it had been a sacred trust and should only be used for doing good. Well, a small feast at Christmas had felt good and she prayed that God would understand. But she didn't want Father Afonso in the house because she knew that he would sense her guilt.

Besides, he had lost the gift that she had left for him. He'd had no time to talk to her then but now that he wanted something he had found time. He was too young; what did he know of life? He had never suffered, never been poor. Look at that shiny little car he drives.

If the money had been a test from God she had failed. She had sinned but couldn't confess because it would be to Father Afonso and she didn't want him to know. It felt good to confess. She confessed to Flavia but she couldn't understand or offer absolution. Even so, could confessing to someone without sin be a form of absolution? Flavia is more perfect than you, priest; she is still perfect. The money hasn't tainted her soul. It wasn't her decision to spend any of the money; she is still without sin. God sees everything but few see God.

'Senhora Ramalho?' She snapped out of her internal world at his gentle call. 'Please, I'm only trying to find out about these pilgrims. From what I have heard, it all seems to point to Flavia.'

She thought about how best to respond. She couldn't tell him about the money and, without that, she couldn't tell him that Flavia had been touched by God; she had tried once but he had not been interested. And now the pilgrims.

'Pilgrims. Father, I tell you something. I used to crave the company, but now I'm tired of seeing them. Flavia doesn't even see them any more; once I thought she did. We didn't ask them to come. I want them to go away. We want to be left alone again.'

'I'll do my best, Senhora, but I can't control what people do.' He wished her a happy new year and walked away disappointed.

With the new year came the first coach. It was high and shiny with dark windows; it could have been the love-child of a giant candy bar and a monstrous insect. It hissed to a halt in the car park in the village centre and exhaled. The door opened and the occupants emerged as if disembarking from a spaceship that had kidnapped them for alien experiments. They helped each other out of the coach and looked around. Three asked where the nearest toilet was. The driver busied himself at the baggage compartment and there was a rush to remove a collection of scaffolding which opened up into wheelchairs.

There were forty of them, silver haired and frail, half in wheelchairs or on crutches, making the centre of Carvoeiro resemble the evacuation of Sarajevo. They were led by a large red-faced man dressed in a clerical suit. He raised his hands and they were silent.

'Gen'l people! Mah brothers and sisters,' he declared in a strong southern American accent. 'The Load welcomes you to Carveera. Praise the Load!' They praised the Lord. 'Now before we partake of the good mercy of the Load and drink from His blessed table.......' He was interrupted by a bent old man on crutches who whispered in his ear. The preacher looked around and pointed towards the toilets on the beach and the old man was helped towards them. Others followed as the preacher watched them, raising a hand. 'Five minutes, ladies and gennelmen. Five minutes.'

'You'll be lucky,' said a voice but the preacher couldn't tell who had said it.

Rui was at the newsagents buying a paper and watched the people, hobbling on crutches, wheeling, being pushed. He saw Carlos walking over to the preacher and followed to see what was happening. As he got closer, he could hear Carlos talking Portuguese to the American.

'Can I translate?' he asked politely. Carlos looked embarrassed when he saw Rui and explained the problem in Portuguese.

'He says you can't leave the coach here,' said Rui to the preacher. 'It's a parking area for cars and there's a coach park further up the hill.' Carlos saluted and left. Rui scowled at him.

'Actually, he speaks perfect English,' said Rui. 'He was just joshing with you.'

'Hey, you from Australia?'

He had had the same question from Americans all around the world and had given up trying to explain about being a Portuguese from South Africa. Americans viewed the world as the great US of A with a few countries dotted around them. Any other concept caused too much confusion.

'Yeah, near there.'

'Thought I recognised the accent. Never wrong, me,' said the preacher, straightening his azure stole. 'You live here?'

Rui nodded.

'You must be proud to live in such a historic place. How old is it? A thousand years?'

Rui had never really considered Carvoeiro interesting in the historical sense.

'Er....I think that some of the buildings may date back to 1900......'

'Yes, siree,' the preacher continued as if not having heard Rui, surveying the square. 'Love history, me. Love Europe. Now, I wonder if you could help me. Where is the Cathedral?'

'Cathedral?' asked Rui incredulously. 'This is only a village. There's a small church at the top of the hill. That was built in about 1910 I think.'

The preacher looked towards the steep hill and frowned. 'That's gotta be one in eight. How're they gonna get up there? Most of them can't walk on the level. We only got an hour.'

'I wouldn't bother, Reverend. The church isn't much to look at. Small. You probably wouldn't all fit in. Anyway, it's closed today.'

'Yeah but we came all the way from Fátima. Had to do Carveera; We done Leweds and Santiago de Campos. We added this at the last minute. Must be a popular place.'

'Well, it's getting more popular,' said Rui. 'What did you come here for? I mean, you can see what we have. It's only a small village, out of season.'

'Ah, small in yo' eyes, Sir, but not in the Load's,' said the preacher with gravity. 'He has blessed this place. Yes, Sir, blessed it in His infinite mercy.'

'I'm sorry, I don't really understand,' mumbled Rui. 'What do you know that we don't know?'

'Oh, come on. Now you're joshin' with me. I can take a joke. The Load can take a joke.'

'OK, humour me.'

The preacher drew himself up to his full height and declaimed majestically, 'My friend, this holy place has been chosen by the Load for His first miracle of the twenty-first century. How blessed you must feel, to be so close to His presence. To know that the Load has worked his marvels on this very spot. This blessed spot.'

There was a shout behind the coach and angry words, then Flavia appeared, waving her arms, followed some distance behind by Senhora Ramalho and eight other women. The preacher looked at her with pity and shook his head.

'Oh, the poor soul. We get them back home as well. The Load surely works in mysterious ways, Sir. Why is that poor girl here? Shouldn't she be in a home?'

Roger Hardy

Seven

The winter was nearly over and the sky was clear and brilliant. Senhor Luis da Silva, Mayor of Lagoa, was looking out of the lounge of his villa at Silves. The window ran the full width of the room and framed the red ochre Moorish castle which, along with the Cathedral, formed the centre piece of the town. Surrounding the castle were trees, thick with bird song. Jumbled white-painted Lego houses lined the roads running up the hill. The Mayor saw a car pull up outside and went to the door with childlike enthusiasm.

'António, come in.' He smiled and put his arm around his visitor's shoulder, leading him into the lounge. The visitor, António Amores, was a man with a presence. The kind of man that people respect or fear without knowing why. He was not tall, not good-looking, but had an air of being in control, simply by the way he moved. His hair was thick, black and glossy. He had the eyes of a predator, intense, unblinking.

'Have you seen the paper? There, on page three,' said Mayor Luis.

Amores opened the 'Portugal News' and took in the small photograph of a topless page three girl and details of the proposed new shop:

Roger Hardy

'SEX SHOP TO OPEN IN CARVOEIRO

It was announced in the Camara at Lagoa yesterday that a trading licence had been granted to a new sex shop to open in the Algarve village of Carvoeiro. It is expected that the shop will be open in six weeks. Father Afonso Gonçalves Mendonça, officiating priest of the chapel on Rampa da Nossa Senhora da Encarnação in the village, is quoted as saying:

'The Church will oppose this blight on the face of Carvoeiro. There has never been a need for such an affront to common decency in this village and there is no need for it now. It will offend decent people and is offensive in the sight of God.'

'Isn't it fabulous?' said the Mayor. 'How did you persuade the Englishman to part with ten thousand Euros, António? It was a stroke of genius.'

'It was easy,' Amores said with a modest shrug. 'When he came to see me, I took out a whole sheaf of application forms for building land and property extensions and put them in front of him. He looked at them like a blind man; he doesn't speak a word of Portuguese, like most of the expats. They think that mastering '*Obrigado*' is enough and they usually get that wrong. Anyway, I said that I'd fill them all in and walk it through the town hall but that there would be opposition to something as outrageous as a sex shop and that I might need to persuade a few of your officials. The next day he turned up with a large brown envelope stuffed with ten thousand Euros. I couldn't believe it. He thinks that this is a third world country. Of course, he's rich and it's small change to him…….oh, by the way, before I forget…..' He took out a small blank envelope and handed it to the Mayor who smiled and put it in his inside pocket. 'Anyway the rest is history, with your efficient cooperation, of course. And now we have the publicity and church opposition. It's all working exactly as you predicted, Luis. Congratulations!'

'Oh, I can just see it now. A protest outside, TV cameras, publicity,' said the Mayor. 'Publicity that we couldn't buy! Whisky?'

'Please.'

The Mayor poured the malt and handed one to Amores.

'How did you know how Afonso would react?' Amores asked, taking an appreciative sip from his glass.

'Oh, he's predictable; you know Afonso. Only wants to make the church relevant to the people. Now he has his chance, the revolutionary hot-head.'

'Oh, Luis I'm counting the extra money already......' Amores chuckled.

'From the publicity?'

'No, I'm thinking about how much Hallworth will pay to stop us rescinding the licence on the grounds of outraging public decency.....He paid us to set it up and he'll pay to keep it open. He has to; he's invested too much to see it close. You can rescind the license a few days after the shop opens, blame the Bishop or something like that; Hallworth needs to understand that he can't do anything without us. He'll keep paying.'

The Mayor nodded in approval. 'Yes, I understand. I think that will be no problem. But I was also thinking about tourism; attracting more visitors to Carvoeiro. That's good for the village and good for my re-election.'

'Ah, you politicians,' mused Amores. 'A sex shop isn't going to attract more visitors; it will only make sure that the ones you have are a bit happier. What about the pilgrims?'

'Oh that bunch of nutters. What were you thinking?'

'Well, it's obvious. Have you been to Fátima? It's full of shops selling religious tack. That's my next plan. I'm going to open a Christian shop. It'll make a fortune.'

'Sounds fabulous,' said Mayor Luis with a lascivious grin.

'I assume the licence will be no problem?'

'Please, António. You merely have to say the word.' The Mayor drained his glass before moving onto the next point of his strategy. 'I hear that the Bishop is not happy with Carvoeiro becoming another Fátima. Personally, I have nothing against him, but it occurs to me that whilst we've got the TV cameras here, why not wheel out that girl they're all trying to worship? Then word will really get about. More pressure on the sex shop.'

'Publicity for the cult.'

'More money from Hallworth,' said Mayor Luis, reading Amores's mind

'More visitors for Carvoeiro,' said Amores, imagining himself as Mayor.

'....and bugger the Bishop!' said Mayor Luis, who was so happy he wanted to dance. Or at least give thanks to a bountiful God who would make it all possible.

Six weeks later Cockatoo was ready to be exposed to the world. The outfitters had finished, the stock had arrived from Ann Summers and Beate Uhse. The location was near the top of Rua do Farol, restaurant hill, and the shop front had been dressed by Rui, who had taken a tremendous pride in the colour-coordination; white, red and black, but tasteful so as not to offend the squeamish. A large sign proclaimed 'Cockatoo' with a winking art deco parrot on either side to ensure that everyone would understand the innuendo. Ursula was putting the finishing touches to the interior, which would be a shop for sexy underwear with the more risqué items in the back room. The champagne was on ice and the team had been assembled.

'Everything's perfect,' said Peter, surveying his masterpiece.

'Perfect,' said Ursula, putting her arm around Peter.

'C'est parfait,' said Rui and put his arm around Tim.

Two waiters dressed in white jackets stood guard at the door, armed with silver trays loaded with glasses of champagne.

'We haven't forgotten anything, have we?' asked Rui.

'Nah,' said Peter. 'All we have to do now is wait for the arrival of the invitees and the press. There should be about twenty, including the Mayor.' They went inside.

'You sure that there won't be any problems?' asked Tim.

'Oh, no. We got the licence didn't we? They wouldn't have given us the licence if they thought there would be a problem. This is a cosmopolitan village; half the people here are expats anyway. There's even a strip club here. What were you worried about? A sit-down protest? I don't think so.' He chuckled.

A few minutes later Ursula heard the sound of shouting from the bottom of the hill and went outside to see what the noise was.

'You won't believe this,' she called, looking back over her shoulder. 'Come out here and see what I can see.'

A small tide of black was surging up the hill holding banners. A priest in full regalia was in the lead, followed by members of his congregation and a hundred or so onlookers. Held high in the centre of the procession was the effigy of Nossa Senhora da Encarnação herself; the mother of God. Behind her, holding crosses high in the air, were two sinister representatives of the medieval Church wearing white conical hats with holes cut for the eyes. Bringing up the rear was a party of pilgrims in wheelchairs. Large scallop shells hung around their necks. They were all singing.

'Jesus, Joseph and Mary,' exclaimed Peter. 'It's the bleedin' Spanish Inquisition.'

By the time the procession had reached the shop, the road was in chaos with cars and two grumbling coaches trying to reverse but blocked by more traffic from the rear. Horns blared, drowning the singing. Walking alongside was a television crew carrying a large hand-held camera and a female reporter in an elegant grey suit wielding a large black spongy microphone.

'My God,' said Tim. 'TV cameras. Did you expect TV cameras?'

'No, I bloody didn't,' Peter exclaimed. 'Thought we'd be lucky to get a local journalist with a fuckin' Polaroid.'

'What are we going to do?' Ursula twittered.

'Dunno, my love. Let's ride it out. You know what they say? There's no such thing as bad publicity.'

'I think we're about to prove them wrong,' muttered Tim.

At that moment, Father Afonso walked over to the group standing outside the shop, champagne glasses in hand. He declaimed loud enough for the TV crew to catch his words.

'I am Father Afonso Gonçalves Mendonça of the church of Nossa Senhora da Encarnação and we are here to formally protest at the opening of this shop on the grounds of indecency.'

Peter kept his composure. 'Nice to meet you Father; my name's Peter Hallworth. Would you and your friends like to join us for some champagne?'

Whilst Afonso was trying to think of a dignified way to refuse, they were disturbed by shouting at the back of the procession and turned to see who it was.

'Let me through...let me through.' Mayor Luis had arrived. 'My damned car couldn't get through; had to walk....'

'I'm sorry, Senhor Mayor, I had no idea that our opening would be so popular,' said Peter.

'But they've blocked the entire centre of the village....,' complained the Mayor looking down the street.

'Peaceful protest; it's our democratic right, Senhor Mayor,' said Father Afonso serenely.

'Not in my bloody town it isn't,' said the Mayor and opened his mobile phone and called the GNR. Ignoring Father Afonso, he turned to Ursula and said, 'Now where is that champagne?'

Peter surveyed the demonstrators now sitting in the road when he heard a whispered voice behind him.

'Don't worry, Peter.'

He spun round and saw António Amores standing next to him.

'Don't worry,' he continued. 'It'll blow over. If they try to rescind the licence, I'll sort it out. They'll soon forget about it. Please don't worry.'

'You're a good man António,' said Peter with relief.

Twenty women, some middle-aged, some frail little old ladies were sitting down in the road. A few children ran in and out of them shouting and laughing. Surrounding them all were more pilgrims in wheelchairs, glaring at Peter with ancient offended eyes. In the centre, squatting by Nossa Senhora da Encarnação, was Father Afonso, like the swan in the middle of a medieval banqueting table. The Spanish Inquisition men had taken off their spiky hats and were cooling themselves with them. While no one was looking, they went into a bar on the other side of the road and ordered a couple of cold beers.

The TV crew mingled amongst the protesters as the police arrived, five in all, led by their sergeant, Carlos at his right hand side. Ursula's eyes brightened when she saw him. She raised her eyebrows in salute and he returned the gesture with an elfin smile. The sergeant turned to face the protesters, cleared his throat and asked them to disperse.

The protesters exchanged glances, then looked at the impassive figure of Father Afonso. No one moved. The sergeant surveyed their revolutionary faces and shuffled nervously, waiting for the first sign of weakness. The rest would surely follow, but nobody made the first move and they appeared to be resolute. He tried again. Again, nobody moved. The sergeant signalled to two of his officers who politely raised one of the women.

'Please, Dona Maria, you can't stay here,' he said, as his men carried her in silence to the side of the road. The hush was broken by a loud cheer from the crowd, saluting the protesters, encouraging them. The men went back for another and another until they had cleared three quarters of the protesters to the cheers of the growing crowd under the eyes of the cameras.

The next woman was about seventy. When two of the men came to her they were intimidated by the resolute expression on her face; gaze directly forward, wrinkled mouth clamped firmly closed. The police stood around her and then looked to the sergeant for inspiration. The old woman broke the silence and said simply,

'Carlos.'

The two men looked at each other, then back at her.

'Pardon, Senhora?'

'Are you deaf, Manuelo? I said Carlos. I want Carlos,' she said with dignity, still looking directly ahead.

They turned and shouted to Carlos.

'Carlos, she wants you for some reason.'

Carlos was by now hot and sweating and walked over to her like John Wayne entering a bar.

'I want you to take me, Carlos,' she whispered. He smiled, bent down, lifted her up and carried her, light as a feather, to the side of the road. As he put her down to the cheers of the crowd she whispered to a friend, 'Micaela, Micaela.......I...I....I think I just had an orgasm....,' She cackled hysterically.

The next woman remaining on the road said loudly, 'I want Carlos as well.' To the cheers from the crowd Carlos picked her up while the other policemen tried to persuade the remaining women to move. They all called for him noisily, 'Me next, Carlos! Me next....' Carlos smiled as the crowd cheered. He waved in acknowledgement. In the end there was only Father Afonso left sitting in the middle of the road. The policemen stood around the defiant figure.

At that moment, there was a shout from the edge of the crowd; Senhora Ramalho and Flavia appeared and silence descended like a shroud. The children stopped running and went to their mothers. The people parted as the pair walked slowly forward towards Afonso, Flavia looking at her fingers, wiggling them in front of her face. The only sound came from a few car engines at idle; the police were rooted to the spot as if to move would be sacrilege. A number of the people went down on their knees as she passed. Mother and daughter walked towards Afonso and sat down next to him. Flavia played with her shoelaces. The overcast sky broke momentarily and a shaft of sunlight illuminated the three of them; they looked up at the brilliant light. Flavia smiled; it was so beautiful. The TV cameras continued to roll.

Eight

Father Afonso felt as if he was being court-martialled. The Bishop was incandescent with rage as he paced up and down. Afonso had not been asked to sit.

'What possessed you to do such a thing? A sit down protest. I mean, really…..to behave like a bunch of bolshy students in front of television cameras. Really, Father; we'll never hear the end of this.'

'I am so sorry, Eminence. I thought that it would unite the congregation and make the church more relevant to their lives. It was an issue of principle. I didn't know the television cameras would be there.'

It hadn't seemed possible but the Bishop's face turned even redder.

'But you should have known that it would get out of control. Control, Father, that is what it's all about and you have failed miserably.' He paused to gather his thoughts then spoke in an icy tone. 'Have you ever considered a future in missionary work in Angola?'

Afonso was desolate; his intention had been good, but the reality had not been what he had expected; he had unleashed something terrible. Angola. Oh, please, God, no. The Bishop paced, trying to put his thoughts in order.

'To make matters worse, the day of the protest was a no-news day. Do you know what happens on no-news days, Father?'

'No, Eminence.' Afonso was sure that it would only be bad news for him.

'Well, let me tell you for future reference. When there are no big news stories, national TV companies look for something unusual at the local level. Then the global players start to get interested......'

'Global players, Eminence?' Afonso could see his career sinking without trace. No one would ever know that he had existed; his only mark on the world would be a neglected gravestone in some forgotten corner of Africa.

'Yes, you know, CNN, Al-Jazeerah, BBC World.'

Afonso swallowed. His mouth went completely dry.

The Bishop strode towards the window as if surveying a disappearing world. 'I hate CNN, but there are some that like it. Apparently, even in the Vatican there are those interested in what is happening outside those domed palaces.'

Afonso wanted to sink into the floor.

'Father,' the Bishop was now starting to sound weary and sat down behind his desk putting his head in his hands. He looked up and said quietly, 'Amongst those that like CNN, I regret to say, is his Holiness the Pope.'

Afonso wondered what Angola would be like.

The Bishop was silent for a moment, then raised his head and stared at Afonso.

'Oh, sit, for the love of God,' he snapped and Afonso sat. 'So, what are we going to do now?'

Afonso dredged his brain for an idea; something brilliant and intuitive. He prayed silently for the Holy Virgin to send inspiration. She did not reply.

'Eminence,' he stuttered, 'I thought I was doing the right thing. The sex shop is an affront......'

The Bishop sighed in frustration. 'I'm not talking about the sex shop, Father. I'm talking about your pilgrims. What are we going to do about your second headache?'

Afonso was taken aback. 'I don't know, Eminence. I've tried to talk to them and tell them that there's been no miracle and they smile knowingly as if I'm keeping some divine secret from them.'

'OK, let's try to list what we know,' said the Bishop, strumming his fingers on his desk top.

'Well, the first thing is the girl, Flavia,' said Afonso. 'People follow her about as if she's holy in some way. She was the girl who appeared at the end of the protest....'

'Yes, of course. How could I forget it?'

'She's one of my parishioners. Severely autistic.'

'OK,' said the Bishop, thoughtfully. 'Let's come back to her in a moment. I'm looking for something with more of a theological basis.'

'Well, there was Senhora Thérèse's cure, but that was put down to spontaneous remission. Believe me, Eminence, if the good Lord was going to favour anyone with a miracle, she would be close to the bottom of the list.'

'And?' The Bishop reached for a pencil and tapped it on the table.

'There's a belief that praying to the Holy Mother will bring riches.'

'Money or riches for the soul?'

'Money. In this world.'

'Ah....the love of money; the root of all evil. Is that it? There have been no visions?'

'Not as far as I am aware, Eminence.'

The Bishop put his pencil down and leaned forward towards Afonso. 'What about Saint James, Santiago?'

'Santiago, Eminence? I've never heard his name connected with the village. Santiago de Compostela, yes, but not in Carvoeiro.'

'The Vatican has heard differently,' said the Bishop, leaning back in his chair. 'You know, it was never confirmed that the bones at Compostela were those of Santiago. Legend has it that Santiago's remains were carried from Jerusalem to Northern Spain, but there are those who claim those to be the bones of Priscillian, a fourth century leader of an ascetic Christian sect. Executed for his beliefs.'

'But, Eminence, it's all legends and superstition. A relic of medieval beliefs that have survived because.....'

'Because the faithful want them to survive, Father. It's they who keep these things alive.' The Bishop stood up and started pacing again, stopping by the window, looking out of it.

'But what connection can Carvoeiro have to Santiago?' asked Afonso.

He turned back to Afonso. 'Apparently, according to the Vatican, there are rumours that his bones are resting in Carvoeiro somewhere.'

Afonso looked shocked.

'Can we be sure?'

The Bishop returned to his chair and resumed his pencil tapping. 'No, of course not. It's what they believe. Remember the scallop shells the pilgrims were wearing at your protest? They are the symbols of the pilgrimage to Santiago de Compostela. I'm sure you know that. The symbols of Santiago himself.'

'But, what if there's no foundation in fact, Eminence?'

'Believe me, Father, that won't stop them. If we don't react to this, we will have another Fátima on our hands.

Afonso slumped. This meeting was something that he had never envisaged when he had chosen to become a priest.

'So, what can we do?' he asked.

'Well, I think that doing nothing is now no longer an option.' The Bishop pursed his lips as he mulled through the choices. 'The girl. The autistic girl. Tell me about her.'

'Eminence. I've just remembered something.' The Bishop looked up expectantly as Afonso continued. 'Her mother once asked me whether someone like her could have no sin.'

The Bishop raised an eyebrow. 'Interesting concept. What did you say?'

'I can't remember exactly. Eminence. I think I said that it was a Muslim belief.'

The Bishop threw up his hands in frustration.

'And you wonder why they don't trust you?'

'I'm sorry. At the time I was late for the service. I didn't think. But the girl has followers, Eminence. One of them asked whether I could see the light coming from within her.'

'I don't see much light coming from you, Father, but I wonder if she is not the source of our problem.'

'You mean, that the pilgrims coming from outside could be coming to see her?' Afonso thought for a few seconds. 'Actually, they seem to show no interest in the girl. They come, they pray, they touch the shrine at the side of the beach, then they go. No one seems interested in an autistic girl except the people who hang about outside her house.'

'I suspect that your parishioners are protecting her from the pilgrims....... and possibly from you.'

'But her mother simply wants it all to end. She told me so.'

'OK, let's look at the options,' said the Bishop. He fell silent as he thought. Afonso waited for inspiration. The Bishop drew in his breath. Afonso saw him close his eyes in prayer and did the same.

After a while the Bishop opened his eyes and continued, in a voice sounding refreshed.

'I have it. There is only one option. We cannot wheel out a girl afflicted with severe autism as an example of God's infinite mercy. It would bring the Church into ridicule. There would be moves to beatify her. No, it would be too dreadful. We have to follow the mood of the moment and divert them.'

Afonso frowned, trying to follow the Bishop's line of thought.

'How do you mean, Eminence?'

'You have a shrine on the side of the cliff facing the beach, don't you?'

'Yes.....Nossa Senhora da Encarnação. It's a shrine for the fishermen. She watches over the sea.'

'Perfect. The healing waters. Encourage your pilgrims to focus on that. No commitment, no promises. They will provide that for themselves. As long as they can touch something and pray, they'll be content. Ordinary doctrine can be used, you don't have to invent anything, not that the Church would condone that, of course. They will only be asking for the intervention of the Holy Mother. They can do that anywhere they want, even on the street. In time, the whole affair will just wither away.'

Afonso was not sure that his parishioners would be so easily diverted, but was relieved that the Bishop was no longer talking about Angola.

'And Santiago?' he asked.

'Needs further investigation, Father. That's the next hurdle for us to overcome in our mission to control this phenomenon.' He stood up and walked to the window. 'Mission impossible,' he muttered under his breath.

Rui and Tim sat at the beach bar with Ursula, a jug of sangria, frosted and dripping, citrus-sweet, in the centre of the table. The spring sunshine blessed the beach, alive with children hooting and roaring. Next to the sunbathers a party of pilgrims was holding a prayer service whilst the invalids watched from their wheelchairs on the square.

At the table next to them sat an earnest young woman in a grey suit, sipping an orange cocktail with a miniature umbrella poking her in the nose as she read her book.

'...and what about that shaft of light?' said Rui. 'Stage-managed or what?'

'It even made Al-Jazeerah,' said Ursula.

The woman on the next table closed her book, turned to them and pushed her sunglasses down her nose.

'Excuse me, are you talking about the protest?'

Rui nodded.

'I was there,' she said.

Rui realised where he had seen her before. 'Yes, of course! You were the reporter with the television crew weren't you?' he said.

'Guilty as charged.' She smiled and extended an elegant hand with devilish red fingernails. 'Cristina. Cristina Soares.'

Rui took her hand, asked her to join them and introductions were made. Her face had a few of tracks of experience but her style spoke of Paris and Milan; she was as understated as a countess, conspicuously out of place amongst the shorts-and-teeshirt holidaymakers. A row of pearls hung around her neck; not too small to be unnoticed, not too big to be ostentatious.

'I know what you're thinking,' she said. 'Air-head from the TV. 'Actually,' she went on, 'I'm an investigative journalist and I'm keen to do an in-depth piece on the phenomenon that has gripped your village. I'll be staying for a few days.'

'Do you need somewhere to stay?' asked Rui.

'Yes. I didn't really have any plans. I suppose there's plenty of accommodation here.'

'There's a beautiful place on the top of the hill. It's absolutely fabulous. Wonderful sea views, everything,' said Rui enthusiastically.

'And a charming, if erratic, host,' added Tim.

Cristina got the message.

'Sounds like that's decided,' she said, smiling.

'Anyway, what kind of piece is it going to be?' asked Ursula. 'About the sex shop?'

'No, except in passing of course.' Ursula looked disappointed. 'No, I want to talk to anyone who knows about this miracle of yours. The pilgrims. Do you think the priest will talk to me? Do you know him?'

'The priest,' said Ursula in disgust. 'Hmmph.'

'Oh, yes,' said Tim. 'Everyone knows Afonso. He's a bloody trouble-maker.'

'Organised the protest over my shop,' said Ursula, resentfully.

'Your shop?'

'Yes. My shop. My own little project. Now no one dares to come in. We only took fifteen Euros yesterday. I'd hate the bloody priest if only he wasn't so cute.'

'And unmarried,' added Tim.

'OK, that's an interesting angle,' said Cristina, thinking it through. 'English entrepreneur defeated by conservative village. Wants to seduce local priest. Conflict between expats and locals. That's good, but it's not really what I wanted. I'm far more interested in the miracle.'

'As far as we can make out, there hasn't been a miracle,' said Tim. 'Only a load of pilgrims who think there's been one. Even they don't know what they're coming here for, but it's developed a life of its own. If there's been no miracle, I think they'd create one.'

'But, you know as well as I do that there's no smoke without fire,' prompted Cristina.

'It's nothing but superstitious nonsense,' said Ursula.

'Spoken like a true protestant,' Rui laughed.

'You don't believe in all that claptrap do you?'

'I'm Portuguese, I was brought up a Catholic……'

'Hmm,' said Cristina. 'I'm beginning to get a nice new slant on this whole story. Ursula, was it the sex shop that started all this?'

'No,' interjected Rui. 'It all started last year when my neighbour, the saintly mother Thérèse, found that she was able to walk again. She'd been a cripple.'

'Well, that's almost biblical,' said Cristina. 'Tell me more. Is she the focus for this adoration?'

'God, no,' said Tim. 'She's a witch. It was spontaneous remission, apparently. Anyway, mother Thérèse is not exactly the kind of woman who God would choose for a miracle, unless it was to cause her to spontaneously combust. She should be burnt at the stake.'

'She's not religious?'

'Oh yes, she worships all right; she worships money,' said Rui bitterly. 'She accused me of stealing two thousand Euros from her. That's never been solved. Another bloody miracle.'

'Ah, village life,' Cristina mused.

George Hatton was a dapper man in his sixties who ran the English language bookshop in the village. Books were his life and he loved to be surrounded by them; they were like children and he almost resented it when someone came into the shop to foster some of them. It was small and as untidy as any bookshop dating from the time before Waterstone's and had that indefinable smell of age and intellect particular to a library; an aroma that asks to be breathed, as if the spirits within the books' covers could be inhaled. There were bookracks against all the walls and others in the centre of the shop making progress around the shop difficult. More books stood in unstable and irregular piles surrounding the desk. Sitting on the only other chair was a world-weary Peter. George emerged from the back room with two cups of steaming coffee and joined him.

'He isn't a bad man, you know,' said George.

'He's a fucking priest, I'm not saying he's bad, he's got God on his side; I just wish he'd get out of my face. We didn't need that protest; it completely fucked up the opening and made us look stupid. Ursula says that everyone's too frightened to come into the shop now.'

'You need to see things from Afonso's perspective,' said George. 'I've known him since he was a teenager and I've been here long enough to know the mentality. You know, they're torn between wanting the money that tourism brings but not wanting to lose something precious that the Portuguese have. You mustn't underestimate the resentment here against expats. I've been here for twenty years, but I'm still not a local. Never will be.'

'Well, how long will it take them to change?' asked Peter.

'Do you really want them to change?' said George with raised eyebrows. 'Think about it. You are here rather than being in England; so am I. We choose to live here. Why? Even if we are not consciously aware of it, we are tacitly accepting that they have a point. Frankly I think that if Portugal became like France or Germany, it would lose its charm. If everything worked like in Germany or people were punctual or reliable…..we're trying to impose our values on them. Don't do it, accept their values and you'll be much happier, believe me.'

'I only wanted to set up a small shop,' Peter protested. 'Surely even the Catholics have sex.'

'Maybe, but the birth rate is falling and they point to condoms and liberal values. It's the beginning of the end for them. In thirty, even twenty, years the country will be quite different. Glad I won't be here to see it, quite frankly,' said George, looking out of the window.

'You're not blaming us, surely? It's only a small shop……..'

'No, of course not, but it's a focus for their resentment, Peter. Be careful. Don't make them hate you.'

The phone rang and George answered it, then looked surprised.

'It's for you, Peter.'

Peter took the receiver and listened.

'No, no…it's not possible….after only four days?… the Bishop? What's it got to do with the fucking Bishop?…….I don't believe it……..OK, I'll be over in a few minutes.'

'Not bad news I hope,' said George, his brow furrowed.

'The worst kind, George,' Peter said angrily, standing up. 'Apparently a man from the *Camara* was at the shop five minutes ago and closed it; the licence has been rescinded.'

Two weeks later, the sign outside Cockatoo was still dark and large sheets of paper had been placed over the windows; a shop in mourning, passively defending itself against the world. The unit next door was a complete contrast, buzzing with activity. The door was open and from the lit interior came the shrieking sounds of power tools and hammering, music and animated conversation.

Rui and Tim were making their way up the hill towards Cockatoo and Tim paused to peer in through the slightly open door.

'It's going to be the new Christian shop,' explained Rui.

They continued to Cockatoo. Rui pushed open the door and Tim followed him in. Ursula was sitting behind the desk like a queen bee and stood up to greet them effusively. After placing a livid red lipstick imprint on Tim's cheek, she wagged her finger to caution him against wiping it off before returning to her desk where she resumed tapping on the keyboard with long finger nails.

Cockatoo had become an outpost for George's mail order business. For him, the interest was in tracking down hard-to-find books but he couldn't be bothered with all the parcelling up and posting, so had asked Rui to do it. As there was no spare space in George's shop, Rui handled it from the back room of the redundant sex shop. It allowed George to read and drink coffee whilst providing a little pocket money for Rui. It was a good arrangement.

When Rui had told Peter and Ursula, they'd been forced to agree. In fact, they thought that it was such a good idea that they decided to take a leaf out of George's book. Internet businesses don't need licenses, they can't cause offence to the feeble-minded and, in addition, it would be difficult for the Church to organise a sit-down protest in cyberspace. Ursula had rapidly become computer-literate.

'Come on, you can help me with George's backlog,' said Rui, leading Tim into the back room.

Tim surveyed the piles of books in one corner of the room and his eyes wandered to the sexy boxes on the table, waiting to be parcelled up. He raised his eyebrows in approval.

'Can I have a look at the Cockatoo website?' he asked. Ursula overheard him.

'Yeah, I'll find it for you,' said Ursula, untangling the mouse. 'Come and have a look,' she said as Tim joined her, craning over her shoulder. Changing places with Ursula, his face glowed in the reflected light from the screen.

'Oh, yes, this is good. Who put this together?'

'Company in Lagoa,' said Ursula nonchalantly.

'Ah, nice pix of the girls. Who did the photography? Ann Summers?'

'No, actually it was done by Carmencita. You know, the stripper. In addition to having prize-winning tits, she's also a prize-winning photographer.'

'Ah!' exclaimed Tim. 'Who's the guy? You can't see his face.' He tabbed from page to page.

'I thought you might like him,' said Ursula playfully.

'Yeah, but who is it?' asked Tim

'I think he's someone that Carmencita knows,' said Ursula. Tim looked at her and waited for more but all he got was an evasive glance and a suppressed smile which made the corners of her mouth pucker. He turned back to the screen as Rui joined him.

'Jeesus. An orgasm with every mouse-click,' said Tim slightly out of breath. 'Sexy guy. He's probably frightened that he'll be declared a god and have pilgrims trailing after him all over town on their hands and knees.....and I'd probably be one of them.'

Rui glowered at him.

The response to the Cockatoo internet business had been so good that, within two weeks, they'd placed an order for additional stock, Ursula hoped it would arrive on time to meet their orders. Rui was still processing the remainder of George's orders which were being pushed more and more into the corner of the stock room.

Ursula collapsed into her chair behind the unused counter and fiddled with the mouse, wondering whether she should turn the computer off to stop the flow of work.

'Rui, I'm exhausted,' she moaned. 'Five more orders have just come in.'

At that moment George came in with a pile of books and handed them to Rui.

'Sorry for these coming in late, but they've only just arrived.' He put them down on the floor and picked one from the top of the pile. 'This is a book on the Spanish Inquisition for Father Afonso. He's been waiting for it for weeks.'

By the end of the day, all the packages were in a large pile by the door, waiting to be taken to the post office. Rui stood up, stretched and loaded the Rav, then clambered in, revved up and was off down the road in a trail of dust.

Ursula sat down behind the computer to check if there were any more orders. Her fingers froze on the keyboard as a terrible thought occurred to her. She hurried back into the stock room, shuffling through the debris of paper and handwritten notes.

When Rui got back, he found her wide-eyed and flustered, 'Rui, I've had a horrible premonition. You know how we write the order number on the parcel, then cover it up with the address label....'

'Yes,' he said slowly almost as a question.

'Well, I wrote some and you wrote some; we couldn't have got confused could we?'

'How? It's a perfect system. It's foolproof.'

'Yeah, I thought so too....but with our different ways of writing '1' and '7.''

Rui felt the first stirrings of doubt.

'Shall we check the paperwork? Just to be safe?'

They checked through the pile of orders and invoices. At first they seemed to be OK, then Ursula came across one where the numbers did not tally, then another, then another.

'Rui, what is Georges's stock number 101?'

Rui searched for it on the computer. 'It's, let me get this right, the *'Historical Revision of the Spanish Inquisition'* by Kamen, Henry. Sounds like a load of laughs.'

'Rui, what's our stock number 707?'

'It's Big Ben.'

'Big Ben?'

'Yes, a ten inch black silicon rubber dildo.'

'And who is customer number 7108?'

'Cockatoo doesn't have a customer 7108. We haven't been in business that long.'

Ursula gulped as the full horror hit her.

'So,' she swallowed, 'I don't really want to ask this question....'

'I think you should...' said Rui.

'Who is Georges's customer 7108?'

Rui searched again on the computer. A name appeared on the screen. His expression turned to one of impotent panic.

'Oh shit, Oh God, Oh buggery buggery bugger....' he gasped. 'It's Father bloody Afonso Gonçalves Mendonça.'

Nine

Rui hared over to the Post Office but, for once, the mail had left on time. He cursed and fumed his way back to Cockatoo.

'Well, this will probably be our last day in business,' he said gloomily, slamming the door behind him to keep the world away. Ursula had been checking the paperwork again.

'What's the damage?' asked Rui.

'It reads like a charge sheet,' Ursula groaned. 'First, a ten inch black silicon rubber dildo to God's representative on earth and our greatest enemy in the world. I can feel the wrath of all the angels in heaven as we speak; the chanting of demons and the crackling of the flames of hell. He'll never believe that it was a mistake.'

'Next?' asked Rui, not really wanting to know the full scale of the disaster.

'Oh, I can hear the judge reading this one,' she said putting her handkerchief on her head. 'Rui Fernandes, did you or did you not on the fifteenth of April, with malice aforethought, supply to The Right Honourable Mr Sebastian Prendergast, MP (retired) a Cherry Picking Cami Suspender Basque, Red, and Pipa Crotchless Skirt when he had, in fact, ordered the book *The Shock Doctrine; the Rise of Disaster Capitalism* by Naomi Klein?'

'Guilty, m'lud,' pleaded Rui, then as an aside, 'but I imagine his wife will be pleased.'

Ursula picked up another order form.

'Come on,' said Rui. 'Let's hear the full charge sheet.'

'Are you ready for this? OK, here we go. Seven-piece fantasy kit and fur love cuffs in place of *Maximum Ride: School's Out*, Rampant rabbit three-way in place of *Watership Down*, Durex tingle, tingle condoms and little gem in place of *An analysis and History of Inflation*, edible cock ring in lieu of *Harry Potter* collector's set. There are more. Shall I go on?'

'Have you got a letter opener so I can slash my wrists?' asked Rui.

'Yes, but I think it's too blunt.'

'That's OK, it's only a cry for help.'

'What shall we do? Do you think we should tell George?' muttered Ursula without conviction.

'What? And give him a heart attack?'

'What about Father Afonso, then?'

Rui tried to picture the scene. It was too horrible to contemplate. He sank into the chair and put his head in his hands.

'Let's see what happens *amanha*.'

'*Amanha*?' asked Ursula.

'It's like *mañana* but without the same sense of urgency,' explained Rui.

'Well, there's nothing we can do now except wait for the phone to ring or the police to call round. We've got about three days of freedom left,' sighed Ursula in a voice full of resignation, 'then it's a long sentence in the gulag followed by eternity in hell.'

The next day, Ursula was sitting in Cockatoo miserably contemplating her fate that was dependent only on the delivery time of the Portuguese mail service. She knew that she was in the eye of the hurricane. Sounds of activity were emanating from the Christian shop next door. Rui walked in, looking more cheerful than was strictly necessary, like a man with a revolving bowtie at a funeral.

'Hello darling.' Ursula pouted. 'Come and cheer me up.'

Rui gave her a big hug and she smiled.

'What's happening next door?'

'The God Squad. They've just taken delivery of some stock. Opening tomorrow, apparently. Cristina's very interested. She says it will give her story a new slant. You know, sex shop against Church, expats against locals.'

'Is she still staying with you?'

'Yes, she loves it. But I think that what she loves most is seeing Carlos.'

'Carlos?' said Ursula abruptly.

'Yeah. You know he comes around every day on patrol, but it's really to see Paula. She's still playing hard to get. God knows why. I mean, I'd shag him without a second thought, but she says she wants it to be special. She'd better make her move soon or he's going to drift off.'

'In the direction of Cristina?' asked Ursula, a tone of jealousy in her voice.

'Oh I don't know. Cristina knows about Paula, of course, but she's a sophisticated woman. She's one of those types who sees what she wants and goes for it. Bit like you, I suppose.'

'Too much like me,' muttered Ursula.

As he left, Rui paused by the Christian shop. The paper had been taken down from the window to reveal a display of bibles, lurid crucifixes and statuettes of Our Lady of Fátima. The door was open and he peered in curiously. Inside were two men, the shorter one dapper in a suit and the other in jeans and teeshirt, his broad back towards Rui.

'Can I help you?' asked the suit, noticing Rui.

'Just curious,' said Rui. The second man turned around and Rui recognised Ben Chilcott.

'Ben? Ben! What are you doing here?' asked Rui in astonishment.

'Rui?' Chilcott was hesitant, fighting for words. 'I....I......what are you doing here?'

'I live here. Remember?'

The suit stepped in. 'We're business associates. And you are?'

Ben had recovered his composure. 'He's Rui Fernandes. He's an old mate from South Africa, aren't you Bro?'

Rui had a dark premonition of Chilcott meeting Tim and realised that the threat was now in his own village.

'Are you just visiting, Ben?'

'Yeah. Foreign soil. Dr Amores and I do a little business together. We had a business meeting.'

'Dr António Amores?' asked Rui.

The suit was surprised. 'Yes, I'm António Amores. How do you know my name?'

'Through Peter. Peter Hallworth. You arranged for the licence for the sex shop. He speaks very highly of you.'

Something flickered in Amores's eyes.

'Yes. I'm sorry to hear the bad news. I'm sure we can sort something out over the licence. I recommend that you give it time.' He smiled like a snake. 'Do you work at the sex shop?'

'No, not really. Well, yes, I suppose so…in a way.'

As he spoke a small smartly dressed young woman entered and set her handbag on the counter.

'The new manageress,' said Amores. 'Would you excuse us?'

Rui left in a state of confusion. What was Ben Chilcott doing with Amores, respected top solicitor Dr Amores, a pillar of local society? What was he doing in Carvoeiro? What could they possibly have in common? Then he remembered Tim again. Shit, Ben in Carvoeiro. He resolved again that the two would never meet. But it was going to be harder and harder now.

After Rui had left, Amores ushered Chilcott into the stockroom.

'OK. Who is he?' he snapped.

'Like I said, António, he's an old friend,' said Chilcott in a conciliatory tone.

'Friend? I thought you didn't have friends.'

'Oh, nasty,' said Chilcott. 'Acquaintance, then. Our paths crossed in South Africa.'

'Did you know him well?'

Chilcott gave a bark of laughter.

'Yeah, better than he knows.'

'And he knows you?' asked Amores.

'Oh, yeah. He had a few bad habits; the kind that got him into trouble.' Chilcott lit a cigarette and offered one to Amores, who took it wordlessly.

'Drugs?'

'Yeah. Amongst other things. He didn't know it, but I was his supplier. He was an escort. A rent boy. He was popular, his customers liked drugs. I did quite well out of him.'

Amores narrowed his eyes.

'Well I'm concerned about what he might know; what he might remember about you.'

'He knows nothing. He can't even remember me, he was so fucked in the head in Johannesburg, believe me. He's still trying to work out who I am.' Chilcott chuckled.

'So he's not going to see you and me talking business in a shop selling Christian tack and put two and two together? Exactly how stupid do you think I am?' spat Amores.

'António, believe me. Take it easy. He's a lot more dumb than you could believe. Christ. He even drove through Soweto with his doors unlocked.'

'How do you know that?'

'Because it was my guys that carjacked him and almost killed him. He had been sourcing his own drugs and started treading on our toes, so I organised a few kaffers to teach him a lesson.'

'He didn't know it was you?'

'No, he has no idea. We're best mates, drinking buddies now, António.'

'What, here?'

'No, in Portimão. Whenever his boyfriend's not here. He's shit scared I'll meet the boyfriend. It's pathetic really; I can see it in his eyes. I mention his past every time, simply to see that look of fear. I'm sure that the boyfriend has no idea what he was getting up to in

Jo'burg. Anyway, Rui has actually been cooperative; he even gave me the contact details of someone who's been muscling in on our turf.'

'That was kind of him. Who is it?'

'Small dealer, name of Chico; I'll sort him out.'

Amores was silent for a moment. 'You're not sleeping with Fernandes are you?'

'No, that was only a fling; all in the past.' Then he hesitated and looked at Amores. 'You're not jealous are you?'

Three days later the phone started to ring. Ursula answered the first call.

'Yes, certainly madam. I'll do that. Good bye.' She put the phone down, looking confused.

'Well, well, tell me….tell me….' said Rui.

'That was Dona Ana Costa complaining that her underwear didn't arrive and could we please send her some more.'

'Well, that's very reasonable. But wait until the Rt Hon Sebastian Prendergast phones.'

But after a week, the Rt Hon Sebastian Prendergast still hadn't phoned. The only calls were from people who had not received the clothes and toys that they had ordered.

The door jingled open and a bow-tied George came in with another pile of books and paperwork.

'Hello, morning, how's business?'

'OK….' said Ursula nervously. 'George, have you had any complaints?'

'Well yes, now that you mention it. There were a couple from people who had received books that they hadn't ordered, but they blamed the post and are sending them back. Is everything all right?'

'Oh, yes, George,' said Ursula. 'Everything's perfect.'

António Amores arrived in his office and his secretary told him that a parcel had been delivered. He examined it; it felt like a book.

Unwrapping it, he saw that it was indeed a book. *Cocaine Nights; J G Ballard.* He flicked through the pages and read the synopsis on the flysheet. His secretary leaned over.

'Oh, that's very good, Doctor, I read it last year. Very dark. You'll enjoy it.'

He ignored her and continued reading. As soon as his secretary left, he picked up the phone.

'Ben, Ben, it's a crisis; we need to take action soon. They're onto us. I've had a threat in the post.'

Rui, Tim, Ursula, Peter were sitting with friends under the gazebo outside Scamps, their faces dappled by the shadows and colours filtering through the canopy. A cooling spring breeze drifted in from the sea, which lapped lazily, sparkling in the sunlight. More drinks arrived and were distributed around the table. Rui was devouring a packet of Nachos.

'So the crisis is over,' said Peter, almost as a question.

'So it seems. There was no crisis in the end,' said Ursula. 'We waited by the phone. Manning the barricades to repel boarders, and nothing happened. We thought that the sky would fall in but it just stayed there, all blue and gorgeous. I really don't understand it.'

'...and there was no comeback from Father Afonso?' continued Peter. 'I really can't believe that. Maybe the dildo got lost in the post. Gawd, that was my worst nightmare come true.'

'Well, maybe someone up there likes us,' said Ursula, stirring her cocktail. 'And George didn't seem that bothered either. Says all his customers have turned into the Stepford Wives. Personally I think it's something in the water.'

George appeared, coming up the stairs followed by a figure in black; it was Father Afonso.

'Oh gawd,' said Peter under his breath, 'look what George's dragged in. What the fuck does he think he's doing?'

'Ladies and gentlemen,' said George, standing in front of them. 'I have decided that it was about time you found out what a nice chap Father Afonso really is. Please be gentle with him; he's fragile and outnumbered. Besides which, he has been addressing his congregation and is in need of some sustenance.'

'........and don't mention anything about dildos...... Schtum,' whispered Peter to Ursula.

Father Afonso looked like a Papal emissary. He smiled at them weakly and appeared self-conscious as he sat down next to Ursula. Removing his jacket, he revealed a short-sleeved white shirt and pale hairy forearms. Next to come off was his waistcoat and dog collar and he undid the top two buttons of his shirt. He was as pale as the high-born Portuguese whose bloodline had never been tainted by the continent to the south. Ursula was always interested in new young men, especially when one had metamorphosed in a few seconds from caterpillar to butterfly right in front of her eyes. Even one that she would, in other circumstances, want to kill.

'Father,' said Ursula, 'I should hate you for what you did to my shop.'

Afonso looked sheepish and ill at ease. She continued after letting her words sink in. 'But George has presented you as a peace offering and the best we can do is to be business-like. Now, answer me one question,' she said, glancing around at the others. 'Are you married?' A wicked grin spread over her face.

Afonso realised that the ice had been broken and sighed with relief.

'Madame, I am completely chaste,' he said in a perfect English accent.

'Chaste or chased?' asked Ursula.

'Well, maybe a bit of both,' suggested George, smiling. 'Please excuse them, Afonso, they've been drinking.'

'How come you speak such perfect English?' asked Ursula, edging closer to Afonso.

He twitched as one of her breasts touched his arm. 'I studied in England for two years; Worth Abbey. Benedictine monastery. I really enjoyed it; beautiful countryside, lovely people.'

'Got over the protest yet, Father?' asked Peter, bypassing pleasantries. He still harboured a grudge and blamed Afonso for the closure of the shop.

'The less said about that, the better, Mr Hallworth. In retrospect, it was a mistake and I apologise. George has told me, and I agree with him, that this is a village and it would be better if everyone got on together. I don't know about you, but I think that we have to separate the issues from the people. We can disagree on issues but I hope that perhaps we can be friends.' George applauded.

'Oh…..I hope so, Afonso,' said Ursula, fluttering her large false eyelashes. Peter looked worried.

Ursula turned to Rui and whispered, 'Rui, he's gorgeous, just gorgeous! I've never really seen him close-up before. Now that he's stripped off, he's lovely. I want to take him home and put him on a silk cushion!'

Turning to Afonso, Rui said, 'There's something I've always wanted to ask a priest…..the celibacy…Afonso. That must be such a turn-off.' He believed that all priests were gay and that was why no fuss had been made over the dildo.

Afonso shrugged. 'Uh, yes, of course. But you have to understand that being a priest is a vocation. It's God's work and you have to accept God's Will. I mean, I'd love to have a wife and children, but I love God more.'

'It's the church's will, Afonso,' said Tim. 'Jesus never said to St Peter, 'My father gave you a penis but you're not allowed to use it' did he? Even Popes had families a few hundred years ago.'

'Did somebody say penis?' said Ursula, taking a sudden interest in philosophy.

'We're discussing the fact that God gave priests penises but does not allow them to use them,' explained Tim, succinctly.

'In most cases it wouldn't make any difference,' she said to Afonso, her hand resting on his thigh, 'but in your case, darling, it's a crime against humanity.'

Afonso blushed, as bashful as a schoolboy. She continued, 'Afonso, darling, I've decided to become a nun. I urgently need some instruction. Will you come back to my place later and we can discuss it?'

Afonso glanced towards Peter who smiled condescendingly as if he'd heard her trying to seduce a priest every day.

'But speaking of penises,' said George, 'I believe that Afonso has something of yours, Peter.'

Afonso glanced at George, then away. All eyes were on him.

'Come on Afonso, we're waiting,' said George impatiently. Afonso seemed frozen, so George took the priest's briefcase, opened it theatrically and pulled out a long box. With the full attention of everyone round the table, he opened the box slowly and pulled out an enormous black dildo, raised it high so that everyone in the bar could see it, then placed it ceremoniously rampant on the table. He sat back and looked at it with a self-satisfied expression. People craned in their direction and the conversation went quiet. Rui squirmed in his seat and slowly raised his hand. Afonso lifted his eyebrows in expectation. He was starting to enjoy himself.

'Er; it wasn't Peter,' said Rui. 'It was me....it was a mistake; no one intended for it to happen. Mix-up in the post.'

'Ah,' said Afonso, savouring the moment. 'The road to hell is paved with good intentions. But the Church is forgiving. God's mercy is limitless.'

'And yours?' asked Peter.

'Likewise. And the church has a way of dealing with such sins.'

'Eternity in Purgatory?' asked Tim.

'No, my son. Confession,' said Afonso, correcting him with a raised finger.

'What? Here?' asked Rui.

'God is in all places, my son,' he said in his best pulpit voice.

'Ah,' said Rui. Everyone waited. The dildo waited.

Rui realised that there was no escape, took a deep breath and said, 'Fatherforgivemeforlhavesinned.'

Father Afonso sat back, rubbed his chin and said, with an expression of immense seriousness, 'And how long has it been since your last confession, my son?'

'I can't exactly remember, but Abba were in the charts, Father.'

Afonso smiled. '....and what is the nature of your sin, my son?'

Rui pointed at the dildo and looked at Afonso with the expression of a chastised puppy.

'And, are you truly sorry?' said Afonso with gravity.

Rui nodded but would have been happier hiding under the table.

'My son, God forgives those who truly repent. Your sins are forgiven. For your penance you will purchase for me one copy of *'Historical Revision of the Spanish Inquisition'* by Henry Kamen, and recite twenty Hail Marys,' then aside he said to the crowd, 'but in this instance sentence will be commuted to one, as long as I get the book within seven days.'

Rui's expression changed to one of uncertainty.

'I'm waiting, my son,' said Afonso and sat back in anticipation.

Rui realised that he was serious and took a deep breath.

'*Ave Maria, gratia plena, Dominus tecum. Benedicta tu in mulieribus, et benedictus fructus ventris tui, Iesus.* Taking another deep breath, he continued, '*Sancta Maria, Mater Dei, ora pro nobis peccatoribus, nunc et in hora mortis nostrae. Amen.*' He finished breathlessly and the bar erupted in applause.

Senhora Ramalho was counting the money in a sombre corner of her apartment; seventeen hundred Euros were left. She glanced out of her window at the shadowy forms moving past her net curtains like spectres. She felt trapped and Flavia was fractious; it was getting more and more difficult to leave the place because of the adoration of the pilgrims. She wanted things to be as they were, when they could walk around the village unnoticed or at least unmolested. If she had to choose between the isolation before to her present situation, she would take isolation.

She looked at the money and it looked back at her. She thought that it had been a gift from God, but she now knew that it had been a test. A test of her faith and fortitude. What should she do with it? She could spend it, of course, but when it was gone it would be gone and so would be evidence of the gift or the test, whichever it was, and she would have failed. What did God want her to do? A thought occurred to her. There was a better way. She would give it to Father Afonso. He could use it for some purpose that God would approve of; then the holy money would find a sacred home and she would be free of it; her soul intact.

She gathered the notes together, put them in a plastic supermarket bag and dressed Flavia.

'Come, *queridinha*, we are going to see Father Afonso.'

Later that day, Rui was sitting with Afonso in his apartment, downing a coffee as the sun poured through the window. After the dildo episode they had become unlikely friends. How bizarre that a lapsed catholic and a priest could have formed a relationship over a plastic penis. Afonso was smiling like a small boy on Christmas day.

'So she gave you all that money?' said Rui. 'Seventeen hundred Euros? But she doesn't have two beans. Where did she get it from?'

Afonso shrugged.

'She told me that it was a gift from God to Flavia. Then she said that she wanted to give it to the Church because it might make the pilgrims leave her alone.' Afonso seemed satisfied with the outcome.

'Oh, I don't think the Lord would bother printing money,' said Rui. 'I wouldn't ask where it came from. I think I'd spend it.'

'Yes, but, come on, Rui. We're rational people. Whilst I like to believe in the infinite bounty of the Lord's love, it's far more likely that this money belongs to someone else, isn't it?'

'Ah, yes! Now you mention it, I lost seventeen hundred Euros……..' Afonso gave him a sceptical look. Rui hesitated as a thought came to him. 'Actually, Afonso, I do know of someone who lost some money last year…….Thérèse next door; she lost two thousand Euros.'

Afonso looked grim.

'Do you think we should get some advice from the professionals?' he asked.

Carlos arrived thirty minutes later and counted the money.

'We should talk to Thérèse, Afonso. She's the only person in the village who has reported a theft of this size.'

All three went around to Thérèse's house and pushed their way past a group of pilgrims stationed outside her house. Four were in wheelchairs. Three more were on their hands and knees crawling up the hill.

Thérèse came to the door, furious.

'Yes, what do you want?'

'We wanted to talk to you, Senhora,' said Carlos, removing his cap.

'And I want to talk to you. Those bloody pilgrims. Always standing outside my house. Their wheelchairs are stopping my guests from parking. I found one this morning trying to remove one of my scallops. I really don't know what's going on. I need a police guard outside, Carlos, that's what I need. Do you know, two of them tried to stay in my rooms yesterday. They wanted to get inside the house. As soon as I found out, I threw them out. After they'd paid, of course.'

Afonso looked at the pilgrims. 'But Senhora, don't you feel any sympathy for them? You were crippled once yourself.'

'Yes, I was, and I got better on my own. And I didn't stand outside someone else's house, stealing seashells, muttering and praying to Mother Mary.' Afonso sighed and shook his head.

'Senhora,' said Carlos. 'I think we have some good news for you.' He proudly presented the money. She gazed at it in delight.

'Yes, Carlos, it's mine. Look. I put a little mark on the corner of each hundred Euro note in case there are any misunderstandings when I am in a shop; once I handed one over and the shopkeeper said it was only a fifty; I couldn't prove him wrong.'

With great reluctance, Afonso handed over the money, hoping that Thérèse might make a generous donation to the church that had recovered it. Thérèse gathered the notes together and took out her cash box, opening the lid.

Rui recognised the old cash box.

'I thought that cash box had been stolen, Thérèse.'

'Yes it was, but Carlos found it and brought it to me…..oh……months ago.'

'But you accused me of taking it…….' said Rui.

'Rui, I did not,' said Thérèse in protest. 'The police thought that you were the most likely suspect. I had nothing to do with it.'

Bitch, thought Rui. He turned to Carlos.

'Carlos? You didn't tell me that the box had been found....'

'I must have forgotten, Rui.'

Yes, you bastard, thought Rui. You forgot it all the time you were shoving my money up your nose. All those months and you knew that I wasn't guilty or even a suspect. Carlos avoided his glowering stare.

'Carlos,' said Thérèse, 'you told me that you found fingerprints on the box.'

'Yes, yours and mine and some we haven't been able to identify.'

'Well there's still two hundred Euros missing. Don't you think that the woman who gave the money to Father Afonso should have her fingerprints taken? She's the thief and she's probably got my other two hundred Euros.'

'Well, then what, Thérèse?' said Carlos. 'You have most of the money. Can't we leave it at that?'

'Carlos. You are a policeman and you know that whether I have the money or not is immaterial; a crime has been committed. She's a thief. She should be prosecuted. Perhaps it was that idiot daughter of hers.'

Carlos raised his eyes to heaven for inspiration.

'Hey, Carlos,' said Rui, 'You know what this means don't you? You've solved your first case. Congratulations. And please note that it wasn't me.'

Carlos shrugged, trying to avoid Rui's accusing stare.

'I'm not sure whether I can claim that, Rui. It was Father Afonso who recovered the money. In a way, the crime solved itself,' said Carlos.

Rui realised that he wasn't going to get an apology. He was disappointed in Carlos and angry at his own stupidity for having allowed their little arrangement to carry on for so long. Afonso looked disappointed too and Rui thought the cause might be more than having to hand over the cash. Then he realised what it was; the money part of the mystery was all over. Perhaps Afonso had secretly wanted it to be true, something to reinforce his faith; the first miracle of the twenty-first century. But it was just a few Euro notes, stolen but recovered. No miracle at all.

'Cheer up, Afonso,' said Rui.

'What do you mean?'

'There's still Santiago,' said Rui alluding to what remained of the miracle.

'And the healing,' said Afonso.

'Claptrap,' said Thérèse sharply.

They watched her sorting the notes into her box, Afonso's eyes following her every move.

'Oh, Father, there's one more thing. I have a small donation to make,' said Thérèse. Afonso's expression changed. His prayers had been answered.

She delved into the bottom of the cash box and pulled out a tiny object. 'It's this little crucifix that was in the cash box when Carlos returned it. I thought you might like it.'

Cristina was upstairs on the balcony when Rui returned. She was sitting under her blue umbrella in bikini and elegant shades, sipping from a chilled glass. Rui breezed in and slumped into the other chair and updated her.

'Senhora Ramalho still claims that it was a gift from God,' said Rui. 'She says it appeared, out of the blue.'

'It was probably Flavia, wasn't it?'

'Yes, almost certainly. But she can't talk, so I guess that will remain part of the mystery.'

'So the case is closed?' asked Cristina, disappointed.

Rui shook his head with a grimace.

'No, not really. Thérèse wants to have Senhora Ramalho prosecuted.'

'My God. The evil bitch. Village life! I thought we had it all in Lisbon but this place is so much more interesting. And the police? What does Carlos think?'

Rui looked at her and wondered how deeply she had insinuated her way into the life of the village. 'You don't mind my asking, Cristina, but have you……….?'

He detected a suggestion of satisfaction on her half-smiling lips. They parted as if she was going to say something, then closed again and she grinned more broadly, concealing something deliciously covert. She took a sip of her drink, trying to force back a laugh, then raised her eyes to him again, composure restored.

'We're getting off the subject, Rui. What do you think the police will do now?'

'Oh I think Carlos intends to celebrate. It's his first case and he solved it. He's been trying to shag Paula for months. Tonight could be the night.'

'Lucky girl,' said Cristina, but she said it in a way that hinted at prior possession; the slightest intimation of jealousy.

'Lucky boy,' said Rui, to set the record straight.

Paula waited expectantly by the window, dressed in a crimson printed blouse that flattered her breasts and knew that she looked good. Her make-up was impeccable and she had put on her most expensive perfume. Part of her was nervous with anticipation but she was excited at the same time. In the past, when she had been out with boys, she hadn't felt like this; it had been pleasant, but she had never felt such a magnetic attraction. Sex had been recreational, almost mechanical; not the earth-moving experience that she knew was out there. Whenever she felt Carlos's eyes on her, she felt a frisson of excitement, as if destiny had a grander plan for them. Of course, he was attractive; he was probably the best looking man in Carvoeiro. Knowing that she could see past superficiality, she wasn't sure what she would find on the other side. It was not going to be an ordinary evening. But she didn't know how Carlos would behave. He could irritate her with talk of football and macho idiocy; she had no control over him. But why should she simply follow the male lead? Why always go with the flow and do what the man wanted? Why not take control herself? She would be her own master; make her own decisions. Yes, it was going to be an exciting evening.

Carlos arrived smelling of shower gel and Eau Sauvage, wearing low-rise jeans, tight on his arse and a fitted short-sleeved white shirt buttoned only as far as decency required. He was trying to look at her face but she knew that her blouse made it difficult for him to concentrate; she smiled at how easy it was to manipulate a man. He put his arm around her to keep her warm in the chill of the evening air and his hand brushed almost accidentally against her breast as he led her to his battered old Fiesta.

Paula glanced sideways at his perfectly trimmed sideburns and freshly shaved face, then down his cleavage. He looked like an actor from a Brazilian *telenovela*. Catching her glance, he smiled back and opened the door for her. It opened with a strident creaking sound.

'Carlos,' she said crinkling her nose, 'have you been using this car for fishing?'

'That was yesterday,' he admitted, 'but I cleaned it out thoroughly.'

She was less than impressed; so much for perfection. 'Where shall we go?' she asked.

'I thought maybe the Sports Bar in Portimão,' he said settling into the driver's seat. 'I think they have Latin-American dancing tonight.'

Paula wondered why he hadn't chosen somewhere in Carvoeiro but remembered his reputation and guessed that he probably didn't want to be seen there with another woman. Never mind. The salsa night would take her back to the streets of Rio, the resonance of carnival in her mind; she liked to be infused with a mixture of *saudades* and euphoria; the untamed music and rhythms were part of her and she wanted to share them with Carlos so she could Brazilianize his world, one day at a time. She wanted him to understand her and know what made her; she wanted this to be a passage of discovery for them both.

They negotiated the narrow cobbled back streets of Portimão and finally found somewhere to leave the car. As they approached the Sports Bar, Paula's heart sank. Football. The place was a large brightly-lit bar on two floors with massive back-projection television screens in each bar. Normally the dancing would start at 10 pm and at least one room would be football-free. The bar was humid and crowded with a noisy good-natured throng watching the night's Benfica match. There was no sign of the Cuban dancer who would normally be setting up his sound system and Paula resigned herself to the fact that the dancing had probably been sacrificed. Carlos ordered a couple of drinks, a white wine for her, a beer for him, and waved to some friends across the bar to make sure that they realised that the beautiful creature next to him was his partner for the evening.

'Have you heard the news, Paula?' he said excitedly.

She shook her head. His shirt was tight across his back as he leant forward and his shoulder muscles strained against the fabric. His arms looked warm to touch; she could see the blood vessels below the surface and almost see his pulse. She wanted to touch them and feel their warmth…… and that chest hair, not too much, flat against the muscles of his chest, a hint of the satin sheen of sweat, the fragrance of male musk. Romance me, she thought. Romance me.

'I've solved the cash box crime, well, almost at any rate. It was the autistic girl's mother. We got the money back today. My first case; I'm so pleased!'

'Congratulations, Carlos; I'm so proud of you.' She held his hand and kissed his lips; it wasn't quite romance but it was a start. She looked around the bar. 'Carlos, do you really want to watch football tonight? Could something else take the place of football?'

Carlos was taken aback. 'Uh……actually, I wasn't thinking about football at all.'

'What would you really like to do, if you could do anything in the world?'

'Paula.........honest answer?' He sounded almost shy. A hint of guilt came across his face, as if he were disappointed with himself. As if something in his eyes had given him away.

'Hey, I can't read your mind, you know,' she said taking his other hand in hers. His was warm and strong; long square fingers, the back of his hand with a sparse covering of fine hair flowing neatly from his forearm; hers, slim, elegant and Art Nouveau with artist's fingers and scarlet-painted nails, a twirl of tiny gemstones inset. Their hands linked gently and silently under a timeless intoxication.

If only you could read my mind, she thought, how I had always promised myself that I would resist you, how I would make sure that I was not just another one of your conquests, how I wanted to be treated like a human being first and a woman second. Now she realised that he didn't have to do anything except be himself. She looked into his eyes, brown flecked with gold, as if into a crystal ball and saw his gentleness. He didn't blink as she plunged deep into his soul; feeling as if she was looking into the eyes of a child, full of love and trust, then those of an old man, still lively and sparkling, and then the clean, fresh and innocent eyes of her own baby. She looked away, breaking the spell and swallowed involuntarily.

'Paula,' Carlos whispered, touching her face with the tips of his fingers. He saw what he thought was a tiny teardrop about to roll down her cheek.

They drove back to Carvoeiro listening to a Shakira CD at maximum volume and entered the village bass-booming while Paula danced in her seat. They drove up restaurant hill, took the short-cut to the church and left the car in the deserted car park. The Alfanzina lighthouse was flashing and they could just make out the one at Sagres in the far west. Paula wrapped her jacket tighter then grabbed Carlos from behind, holding him in a bear hug. He struggled to get the key from his pocket and hushed her as he fumbled to put it in the door of the coastguard lookout office. Opening the door, he turned on the light.

'This is our refuge,' he said proudly and smiled.

He went to the sofa, clicked the release catch and presented the bed with a fanfare like a magician.

'You said you wanted somewhere comfortable; we can't go to your place and we can't go to mine....' Opening the fridge, he pulled out a bottle of wine. There were two glasses on the desk, ready and waiting. The Shakira CD went into the machine and there was music. Carlos went to the toilet and gave thanks to the Lord for his little arrangement with Rui; this was a night for something up the nose and he was sure that Paula would not be interested. As he snorted he felt a twinge of selfishness.

When he came back into the room, Paula was smiling broadly.

'Oh, I'm so proud of you, Carlos, you've really been busy; it's fabulous.' She draped herself on the bed while he filled the glasses and brought them over. The coke hit him and his head started to spin. Carlos ran his hands down her legs and she beamed, showing a row of perfect teeth. She opened her mouth slightly and put her tongue between them, then ran it over her lips.

A delicious urge came over Paula to take the initiative. 'Carlos Da Silva,' she said with emphasis fuelled by wine, 'I am going to seduce you.'

'Oh...yes please....' he breathed.

'But on one condition……..' her teeth bit the tip of her tongue. He gazed at her. 'Anything,' he said, his voice trembling.

'You have to keep your hands to yourself until I say…….'

She put her drink down and stood directly in front of him, moving in time to the music, like Shakira, only better, real, close to him, snaky, sexy, close enough for him to smell and feel her heat. Unbuttoning her blouse, she took it off and threw it to him. He reached out for her but she wagged her finger and shook her head in time to the music. Then she unfastened her bra and it fell to the floor revealing perfect firm breasts like ripe oranges. Her stomach was as smooth as milk and curved like the music swirling around them as she moved with the rhythm. Her nipples were erect and Carlos wanted to sink his teeth into them; his dick so stiff that it hurt. She gyrated in front of his face, took a mouthful of wine, bent down, breathed a sweet perfumed breath on him, then brushed her lips past his before kneeling down in front of him. Again he tried to reach for her; again she signalled 'no.' Instead, she unbuttoned his shirt and let it fall to the floor, ran her fingers lightly along his shoulders and over his chest, lingering on his nipples before kissing him on the lips. Carlos was moaning now, his hands reluctantly at his sides. Paula beckoned him to stand and ran her fingers down both sides of his torso from chest to waist, undoing the top button of his jeans, then she unfastened her skirt, letting it fall round her feet. Then she unzipped him and put both her hands down into his warm pubic hair, feeling his solid penis still trapped like a wild animal; she liberated and lightly fondled it, cupping his balls. He pulled off his jeans with her help and stood before her.

Continuing to dance, she slowly removed her knickers and placed them around his neck. He watched her snaking in front of him, mesmerised. She knelt down in front of him, took him in her mouth. When she tasted the salty leakage, she bade him kneel down so that they were both on the floor, face-to-face. Lifting his hands, she placed them on her breasts; now he could be in charge. Once again, she saw him as she had in the bar; the man with the child in his eyes.

Afterwards, he sank wearily onto her and they folded their arms around each other, the sweat slowly evaporating off their bodies, cooling them. Paula smiled, recognising the power that she had released from within her. Not only did she not know him, she did not even know herself.

Ten

Chico looked around nervously and lit his third cigarette in fifteen minutes, trying to stay in the shadows. Business had been slow and he didn't know why; the phone calls had become less frequent. He needed this customer tonight. Cars drove up and down the road next to the car park, but none stopped. Carrying four packets, he was feeling vulnerable. A black face loitering in the same place for too long would attract attention, maybe a phone call and a precautionary visit by a squad car. A young couple walked past arm-in-arm, laughing, and disappeared down one of the side roads leading to the quay.

Headlights illuminated the wall behind him and grew in strength; behind the headlights Chico saw a large black Mercedes with dark tinted windows. The car approached like a ghoul and the engine died. A tall man got out of the back and walked towards Chico; he couldn't see his face with the headlights blinding him. He tried to shut out the lights with his hand until he could see him; it was not a man he recognised. A second man got out of the car on the driver's side and stood by the open door.

'Chico, I presume?' said Chilcott. Chico, his heart thudding, stayed silent for a moment.

'Why do you want to know?' he asked, looking to each side to check that they were still alone.

'Well, it's a little delicate, Chico,' the voice continued, smooth and reasonable. 'You see, I think that we share similar business interests and the people that I work for are not entirely happy with that. Competition is not always good for business; it drives down prices and splits the profits. You understand, I'm sure.'

'Come on,' Chico protested. 'I'm small-time. I'm no serious competition for you guys.'

'Small dealers become big dealers, my friend, and we don't want any other big dealers in this area, do we?' Chilcott took out a packet of cigarettes, removed one and lit it.

'Jesus, I'm just trying to make a living,' said Chico.

'No no, you misunderstand me.' Chilcott's voice changed as he started to lose patience. 'I don't intend to debate about this. Perhaps I need to make myself clearer. I am advising you as strongly as I can not to do anything that might jeopardise the futures of those dearest to you.' He blew a long stream of smoke into Chico's face.

'You bastard,' hissed Chico, moving towards Chilcott who raised his hands in a conciliatory gesture. 'Touch one hair of their heads and you're dead.'

Chilcott laughed and took one step back, his hands still raised in mock submission. 'Chico, please, don't get violent. You're a big guy and I might get hurt. My mother wouldn't like that.' He lowered his hands, raised a finger and wagged it close to Chico's nose. 'Listen, my friend, let me give you some advice. You are not in a bargaining position. You hold none of the cards. I, however, have a winning hand. Who am I?' He spoke very quietly now.

'I don't know,' Chico answered, a tremble in his voice.

'Precisely.' He whispered. 'I, on the other hand, know your name, I know where you live, I know your phone number, I know your wife and daughter and I know all about your business, I know you have drugs in your house. There's so much I know about you, and yet you don't even know my name. Chico, get wise. Do yourself a favour. Do what I ask and you can forget that this night ever happened. It will be like a bad dream and you'll wake up in the morning and it will be a brand new day. Do this for me. Find something else to do. You know it makes sense.'

'You bastard,' hissed Chico.

Chilcott dropped his cigarette and stamped it out as if it were a cockroach. He turned to walk away, then looked back and said,

'I'm feeling generous. You've got a week.' As he reached the car, he turned again and, for the first time, he shouted, '.......That's one week, you fucking kaffer!' He got into the Mercedes, laughing loudly, and the car drove away.

Chico walked back to their apartment slowly, puffing at another cigarette, wondering what he should tell Maria. When he arrived, Maria was nursing Fátima on her lap.

'He didn't turn up, sweets,' he said.

'Oh no, What are we going to do without money?'

As she spoke, her mobile rang and she picked it up.

'Oh, Aleixo, so nice to hear from you. Four people for tonight? OK, twenty minutes? OK? OK.' She beamed a smile. 'Aleixo saves the day.'

Saying nothing, Chico returned to the car park.

Twenty minutes later Aleixo's Vitara pulled up. They exchanged a few words, did the business and the Vitara drove off.

Chico turned to walk home. On the other side of the road a black Mercedes turned on its lights and drove away.

'Shit,' said Chico. 'Shit, shit, shit.'

The following day, Rui finished parcelling up George's books in the sex shop and set off for home. The Christian shop was now decidedly open for business and he popped in to see what was on offer. A large sign radiated the chosen name *'Encarnação'* in sacred light. The shop and was clearly doing good business. Around a dozen pilgrims were inside, admiring the religious kitsch. There were racks of garishly-painted statuettes of Nossa Senhora de Fátima, Saint Sebastians appealing heavenward, peppered with silver darts, expressions of sexual ecstasy on their painted faces, crucifixes of various sizes, portraits of saints, crystal tears melodramatically rolling down their cheeks, rosaries, bibles and other books. Jesus action figures were on another shelf, beneath which were 'Ten Plagues of Egypt' cuddly toys, looking surprisingly wholesome. 'Jesus Saves' money boxes were next to those; he wondered whether Thérèse would like one. They even had soap; 'Wash Away Your Sins'. I could do with some of that, he thought. Car stickers: 'Jesus is coming: Look busy'; 'Work for God; the retirement benefits are great'. Rui was surprised to see teeshirts and underwear as well. A display of girl's knickers was prominent, emblazoned with the logo 'Thongs of Praise'.

Gazing around the shop, he came to the conclusion that it was not so different from the sex shop. There was nudity, sadism, masochism and effigies that looked like vibrators. They even sold sweets, Testamints, like peppermint-flavoured condoms, and bread:

'The Holy Toast'. He looked around to confirm that there were, in fact, no condoms on sale. Turning to walk out, he smiled to himself and bumped into a delivery man carrying a large box. Behind the delivery man stood Dr Amores, staring at Rui. He was not smiling.

A week later, in the lounge of António Amores's villa in Ferragudo, Ben Chilcott sat in the breeze coming through the open veranda doors sipping his whisky. He stubbed out his cigarette in a cut-glass ashtray.

'I put the frighteners on that dealer, Chico. I went back half an hour later to see whether he had got the message but he was dealing again. I gave him a week to get out but I think we're going to have trouble with him. I also gave a tip off to the GNR so they could monitor his mobile number.'

António Amores sat back and drew on his cigar, his head surrounded by a lazy cloud of blue smoke.

'I wouldn't hold out any great hopes with the GNR; they wouldn't recognise a drug dealer if he was operating out of their front office. This Chico may be small time, but he's driving the prices down and getting a reputation. We've been trying to starve him out by cutting prices but that can't go on. I don't want people to get the idea that we're soft on competition. We have to nip it in the bud otherwise everyone will think they can do the same thing.'

'Why not put him on the payroll?'

'No, he's got a wife and kid; he'll always put them first. I don't want people with emotional attachments. They're too vulnerable.' Amores took another puff of his cigar. 'So, you gave him a week.....you're too soft. Don't follow through with the threat to the wife; that'll only make him come gunning for you. No, he's the one we need to remove from the scene.' He stood up and paced towards the window.

'Then there's the matter of that book I got in the post. It's about expats, drugs and murder. That is not exactly a subtle code. To me it says – I know all about you and I am going to be your worst enemy.'

'Who sent it?'

'I went to the bookshop where it came from. It's run by an old Brit. He gave me some rubbish about there being a mix up but I didn't believe him. He told me that the mail order business is handled by someone else.'

'Who?'

'Your friend; your drinking buddy, Rui Fernandes.'

Chilcott paled. 'Oh fuck. Do you think he's onto us?'

'What do you think? He saw me in the shop when the stuff was delivered as well. I'm getting a nasty feeling about him. He's always smiling as if he's hiding something. I never trust anyone who smiles too much.'

'Could there be anyone else in Carvoeiro that has a grudge against you?'

Amores narrowed his eyes.

'Well, yeah, there are a few. Peter Hallworth for one. I conned him out of ten thousand for the opening of his sex shop, then Mayor Luis closed it within a few days. He was spitting feathers.'

'But surely he doesn't know your part in it and thinks he needs your help in re-opening the shop,' said Chilcott.

'Hmm. I thought so too, but then he started the internet business and now he doesn't seem so interested in the shop; he's doing OK without it.'

'So he has a motive as well.'

'Yeah. Maybe. I had him under complete control but now the tables have turned…..and I understand that he has some nasty friends in London,' said Amores.

Chilcott thought through the implications.

'So, it could have been him that sent the book.'

'Yes, I suppose so. But I wouldn't have thought Hallworth would be quite so stylish….nor Fernandes for that matter. But I'm more worried about Fernandes. The fact that he was in the shop when the drop was made.'

Chilcott shook his head.

'He won't suspect anything, António. He's too stupid. It was just a local courier. Good scheme, choosing local deliveries. Christian tack for a Christian shop.'

Amores hesitated as a thought occurred to him. 'This Fernandes. Does he connect you in any way with drugs?'

'No. He never knew in South Africa.'

'And you never supplied him here?'

'Only once. He's been using his friend Chico.'

Amores gasped. 'Oh, Ben, you stupid fuck. Now he knows that you're in the business.'

'I'm sure he thinks that I'm just a user; Christ, António, I can't see the future. How was I to know that he'd turn out to be an enemy? I was doing him a favour, that's all.'

'That was not a smart move. He's right next door to the shop. We don't know what he knows. There's a big shipment coming in the next few days. I'm not taking the risk. We'll arrange the delivery to your place in Portimão. The last thing we need is him mouthing off to his police buddies. We can worry about Hallworth later. Perhaps if we dispose of Fernandes, Hallworth will get the message and back down.'

Chilcott lit another cigarette, frowning. 'And the police?'

'Oh, come on. They already think Fernandes is a crook. If what you say about him is true, they'll do a post-mortem and probably find he's full of drugs anyway. Open-and-shut case. You know they're not bothered when druggies get killed.' He looked Chilcott in the eyes. 'Do it Ben. Do it soon. Do it tonight. For all our sakes.'

'And Chico?'

'Yeah, him as well.'

'It's not been a good year has it?'

Amores looked at him over the rim of his glass. 'It'll get better,' he said.

That evening, Rui and Tim sat bored in the apartment watching television. Rui's mind drifted to Portimão. Although well over the drink-drive limit, he had entered into that mental state in which he often found himself after a bottle of wine. The one where he knew that he was the world's best driver after a few drinks, it would only take twenty minutes and he had earned a bit of relaxation and, after all, bad things only happen to bad people. His horoscope that morning had been good.

'Fancy a little pick-me-up?' he said to Tim.

'If you insist. I'm easy. It's a light day tomorrow.'

'You coming with me?'

Miracle in Carvoeiro

'What? Are you crazy? You know I never get close to those guys. I've got a reputation to think about,' Tim said with an air of arrogance.

'But you're first in line when I get some.'

'It's always your idea. I never encourage you.'

Rui shrugged, opened his phone and called Chico.

Twenty minutes later he drew up in Chico's car park. He could see the lights from the quay and hear the traffic and laughter from the restaurants, but here it was like a graveyard, dark and menacing. It was as if the quayside was a stage with the performance in full swing and here was backstage, waiting for the actors to take their curtain calls and leave to a muffled applause from the auditorium. Getting out of the car, he lit a cigarette and waited. Chico appeared after a few minutes.

'Hey Chico, howzit?' Rui asked, slurring his words slightly.

He couldn't see Chico's expression; black face on a black night. 'Not good, Rui. Not good.' His voice sounded heavy and burdened.

'What's the problem?'

Rui heard Chico sigh. 'Rui, we've decided to get out of this business. I'm being run out of town. I'm getting rid of all the stuff I have and then we'll leave. There's no future here. How many do you want?'

'Two……..Oh, I'm sorry to hear that Chico. What about Maria and Fátima? '

'It's for them that I'm doing it. You can't bring up a child in this kind of life.'

Rui took the wraps and handed over the money.

'Are you in danger?' he asked.

'I'll be OK. I have to get out of this business. Hey, look after yourself. Ciao.'

Rui shook Chico's hand and felt the sweat in his palm. Chico walked off into the darkness and Rui climbed unsteadily back into the Rav. After concealing his two little bags in his underpants, he drove back to the old bridge, unnerved by Chico's agitation.

Without warning, the air was filled with an ear-splitting crash like an exploding bomb and the inside of the car was full of dust and shards of flying glass; then it was over. His ears registered nothing except a ringing sound. Rui was completely disorientated and felt sharp pains on both sides of his face and his shoulder. Glancing in the rear-view mirror, all he could see of the rear window was a ragged curtain like a broken Tiffany lamp, flapping pathetically. Turning his eyes back to the road, he wanted to accelerate but his vision was filled with shattered glass, a large blood-spattered hole in the centre, cracks radiating out like ripples in a pool. He punched out the shattered windscreen which fell onto the bonnet, then accelerated as fast as the car would go.

Fuzzy stationary red lights winked at him from the Ferragudo end of the bridge. His eyesight, blurred by wine and shock, he couldn't make out the source. As he got closer, he realised that it was a police road block. In his shaken state and all he could think of was how to explain to the police that his car had disintegrated. Fuck! That's all I need, he thought. My car has exploded and now a fucking road block.

Something was running down the back of his neck; he was drunk, he had drugs in his pants, one headlight was not working, there was a shower of glass on the seats and his windows had just exploded. A policeman flagged him down with a torch, shining the beam at the remnants of the windscreen as he strode towards Rui's car. Rui took six very deep breaths before opening the window; he had been told that it was a way of cheating the breathalyser. Seeing the state of the car, a drunk driver was the last thing on the policeman's mind.

He shone his torch onto Rui's face. 'Senhor, you're covered in blood…….what's happened?'

Rui was drunk and bewildered. 'Officer….I don't know. I really don't know.' He started shivering uncontrollably and realised he was crying. The policeman opened the door and helped Rui out of the car, calling to the other officer.

'Hey, Paolo, come here quickly. I think he's been shot.'

Back at the car park, Chico was waiting for another rendezvous. He reckoned up the cash from the last week; almost there. Another cigarette.

'Hey kaffer!' a voice called out from the darkness.

He spun round to see Chilcott walking towards him with two other men and felt his mouth go dry. The other two were large and threatening, but the central figure was the one holding all the menace.

'Hey, I'm getting rid of the last of it,' Chico protested. 'I'll be out of your hair soon. Just give me a couple more days…….'

'I gave you a friendly warning,' Chilcott growled, 'and you ignored it, you fucking kaffer.' His eyes glinted in the street light.

'Two days….' said Chico.

'Ah, a pleading kaffer; that's what I like to see,' said Chilcott. 'Two days, what? Shouldn't that be 'Two days, boss'? Go on, say it, kaffer. Say 'Yaz, boss, two days'……oh, and you say it on your knees.'

Chico felt rage growing inside him and knew he was starting to lose control. Recognising the signs, Chilcott continued to pour fuel onto the fire.

'Ah, kaffer, I'm enjoying this so much,' he purred. 'It's giving me an erection, Chico. Do you want to see it? Hey?'

Chico's expression changed from victim to predator as he lunged for Chilcott with his hands clenched together as if in prayer; he swung them up, crunching against his jaw with a loud crack. Taken by surprise, Chilcott reeled back and fell to the ground. Clutching his chin, the blood ran from his mouth over his fingers and he felt loose teeth in his mouth. The other two launched themselves at Chico, but he was a powerful man with the rage of a taunted bull. He was fighting for his life and dignity; they were fighting to order. One tried to grab him from behind, but Chico lurched forward and the man flew over his head and hit the ground with a brain-jarring thud. The other man came toward him, jumped over the two on the ground and tried to land a punch on Chico, who neatly side-stepped it and kicked him in the groin. Seeing his moment, Chico turned and ran as fast as he could into the shadows.

Gasping for breath, he tried not to make a sound. He needed time to think about what to do next. There were no sounds of pursuit; all was quiet, only some cars in the distance. Chico lit a cigarette with shaking fingers and paced up and down, before throwing it away, glowing, half-smoked in the gutter. They would have to leave tomorrow or even tonight. No, that would be impossible, at the very least they needed to pack. They had to find somewhere safe to stay tonight where they couldn't be found, but he couldn't think of anywhere. They had no car; all they had was some money and a few bags of cocaine; just a few bits of paper and some white powder when what they needed was wheels and a safe place to hide. A hideous thought occurred to him. They knew where he lived. Maria and Fátima were there. Alone.

He ran in the direction of his apartment but, as soon as he got close, he could see the car waiting. Two men got out when they saw him. Behind him he could hear the running footsteps, slowing down as they approached, panther-like, their long shadows reaching out to where he stood, like the fingers of death. Chico felt his feet rooted to the ground. Escape was impossible. He felt a wave of panic and regret engulf him.

'Please Holy Mother, look after Maria and Fátima, I beg you,' he prayed. From an open upstairs window Fátima cried in her sleep.

Roger Hardy

Eleven

Tim paced up and down the apartment, looking at his watch, urging Rui to get back. He was two hours late and Tim assumed that he had been stopped by the police. He wondered whether he would be able to get him released on bail. Then the phone rang.

When Tim arrived at the Hospital do Barlovento in Portimão, Rui was propped up in bed, his face pock-marked from the flying glass, his arm in a sling and a large bandage under his arm and over his shoulder. The air smelt heavily of disinfectant. Trolleys rolled past silently on linoleum floors. Tim tried to embrace Rui but it was too difficult, so he settled for a kiss and a weak smile as Rui told him what had happened.

'They said I can go home later today,' said Rui brightly.

'I don't know how you can be so cheerful when you've just been shot,' said Tim.

'Oh, I wasn't actually shot, I was shot at. It was the car that got shot. My poor baby. All I got was cuts and bruises and a bullet graze to the shoulder. And I used to be good-looking before I came to Portugal. Look at my face now. This place is really bad for the health. Hate hospitals. They're full of sick people.'

'My God,' exclaimed Tim. 'Stop complaining! You are lucky to be alive. But Rui, this is serious. Who could have done it?'

'God knows,' said Rui, his smile fading. 'Maybe just a random pot-shot?'

'Oh come on. This isn't Kansas City. We don't get drive-by shootings here. No, it's got to be something else. Have you upset anyone?'

'Me? I never upset anyone. And now some psychopath is trying to kill me.'

Tim squeezed his eyes shut for a moment.

'What have you told the police? What happened?' he asked.

'What can I tell them? I was out scoring drugs then someone took a shot at me?'

Tim glanced round to make sure they couldn't be overheard. The patient in the next bed stirred in his sleep and let out a sigh.

'Well, it was a shooting,' he hissed. 'Surely they must have been slightly curious.'

'Well, yes. But there's no evidence. No leads. I couldn't tell them anything, so they're talking about it as a random event.'

'Well, Cristina told me that she definitely wants to interview you,' Tim sighed. 'She was planning to leave but she's extended. She says she'll get to the bottom of it. It's taken her mind off the miracle.'

Two days later Rui was convalescing in bed back at the guest house, enjoying the rest. It was late when Tim joined him, having

Miracle in Carvoeiro

spent the day doing the work around the guest house. Picking up the unopened newspaper, he lay on the bed next to Rui, turned on the bedside light and read the front page.

'Oh they've pulled a body out of the river in Portimão. The police say he was a drugs dealer.'

Rui felt his stomach clench. 'A drugs dealer? Is there a name?'

'Chico Vaz.' Then a thought occurred to him. 'Isn't that the name of your guy?'

'Oh, fuck,' Rui gasped, putting his hand to his mouth. 'He told me he was being run out of town. The bastards. He told me they were after him.'

'Who was after him?' asked Tim. 'The police?'

'No.....I don't know......' Rui stopped as a horrible thought occurred to him: I gave Chico's phone number to Chilcott. It was only after that that Chico started to have problems. Jesus, was I the start of all this? Did I cause him to be killed? That simple, innocent act? The thought was too horrible to contemplate but he couldn't dismiss it from his mind. But Chilcott was just a user, surely.

There was a link there, but it was a silent link that had to stay in his head. Tim must never know about Chilcott; that would open the door to his past; a past that had to remain firmly locked away. His relationship depended on it. Tim the perfect, Tim, the man who rejects imperfection.

'What's up? asked Tim. 'Who was after him?'

'What? Oh, no, it's nothing,' said Rui trying to cover up. 'When do they think that Chico was killed?'

'Same night that you were shot apparently. Do you think it's a coincidence?'

The ideas flooded through Rui's head. But why anyone would want to shoot him? Tim would probably work it out; he was sharp as a razor. He'd see the links but he must never know about Chilcott. Rui wished that he could talk to him. Then another thought came into his mind.

'Oh, no,' he said. 'What about Maria and Fátima?'

'Who're they?'

'Maria's his wife. Fátima's their little daughter.'

Tim shrugged.

'So, a drug dealer gets killed. Doesn't that come with the territory?'

'Oh, Tim, have a heart. I know it'll sound crazy, but they were hobby drug dealers, doing it to earn a bit of extra money. They were a nice couple, a really nice family. They never even did drugs themselves.'

'You knew them well?'

'Uh-huh.'

'Oh, I'm sorry,' said Tim. 'I guess that makes it personal.'

'It's such a tragedy,' mused Rui, examining his bandaged shoulder.

'Is Portimão a violent town?' asked Tim.

'No, not really.'

Tim's brow furrowed. 'Yet, there's a murder and a shooting in one night? Don't you think they might be connected?'

'Oh, I don't know. Can we talk about it tomorrow?'

'I want to talk about it now. I bet Cristina does as well……'

Rui interrupted him. 'Please Tim, let it go. Chico's just been killed. I'm just so upset about his family. What're they going to do now?' Rui fell back and lay looking at the ceiling.

'It's a dangerous business,' said Tim, folding the newspaper. 'People who get involved in it must understand the risks, surely.'

'Tim, they're human beings,' spat Rui. 'You were their customer too. For you, people are either all-good or all-bad. No one's perfect. Live with a little imperfection, for Christ's sake. If you have a slightly chipped glass you throw it away. It's much more difficult to fix it or live with a little imperfection.'

'Well, I've been living with you for long enough,' Tim blurted, stung into reacting.

'For fuck's sake, Tim. I'm an invalid. You're meant to be feeling sorry for me. Insult me next week.' Rui sulked for a moment. 'You didn't mean that, did you?'

Tim was silent. Rui was proud of his imperfections. Getting involved in other people's problems and lives was perhaps a Portuguese trait, but he was pleased that it made him sympathetic to others. There were times when he wondered whether being opposites would ever really work.

'Where do you think you go when you die?' Rui murmured.

'What brought this on? It's dust-to-dust isn't it?'

'No, the soul, I mean.'

'I'm not sure I believe in a soul,' muttered Tim sleepily.

'I believe in something greater out there,' Rui said after a pause.

'Ah, that new-age shit. Well, I'm an existentialist. I believe what happens to me,' said Tim emphatically.

'Then if there's no soul, there's nothing? What's the point of living?' asked Rui.

'To have fun, make babies, do things that people remember,' Tim yawned.

'So when no one is left who remembers you, it is as if you'd never existed?'

'Well, yes, I guess so. But you're no more forgotten than all those untended gravestones in a churchyard. Can we go to sleep now?'

'I almost prefer the Church's idea,' said Rui.

Tim grunted in irritation. 'That's comfort food; suffer in this life and go on to life everlasting. But when you're dead and you find there's no life everlasting, it's a bit late to have fun. Even worse, heaven might be full of Christians; had you thought of that? Eternity in church! No, thanks. No, become a Buddhist instead; it's healthier and you keep getting reincarnated until you reach Nirvana. Of course you might come back as a cockroach if your karma's bad but, hell, that's life.'

Rui lay on the bed, thinking about life and death. Now it was real and he realised that he was thinking about his own mortality. They lay in silence.

After a few minutes, Rui stirred. 'Talking about good karma, do you think we should offer Maria a job?' he asked.

Tim was now awake and feeling angry; angry because he wanted to sleep and angry at the idea of employing Maria.

'Are you crazy? Giving a job to the wife of a drugs dealer? Do you want to get shot again? You've got to be out of your mind,' he retorted. 'No, absolutely not. I don't even want to meet her.'

He turned over and faced the opposite way without kissing Rui, who lay, staring blankly into the dark space between them.

'You're not perfect, you know.' Rui murmured.

'Gawd, this place is getting like the Queen Vic,' said Peter as Rui, Tim and Cristina came up the stairs to Scamps. They joined them at the table under the gazebo, basking in the midday sun. The canopy cast colours over them, the fringes fluttering gently in the cooling breeze. Sunday lunch at Scamps had become something of a ritual and the bar was packed. English was the only language in the air; roast beef and Yorkshire puddings the only thing on the menu. George was getting a joke update from Ursula.

'What do you do if you're lover is too fat?' she asked, an incipient laugh already on her immaculately painted lips. Without waiting for a reply, she answered so that everyone could hear. 'You get him to walk three miles in the morning and three miles in the evening, then at least by the end of the week the fat bastard will be forty two miles away!' George laughed politely.

'Rui,' asked Peter, tucking into his Yorkshire pudding, flooded with steaming gravy, 'How's the investigation going?' He chewed noisily, open-mouthed.

'I don't think it is really,' Rui answered. 'You'd think that they'd take pity on a man who has just been shot at. And my beautiful little Rav.....it's going to cost a fortune to get it fixed. The cops have no idea who did it, and it looks like there's not much chance of them discovering anything new.'

'But why would anyone want you dead?' asked Ursula.

'God knows,' Rui shrugged. 'Everyone knows I'm a ray of sunlight. Maybe Jesus wants me for a sunbeam.'

'It's a mystery,' said Tim, shaking his head.

'It's a miracle,' Cristina corrected.

'Speaking of miracles, have you made any progress, Cristina?' asked George.

'I saw Father Afonso. He told me about Thérèse and the so-called cure. Then I saw Dr Müller and he confirmed that it was spontaneous remission. The gorgeous Carlos told me that the money was not part of the mystery and had been returned. Senhora Ramalho won't talk to anyone about it because she's being prosecuted by the police and Flavia…..well, Flavia probably knows everything, but……' She threw up her hands in despair.

'What about the Santiago angle?' asked Tim. 'You know, the bones of the saint. That sounded interesting to me.'

'They're at Santiago de Compostela, not here.'

'Do we know that for sure?'

Cristina brushed her hair back from her face.

'Nothing's ever certain where the medieval Church was concerned,' she said. 'But there doesn't see to be any evidence that they're anywhere else.'

'So the pilgrims? Why do they think they're here?' asked Rui, confused.

'Mass hysteria is the best description I can think of,' she said with a sign of resignation. 'Father Afonso told me that he's sanctified the little shrine on the side of the cliff. And the church is now open seven days a week.'

'Sounds good for business,' said Peter.

Cristina laughed. 'He says he's run off his feet and needs help dealing with the pilgrims.'

'Yet there was no miracle?' asked Tim, spearing a roast potato and holding it up on his fork like a trophy.

'He says not,' Cristina replied. 'He reckons that the existence of Jesus Christ and the intercession of the Holy Mother of God is miracle enough. That's all they're promoting. It's impossible to get inside the mind of the Church; you never know what they're thinking. It's like dealing with a multinational. I mean, they denied Fátima for years, and look at it now. The Church only moves when it has no choice.'

'Sounds like business as usual,' said Rui.

'So no story?' asked George with a sympathetic smile.

'No story,' agreed Cristina.

'What about Rui and the shooting? There might be something for you there.' Peter suggested.

'Oh I haven't done crime for a while,' Cristina protested. 'But it is intriguing, I have to admit.'

'OK. Come and plug your brain into this one,' said Peter. 'Let's work out who shot cock robin.'

He turned to Rui. 'Now, Senhor Fernandes, what were you doing in Portimão?'

'Visiting a friend,' said Rui, conscious that the reason why the police investigation would go nowhere was because he could not divulge the real reason for his visit to the town. A drug habit was not one to be shared with friends over Sunday lunch.

'Which friend?' Why wasn't Tim with you?' asked Cristina. 'It was late, wasn't it? After midnight?'

Rui felt himself go cold. She had asked all the wrong questions. Like a surgeon with a scalpel she had gone straight to the root of the issue. Fuck. He saw the whole affair running out of control.

His silence intrigued Cristina. She continued probing. 'And it was the same night that a body was fished out of the river, wasn't it?'

Rui took a breath. He needed to stop this line of questioning and cursed Peter for starting it. 'Oh, please, this isn't going to get us anywhere. I answered all those questions when the police asked me. It didn't get them anywhere either. It's a mystery. Let's leave it at that.'

Cristina eyed him suspiciously. He glanced at her and could see from her journalist's eyes that the matter wasn't over; she had smelt a story and was not going to give it up lightly. She nodded and Rui knew that, in those few seconds, she had put two and two together.

Ursula broke the awkward silence. 'So, Cristina, will you be staying in our little village for a while?'

'Oh yes. Absolutely. I think I may enjoy a little sabbatical,' she drawled. 'There are so many interesting people here. In Lisbon we lose the human scale, but here it's such an eye-opener. And I'm getting an idea for a story. It's just not the story I was expecting to write.' Her eyes never left Rui's.

'So, it's love is it?' asked Rui as Paula sat down for her mid-morning coffee break. They sat on the balcony of the vacant room next to Cristina's.

'Oh, yes,' she said. 'He's beautiful.' She blushed like a schoolgirl. 'It sounds terrible, doesn't it? I mean, talking about a man like a man would talk about a woman.'

'It works both ways,' said Rui, 'if it's the real thing. You don't have to be ashamed. It's a sign that this is the genuine article. Come on, I'm a gay man; I understand.'

'I want to marry him,' she blurted.

'Paula,' cautioned Rui, a note of concern in his voice. 'Having great sex is one thing, but marriage is serious. Are you sure that Carlos is the marrying type?'

She was silent and Rui could see a shadow come over her mind.

'I'm certain that he's been faithful to me since we've been together,' she said. 'And I've been faithful to him. I don't want anything to jeopardise what we have.'

Rui was more aware than Paula of the power of male lust and the weakness of moral fibre that came with it. This seemed to him to be an unequal battle and he didn't want Paula to be sucked into it, have her faith in Carlos betrayed, and lose this great moment in her life. He hated the idea of her being committed to a feckless rampant man just to have her heart broken later.

'Do you think I'm just his latest bed warmer, Rui?' she asked as if she had just read his mind.

'I can't answer that one, Paula,' Rui replied without conviction. 'Have you thought about the realities of life? Carlos has a reputation and there's no smoke without fire. He's Portuguese, you're Brazilian. He's a policeman and you're illegal.'

'I talk to my girl friends about it, but they're all older and think that marriage is a crock of shit. So why do I want something so much that everyone else tells me not to do? It's what I want more than anything else in the world. I don't care what they say, I want to try it for myself and make up my own mind,' she said with determination.

'Paula,' Rui warned, 'Remember that love is a mental illness that makes you ignore the faults of the person you love.'

'Oh, well said!' The voice came from the next room as Cristina emerged onto the balcony. 'Sorry, I wasn't evesdropping, but I can't help being a journalist. That was a good line, Rui, very good. Can I use it?'

Rui smiled. 'Come and join us. I think your advice might be more useful than mine.'

Cristina removed her jacket and pulled up a chair. 'OK, but I have an appointment in twenty minutes. So, what's the excitement?'

'It's love and men,' said Rui. Paula looked embarrassed.

'They're mutually exclusive, my dear. Trust the voice of experience.'

'Cristina, I'm in love and I want to make him marry me. What should I do?' Paula pleaded.

'Oh, come on, are you a child or what? Such a simple question; a simple question with a difficult answer. The answer is you make him fall in love with you and you can decide.'

Paula shook her head. 'It's not so easy. I think we've reached the falling in love bit. It's the next step that's more difficult.'

'Find another lover,' Cristina instructed. 'Drive him crazy with jealousy, then he'll marry you.' She strummed her manicured nails on the table. 'But are you so sure you want marriage? Come on, we're modern girls. Do we need it?'

'I need it.'

'Then you should really talk to someone who's been married. That's not me,' said Cristina.

'Tell me I'm crazy,' Paula protested, 'but this is different.'

'We all think that, but it'll pass. If he won't marry you, live in sin,' said Cristina with a dismissive flick of her hand.

'No, I want more than that. I want a home and children with the man I love. I want him to want that as well. I want him to want it without me telling him that's what he wants. Living in sin is OK for fun, but it's not the future.'

Cristina snorted. 'You're such a good Catholic.'

'It's not the Church,' protested Paula. 'I don't want to do it because it's what the Church says or what my family wants, I want to do it because it's what I want. I want to wake up next to him every day and spend the rest of my life with him.'

'I guess we're talking about Carlos?' Cristina's voice dripped with sarcasm.

'Yes, of course. We've been seeing each other for a few weeks. It's been the most wonderful time of my life.'

'Before you say anything, Cristina,' Rui interrupted, 'I've already told her that he has a reputation.'

'Every man has a reputation,' said Paula, her lips set in a stubborn line. 'I don't hold it against him. Everyone has a past; we should live for the future, don't you think?'

'Love,' Cristina sneered. 'It all comes down to sex and security. Love is security for women and sex for men. That's all.'

Paula looked at the other woman with sympathy.

'Oh, Cristina, that's so cynical; surely it can also build and create; home, family, isn't that what every woman really wants? Don't you want that? Doesn't every man really want that as well?'

'A man only wants it because a man on his own is a sad creature and in the end he hates living with himself,' said Cristina standing up. 'Look, I have to go. I have an appointment.' As an afterthought, she added, 'Buy him a present, Paula. Have a look at the Cockatoo website. There's lots of surprises there, believe me.'

'What did she mean by that?' asked Paula, after Cristina had left.

'Dunno,' said Rui, 'but it's a good website.'

'I've never seen it. Can you show me?'

Rui sat Paula down behind his laptop in his apartment below. She sat concentrating with her tongue licking her upper lip and tapped away for a few minutes in the women's section.

'Oh, really sexy; I'm so jealous. Oh, I want that one....and that.....' She spent a while going through the screens then moved to the menswear.

'Oh, who's the hunk?' She peered closer and looked again, a seed of recognition growing in her mind. Her eyebrows furrowed with the concentration then raised as her eyes opened wide in realisation, her mouth falling open.

Paula tabbed through the other pages to make absolutely sure, but there was no mistaking those buttocks or the shape of his dick caught like an eel in the sheer briefs. She put her hand over her mouth and gasped.

'What is it?' asked Rui.

'It's Carlos,' she breathed. 'That's him in these pictures. Who took them?'

Rui looked over her shoulder, remembering Tim's reaction to the photos.

'That's Carlos?' he exclaimed with a hint of admiration in his voice. 'I think Carmencita took them; she's almost a professional photographer.'

'She's a stripper, Rui,' she said in disgust. 'She's a prostitute.' Already shocked, she reeled as another thought hit her.

'When were these taken?' she breathed.

'Immediately after the sex shop opened, then closed. It had to be done quickly after the shop lost its licence.'

'But he told me that he'd stopped seeing her months ago.'

'I'm sure it was a professional arrangement,' said Rui, sounding unconvinced.

Paula turned to Rui, her face red, her expression somewhere between anger and heartbreak. They heard the front door slam closed above them. Rui peered out of the window. He looked back at Paula and came to a decision.

'Paula, I really shouldn't say this and I won't answer for the consequences but that was Cristina leaving. You might want to follow her.'

Paula followed the elegantly suited woman down the hill. She could almost smell the trail of Dior. Cristina walked with shapely nylon legs and a confident stride. Then she saw Carlos emerge from the GNR building. Something told her to conceal herself, so she made for the gap in the whitewashed wall leading to the little shrine on the side of the cliff. There was a crowd of pilgrims and she merged into them. She saw Carlos wave at Cristina as he passed her, making his way up the hill. As soon as he had gone past, she prised herself away from the pilgrims and saw Cristina at the bottom of the hill, turning to the right. Paula half-ran, not wanting to lose her. As she rounded the corner she saw Cristina turn right again, back up the hill towards the church. It seemed as if the journalist was following a route like three sides of a square, and Paula followed, trying to look nonchalant.

At the top of the hill, behind the school, she watched as Cristina walked up to the Coastguard lookout building and let herself in without a key. Paula's world collapsed around her and she slumped onto a bench outside the school, hot tears rolling down her cheeks. The brilliant sun blessed the ocean but she was impervious. She waited, feeling numb. An hour later, the door opened and Paula leapt up, crossed the road and hid behind the back wall of the church. Cristina sauntered back towards Casa Rui. Paula waited a little longer. Carlos emerged a few minutes later and saw her as she stepped from the shadows.

'Paula…….'

She walked up to him, and, without warning or words, hit him with full force on his face. Taken by surprise, he reeled back, lost his balance and fell to the ground heavily. Paula spat on him with contempt and ran back down the hill in tears.

Twelve

Tim was looking out of the window at a pilgrim on her hands and knees being harassed by one of the street dogs when he saw Paula run past, followed by Carlos who looked dazed and confused.

'I've just seen Paula being pursued by the forces of law and order,' said Tim.

'Oh God,' groaned Rui. 'Was she crying?'

'Buckets.'

Rui sighed. 'Well it's probably for the best. It's better she finds about Carlos now rather than later.'

'Do you think she's discovered him *inflagrante delecto*?'

'I know it.'

Tim turned to Rui with a look of suspicion. 'Did you organise it?'

Rui winced. 'Kind of. I thought it might be for the best.'

'And fuck up Carlos's life at the same time. Was that an itsy-bitsy revenge on him?'

'Maybe,' Rui admitted.

'Bitch,' said Tim with a smile. 'So, was he shagging the lovely Cristina?'

'Amongst others.'

'Who else?'

Rui raised an eyebrow. 'Well, I've got strong suspicions about Ursula.'

'Ursula? Ursula? But she's old enough to be his mother.'

'He's twenty three. He'll fuck anything with a pulse.'

Tim shook his head with a grimace.

'Yes, but, with his looks you'd think he'd be a bit more selective. He can have any girl he wants.'

'Maybe he is being selective,' muttered Rui, thoughtfully.

'What do you mean by that?' asked Tim.

Before he had a chance to answer, there was a knock on the door.

Cristina walked in, a little frayed around the edges and slumped onto the sofa. 'Village life,' she said and sighed. Rui and Tim looked at her expectantly, Rui with accusing eyes.

'I'm not going to say that I'm sorry,' she said abruptly. 'I saw what happened.' She sighed again and glared at Tim and Rui. 'What? Come on, you're gay men. It's Carlos. He's irresistible. Don't blame me, Rui. Look at me….my time's running out. I'm going to get it while I can and I'm not ashamed of it. I'm a career woman. I'm well-known, respected, independent and rich enough. I gave up the possibility of family for this job and I'm not sorry. Not sorry at all.'

For the first time he saw, peering out from under that sophisticated and worldly external shell, a very lonely woman.

'But now Paula is destroyed,' said Tim.

'And Carlos,' added Rui. 'He's just lost Paula.'

Cristina's face twisted. 'You want me to say I'm sorry. OK, I'm sorry for Paula. She's a sweet girl. She deserves better than Carlos.'

She shuffled in discomfort. Rui and Tim looked at her accusingly. 'Look, if they really love each other, they'll get over it. Yes Carlos is upset. But not only about losing Paula. Well, I guess he's sorry about that, but it's too late for regrets and he really only has himself to blame.' She looked pointedly at Rui. 'No, he's most sorry because he's used the last of the coke he got from you.' She let her words sink in. Cristina was again the investigative journalist and they hadn't noticed the transformation. Rui gasped. Tim looked stunned.

'So you know everything, then,' muttered Rui.

'Well, it didn't take Sherlock Holmes to work it out. I was an end user. Carlos is not exactly discrete.'

'You know it was my dealer that was killed?' Rui felt Tim's eyes boring into him.

'I guessed as much.'

'My arrangement with Carlos finished a while ago. He was blackmailing me,' said Rui.

'Oh, come on,' Cristina snapped. 'Blackmail? That's a pretty strong word. He says that you were quite willing; you went along with it.'

'Hmph. Yeah, at first. But he kept stringing it along. Jesus, the guy was bankrupting me. Anyway it's all over. In more ways than one.'

'How do you mean?'

'We've stopped using it. I always thought of coke as a victimless crime, but now Chico's dead.'

Rui glanced at Tim who was slumped in a chair, his head in his hands.

'He was a drug dealer………' said Cristina.

'Christ,' interrupted Rui. 'You're sounding like Tim. Chico was a lovely guy, a really lovely guy. Wife and child. Never used the stuff himself. He was only dealing to support his family. He didn't have a choice and now he's on a slab in the morgue. It's really not worth the shit. So now we don't do it.' He paused to gather his thoughts. 'Sorry,' he continued, 'it's just that I feel quite strongly about it now. It's the first time I've seen what it can lead to.'

Cristina looked down. She was silent for a moment and then the journalist came alive again.

'Well if you feel so strongly about it, why don't you help the police with their enquiries? You're the one who was shot.'

'What? I tell them I was a customer of a drug dealer who was found dead the next day? Probably the last person to see him alive? Come on. I might as well throw myself in prison now. I'd probably be accused of his murder myself.'

'Yeah…..I see your point. OK then, we have our own resources and our own brains. Let's see who we have on our side. We have an investigative journalist, one of the best in the land,' she said with a touch of irony. 'We have an exquisite policeman with his brain in his dick, but we have Euro-brain Tim as compensation and….and…… we have you, Rui. I mean, it seems to me that you can be smelling flowers and a crime will happen somewhere near you. Anyway. The Fantastic Four. We will find out who killed Chico.'

There was something of a fresh sparkle in Rui's eyes. He liked the idea. Then a shadow fell over him; the shadow of Johannesburg. He cast a glance in Tim's direction.

'So, show me the bright lights of Portimão,' said Tim, switching off the TV.

'Bright lights?' said Rui. 'As far as gay life is concerned, it's more like a twenty five watt light bulb. There's only one club and that's always deserted. There are better places at Lagos or Albufeira. Why not go there?'

Tim shrugged. 'Portimão is closer and you've never taken me there.'

'I thought we'd decided that we were getting too old for all that dancing queen shit.'

'Yeah, but I miss Amsterdam.'

'Believe me, there is absolutely no comparison between this place and Amsterdam,' Rui said.

The club in Portimão was the last place that Rui wanted to go to. Over the years he had grown to hate gay clubs where he would find himself surrounded by sweet young things reminding him that he was no longer one of them. But his greatest fear was a big South African. So far, he had managed to avoid Tim meeting Chilcott but he knew that one day or another, their paths would cross, and he dreaded the prospect.

Thirty minutes later, Rui was leading Tim down the narrow cobbled streets of Portimão below the road from the old bridge as the muffled stroke of midnight floated through the sultry night air.

'Oh, they'll all be out tonight. All five of them,' said Rui. He had resolved to show Tim what a shit place the bar was, have a quick beer then go home hoping they wouldn't bump into Chilcott.

'Don't the gays here go out much?' asked Tim.

'They're probably all married and staying at home with their wives and kids. They can't simply tell the wife that they're off for a shag at the local gay bar.'

The bar was nondescript from the outside with only a single light suspended above a large stone doorway to signify that there was life on the other side. There were no windows. The door was imposing, wide and heavy. Rui rang the bell and it creaked open as warm air and the sounds of Abba and laughter flowed out onto the street. Rui was shocked to see that the place was packed, disco lights flashed red, yellow, green, blue in sync with the music and a giant sixties glitterball rotated above their heads like a death star. As Tim ordered the drinks, Rui noticed someone on the other side of the room waving. Rui turned to Tim and took his beer, his heart thumping. A minute later there was a tap on his shoulder and he spun round to see the tall frame of Ben Chilcott standing in front of him, flushed and sweaty.

'Hey Rui, trying to ignore me?' Chilcott breathed beery fumes over them. 'Oh,' he said, 'what happened to the face?

'Wrong moisturiser,' said Rui. The meeting that he had tried to avoid was about to take place.

To prove the point, Chilcott turned to Tim, 'Is this the boyfriend?' They introduced themselves and Rui prayed under his breath that Ben would keep his mouth shut about South Africa but the South African's eyes were like saucers, he was clearly wired and anything could happen.

'Rui and me were old friends in South Africa, weren't we?' he said, slurring his words slightly and revealing a row of teeth that looked too big.

'You've met here before?' asked Tim suspiciously.

'Yeah, we go back a long way, don't we Bro?' Chilcott put his arm around Rui. A feeling of dread came over Rui and he started to sweat.

Tim's eyes said 'who the fuck is that?' Rui knew exactly what he was thinking. An old friend. A secret old friend. Chilcott carried on, oblivious.

'You know South Africans, we all know each other and we're all refugees,' he laughed.

'You're a bit wired tonight,' said Rui, trying to sound casual. 'What're you on?'

Chilcott grinned, his teeth glinting.

'A little snow; want some?' He fumbled in his jeans pocket.

'Nah, I'm kind of off it at the moment.'

Chilcott peered at him. 'Why's that?'

Rui swallowed, but his mouth was dry. 'My dealer was fished out of the river last month,' he said. 'It kind of changes your perspective. Makes you realise it's not worth all the shit.'

The smirk didn't leave Chilcott's face.

'Oh, yeah, I heard about that. Nasty.'

'Yeah, nasty. He was called Chico; I gave you his phone number, remember?'

Chilcott shrugged. 'No. Never heard of him. Must've lost it, sorry Bro.' He looked around the room to see if anyone attractive had come in.

'So what do you do here, Ben?' asked Tim looking at him through narrowed eyes.

'Ah, you don't want to know,' Chilcott replied, returning his attention to them.

'Yeah, I do, go on……' Tim prompted.

Coke is a truth serum and makes people talkative; Rui mentally crossed himself as Chilcott answered Tim.

'I work in a bar here; shit bar but we have a few sidelines…..'

'Sidelines?'

'Yeah, a few girls and a few lines on the side, if you know what I mean. You know the sort of thing; this is a port. P'raps we can go there later. We can get free drinks, though I don't suppose the girls would interest you too much. Might interest Rui, though. Hey Bro, you had a bit of a hetero track record back home didn't you?'

'It was just a phase I was going through,' Rui muttered.

The bar owner appeared on stage, took the microphone and announced the acts. As they watched an emaciated comedienne telling a succession of blue jokes, Rui was aware that Tim was watching him and Chilcott out of the corner of his eye. Looking for signs of affection or good times gone by, no doubt. Oh, God, how was he ever going to explain this? It was approaching three o'clock when Chilcott suggested going to his bar.

'It's open until the last punter leaves, Bro. Let's get some free drinks.'

The bar was deep in the backstreets and didn't look like a bar at all until the door was opened by the bouncer and they entered through a second door. Tim wished he could go home; it was late, he was tired. This bar was like the reception area of a low-class brothel and he felt threatened and uncomfortable. But there were so many questions in his mind. What had Rui been getting up to when Tim was in Amsterdam? Rui had never mentioned Chilcott. An old friend from South Africa and he never so much as mentioned his existence. He would have been over the moon. They would have been drinking buddies. Chilcott was not Tim's type; he was big and butch. More Rui's type, he thought. Bastard.

A fan wobbled uncertainly from the ceiling to no effect. There were half a dozen girls, flitting like painted butterflies between groups of men; Lolita, sultry in a peasant's cheesecloth blouse veiling her bare breasts, Suzie Wong in a silky turquoise chongsam, slit to her waist, Brünnhilde with long waxy bleached hair and lipstick too red, three Carmens and one Violetta. They brought drinks, sat on laps, stroked unshaven faces, thinking about the money, bed and rest. The men were a mixed crowd; young and old, smart and dishevelled, they sat around admiring the girls and fondling them.

Chilcott ordered the drinks. Rui looked around and saw an attractive black girl come into the bar from a door at the back and sat down at a table on her own. His expression lightened to one of recognition, then darkened again in concealment.

'I don't know about you guys, but I'm going to see whether the old hetero magic still works,' he said to Chilcott and Tim. 'See you in a few minutes.' He moved over to the black girl and sat at her table on the far side of the bar.

'Hetero magic, my arse,' said Chilcott, smirking. 'He knows her, doesn't he?'

'No idea,' said Tim, frowning. 'I've never seen her before. Who is she?'

Chilcott chuckled.

'You don't want to know.'

Tim realised that he was alone with Chilcott. This was his opportunity to find out whether there was anything between him and Rui.

'So do you and Rui know each other well?'

'You could say that,' said Chilcott, keeping one eye on Rui and Maria. 'He has quite a past, you know.' He ordered two more beers and repositioning himself at the bar, turning to face Tim. 'You knew about his dancing days?'

'Yes, of course. He danced for five or six years, all over the world.'

Chilcott's grinned. 'Bet he didn't tell you everything.'

Tim's eyebrows raised in anticipation. 'Tell me more,' he said, his heart pounding.

'You don't know the half of it, Bro. Yeah, your Rui was a dance machine and sex machine. He even had sex with the Village People when he was at Sun City. He was the hottest thing in South Africa. He was on television a few times, and his face was on magazine covers.'

Tim fixed a smile on his face, realising that his boyfriend had a past that he knew little about. 'Oh yes,' he lied, 'he told me all about that.'

'Yeah, he had a real stage presence,' mused Chilcott, reminiscing. 'When he was on stage, the audience weren't looking at anyone else. Not the tits and feathers, not even Liza Minelli. She complained about it. When I'm on stage, I want everyone looking at me, she said, so they had to put him at the back.' He took a swig of beer. 'He had something you couldn't put your finger on. He was magic.' He glanced over to Rui and Maria. 'Don't you ever get jealous?'

'I'm not a jealous person,' lied Tim again. He was jealous of all the people who had ever known Rui before they had met; all those lost years when they could have been together, his lover had been shared with the rest of the world. He was jealous that he hadn't been there and was jealous of Chilcott who knew so much more about Rui that he did.

'So, you knew him pretty well,' said Tim, fishing.

'Everyone knew Rui. He's still got a great body, hasn't he? Yeah, he still looks the same as all those years ago. A few more wrinkles, but it's the same old Rui.' He raised his glass in mock salute. 'You're a lucky man. He's a lucky man for meeting you. I think you've kind of saved him from himself.'

'How do you mean?' asked Tim, hardly daring to breathe.

'Oh, it's a long story; I'll tell you one day. If he doesn't tell you first. Let's just say that he got really popular; everyone knew him, everyone wanted him and he was kind of public property for a while before he disappeared. He needed to hide in a hole and what better hole than here?'

'That's not why he's here.'

Chilcott turned to him and said in measured tones, 'That's why we're all here, Bro.'

As Rui sauntered towards Maria, he glanced over to Tim and Ben. They were deep in conversation and Rui shuddered to think that Ben might be spewing out his entire past in his drugged-up haze. Having survived the first meeting between Tim and Chilcott so far unscathed, he realised that he had become a little complacent. The sight of Maria had distracted him, but now he realised that he had done what he had vowed he would never do; leave Tim and Chilcott talking together. He watched them from the corner of his eye. He needed to keep this as quick as possible.

Barry Manilow blasted out over the sound system. The girl behind the bar turned up the volume and started dancing to *Copacabana*. Rui walked over and put his hand on Maria's shoulder. She turned around and her blank expression flickered with recognition. She looked passive, defeated. *Her name was Lola, she was a show-girl.*

'Maria, what are you doing here? You're not working here, surely?'

Maria stared at him with dull eyes.

'I had no choice, Rui. Ben, that bastard Ben over there, he threatened to blackmail me after Chico was killed.'

Rui reeled in shock.

'What? Ben runs this place? He's the pimp? Christ! So that's what he does; a slimy pimp!'

'Pimp, blackmailer, drug dealer, some say he's done worse. You be careful with that guy, Rui. I have my suspicions. One of the girls heard a rumour that he was involved in Chico's murder............'

'Jesus. We've got to find some way to get you out of this.'

'He's a greedy, sadistic bastard; everyone hates him,' Maria spat.

'What about Fátima? This is worse than pushing drugs.......' He thought for a bit and listened to the insistent music involuntarily; '*she lost her looks, she lost her Tony, now she's lost her mind.*' Listen, Maria, I understand what it's like. I've done what you're doing,' he hissed.

'Oh Rui, no,' she said, shocked.

'Yes, it's true. I'm not ashamed of it and I'm not sorry that I did it. At the time I had no choice; it was that or starve. But I'll tell you something; I learnt more about people in those few months than in the rest of my life. For God's sake don't ever mention it to Tim. He's the one standing next to Ben; he's my partner.'

She smiled weakly as if resigned to a future out of her control.

Rui clasped her hand. 'We need to find a way to get you out of Portimão. I promise I'll do everything I can to help. Promise. The air stinks here. I can't stay, I have to get back to the others. You still got the same mobile phone number?' She nodded. 'OK; I'll call you. Maybe Tim will come up with some ideas. Ciao.'

'You didn't tell me about the Village People,' said Tim as they drove home. To his relief, Tim had said he wanted to leave as soon as he had rejoined them.

'Ah, that was fun,' said Rui. 'Of course, it wasn't all four, only two of them. I was water-skiing and got an invitation to join them in their hotel. We had a real party. It'll be engraved on my tombstone!'

'He seemed to be fairly familiar with your body, that Ben; quite a fan of yours.'

Here it comes, thought Rui.

'What do you mean?' he asked, trying to keep his voice light.

'He was telling me about South Africa; you had quite a reputation, it seems.'

Rui felt cold inside; the bastard, he thought. 'What, the dancing queen days?'

'And the rest…..' said Tim. Rui held his breath. Tim carried on. 'I wish I'd seen you on stage; must have been fabulous.' Rui sighed in relief; maybe Ben hadn't told him. He was silent for a moment, thinking about Maria.

'You know that girl I was talking to……' said Rui, trying to change the subject.

'Yeah, the black girl….'

'That's Maria; she's the wife of Chico. They've blackmailed her and now she's on the game. I'm getting a nasty feeling.'

'Ben knew that you knew her,' said Tim darkly.

Rui was silent, trying to work out the implication of that. 'Well, he knew that I was using Chico, so he assumes I knew Maria as well, maybe.'

'But now you know that she's been blackmailed into prostitution. By your friend Ben.'

'He's not my friend. He's an acquaintance,' said Rui. 'I feel so sorry for Maria. I'd like to get her out of that mess regardless of whether or not they find Chico's murderer.'

Tim shrugged. 'She's not our problem. In any case, I think we should not get diverted from the murder and your shooting. The more I think about it the more I'm convinced that they are connected.'

'What makes you say that?' said Rui, turning to Tim, taking his eyes off the road.

'It's just a feeling,' said Tim. 'That, and the coincidence. Now Maria's in Chilcott's place……' He saw the car getting too close to the side of the road and nudged the steering wheel. 'Mind where you're going!'

Rui put his eyes back on the road. 'I don't suppose that the police will be that motivated. As far as the murder is concerned it's criminals killing criminals. It's probably good for the crime statistics in the long term,' said Rui.

'But we agreed with Cristina that we would solve this thing ourselves.' argued Tim.

Rui was silent for a minute as they drove. 'Do you love me?' he said, out of the blue.

Tim looked at Rui's profile, illuminated by passing street lights.

'What brought this on?' he asked.

'Simple question....'

'Of course I do,' said Tim but there was a note of uncertainty in his voice.

'What if I had been a murderer?'

'I hope that's hypothetical, but yes, probably. Don't suppose it would make any difference, unless you were a serial killer of course, or a psychopath.'

Rui kept his gaze on the dark road ahead.

'What if I had been a drugs dealer....hypothetically, of course.'

'That's a different matter; I'm not sure whether anyone can love a drugs dealer.'

'Maria did.'

'Yeah, and now she's a prostitute.'

Rui hesitated for a fraction of a second.

'OK, if I had been a prostitute, then.'

'Now you're getting really hypothetical. I won't dignify that with a reply.'

Tim was silent for several minutes and Rui wondered what was going through his mind.

'What made you decide to have an affair with Chilcott?' said Tim.

Rui was stunned. 'What? What did you say?'

'Oh, come on. I'm not stupid. How long has it been going on?'

'What? Are you crazy? He's a fucking Boer. He's just a mate. Give me some credit. Anyway, how do I know what you were getting up to in Amsterdam? You're the one who had the opportunity. You've seen what a fabulous gay scene we have here.'

'You know I don't do anything; I don't want to,' said Tim, defensively.

'Well, I'm the same here.'

'That's not what he told me. He said he had sex with you,' said Tim coldly.

'Well, he's lying,' said Rui angrily, but inside he was falling apart.

As they drove home in silence, his past was the only thing Rui could think about. He had had a few drinks; maybe too many, and the old guilt came back to him again. He felt that he knew all about Tim; he was an open book and, although he never really acknowledged personal failure, he didn't have much to be ashamed of. Rui was unable to say the same about himself; there was so much that Tim didn't know. A stranger from South Africa knew all about him but his partner did not. The past stood like an indestructible monument, waiting to be discovered. There would always be another Ben to destroy his life. He realised in that moment that he had to tell the truth, regardless of the consequences; his self-respect was more important and he knew now that he wanted honesty in the relationship above anything else, even at the risk of losing everything.

Rui pulled over to the side of the road, stopped the car and turned to Tim.

'Tim,' he said slowly and nervously, 'there's something I have to tell you.'

Roger Hardy

Thirteen

Rui sat in the shade of a rainbow umbrella nursing his beer at the beach restaurant, surrounded by sunburnt and salty holiday makers, eating, drinking, laughing,. Carlos sat opposite looking crestfallen with the brown souvenir of his black eye. Children squealed on the beach; the sea rippled gently and the humid air was still. A street dog came up to Rui and he gave it some crisps.

'OK, now go and chase a pilgrim….good dog.' He turned to Carlos. 'Though I'd prefer it to go and bite Tim,' he added.

'So, he's gone back to Amsterdam?'

Rui looked into his drink. 'He didn't say anything,' he muttered. 'I woke up and he was gone. We're finished. Bastard. All men are bastards. Present company excepted, of course.' Then he thought about it. 'No, cancel that last remark.' Carlos winced.

'What, finished, just like that? After four years? Won't it blow over?' he asked.

Rui looked dejected. 'No, I don't think so. Tim's a perfectionist and he expects everyone to be the same. He's completely inflexible.' He stared into his glass again to see whether his reflection mirrored his mood. Cold-hearted bastard, he thought. Talks to me like my bank manager. How could that warmth and love be swept away as if it had never existed? Bet he doesn't get that empty feeling lying in bed; bet he never cries himself to sleep.

Carlos was still smarting in his own world. 'At least he didn't hit you. How do I explain this?' he asked, pointing to his eye. 'Injured in the line of duty? It's so embarrassing to admit to being floored by a girl.'

Rui sighed. 'Carlos, we've both fucked up. Why can't people accept that everyone has a past and it can't be changed?'

'Yeah,' Carlos sighed, sounding weary. 'I can't get Paula out of my mind. I think about her all the time, but I've been seeing other girls; of course I have.' He looked up at Rui. 'I'll be honest with you; Cristina is just the latest. Now, you'll tell me that wasn't the smartest thing to do, but I had my reasons. Women look at me and I look at them and…..well, it's so easy, Rui. And there's Carmencita; that's being going on for a year and it's not so easy to break it off. The website thing was a bit of a laugh; and she paid me, or rather, Peter did.'

'Yeah, yeah, I know.'

'These women offer themselves to me on a plate. Rui, you're a gay man. Would you say no if a really good-looking man came up to you and offered himself to you on a plate? Would you say no?'

'I suppose not,' he said weakly.

'And you've got a partner,' continued Carlos. 'Come on, you're as bad as me.'

'I don't have a partner, I have an ex-partner. But Carlos, you're never free when somebody loves you. I'm not sure whether Tim ever really loved me. As far as gay life is concerned, it's different; gay people aren't going to get married or have children or become respected pillars of society; we'll always be on the outside. But you're on the inside. You have a beautiful girl who loves you....'

Carlos interrupted him. 'Loves me so much that she gives me this black eye. Anyway, there are lots of girls in the village who probably love me. I'm twenty three. What would you do if you were me?' He fell silent.

Rui realised that, in a way, he admired Carlos. He could see a mirror image of himself as a twenty three year old. At that age, he had chosen a life of excess, dancing and glamour but had fallen spectacularly, destroyed by his own success. Carlos could have done the same, but didn't. He had decided to ignore his looks and become a simple policeman and that showed better judgement than most people would have given him credit for.

'I can't offer any advice, Carlos,' said Rui. 'My own relationship is fucked up, and my only crime was to try to be honest. You know, I have a past that I'm not proud of, but I'm proud of who I am. I only wanted to be honest with Tim. So I told him.'

'Was it so bad?'

Rui grimaced.

'To Tim it was. It was years ago. I gave up the dancing to be with my boyfriend. We had a clothing company together and for two years we were doing great. Then he died. His parents bankrupted me. I had nothing. Then I fell in with the wrong crowd. After that, my life got fucked up by drugs and bad relationships and I found myself on the street; then I got involved in the massage business. Money came in; lots of it. Carlos, I used to take money for sex.' He looked at Carlos for a reaction; Carlos just nodded, encouraging him to say more. 'I had to. I had no choice at the time. Now he accuses me. I mean, where does he think I got my money from anyway? It didn't come out of thin air.'

Carlos gazed at Rui. It was like hearing confession and he wondered if it would be good for the soul. He glanced round, then leant forward and spoke in a quiet voice.

'Rui, will you promise not to tell anyone what I am about to tell you?' Rui nodded. 'I've been saving up to buy a BMW Z3, a beautiful little metallic blue one; only four years old; thirty thousand kilometres. I see all those old men driving around in them and want one before I'm too old to enjoy it. Policemen's wages are shit, you know. I would never have been able to afford it. You've seen my Fiesta.'

Rui had seen the Fiesta and agreed that it was probably worth selling one's soul to get rid of it.

'You've been supplementing your income?'

'Well, yes, in a manner of speaking.'

'Cristina?' Carlos nodded. 'Ursula?' He nodded again.

'There have been others,' he said sheepishly. 'Lots of others. But, you know, it's a funny thing; I can barely remember most of them.'

Rui looked at Carlos, but his mind understood the clarity of forgetfulness.

Carlos continued. 'Oh, come on, Rui. Those women have more money than they know what to do with. It means nothing to them but it means everything to me. You always want what you can't have.'

'In your case, a car; in their case, you?'

Carlos was silent for a while.

'Yeah. But now that I've almost got the money for the car, I can see what it's cost me. I don't want to think about how I earned it and now I've lost Paula. All for the sake of a fucking car.......Losing her has really hurt me. I'd give my life for that woman,' he said in a small voice, as if the realisation had only just occurred to him. 'You never know what you have until it's gone. You do believe me, don't you? Everything I've said?'

'Of course,' said Rui. 'Actually, the only difference between you and me is that you're younger. And here we sit; two single men, crying into our beers. Tell you what, Carlos. Tonight I am going to get seriously pissed. Starting right now.'

As he ordered another round of drinks, a tall attractive middle-aged blonde walked past and waved at Carlos. He waved back.

'You didn't.........' said Rui incredulously and Carlos smiled like a naughty boy.

Ben Chilcott sat in the brothel bar, which was getting busy. The music and conversations mixed with the smell of stale ash that permeated the establishment. Chilcott was on his mobile phone to Amores, his hand over one ear to to cut out the noise. He stood up and moved to a corner.

After listening intently, he closed his phone, lit another cigarette and drew on it deeply. Taking Rui's card from his wallet, he flicked open his mobile and dialled. At that moment the door swung open and Rui staggered in, moving like a ship in a storm, his mobile phone ringing in his hand as he fumbled with the buttons, dropping the phone on the floor where it broke in two pieces.

'Shit, shit, shit, shit,' said Rui.

Chilcott smiled to himself.

'Hey, Rui. Howzit?' he said, retrieving the bits of Rui's phone from the floor.

'Shit, Ben. Get me a fucking drink, won't you?' Rui was unsteady and sat himself next to the bar, swaying. His eyes were glazed and looked unfocussed. He swallowed as if he were about to be sick.

The beer arrived on the counter as Rui perched on a bar stool which wobbled in sympathy. Picking up the glass, he downed half the contents in one go. He looked at Chilcott as if trying to remember something.

'What's up Bro?'

'I jusht wanted to say how much I fucking hate you. You're the cause of all my ……..grief.'

Chilcott didn't attempt to cover his smile.

'What did I do?' he asked.

'Tim's gone,' Rui slurred. 'I'm a batchel…..a bachelor again. We had a fight and he's gone. Forever. Back to Amsterbloodydam. Gone to get his rocks off. Shagging anything that moves. Bastard.'

'What, it's all over? Just like that? I'm sorry, Bro.'

Chilcott's expression said that he wasn't sorry at all. He looked at Rui wobbling unsteadily on his barstool. He looked sad, drunk and sad. Sad and vulnerable.

'Ben,' Rui moaned, 'I'm lonely. You're my mate aren't you? I hate you, but you are my mate, aren't you?'

'Of course, Rui. We go back a long way, mate.'

'Tell me, Ben. That's your name isn't it? Yes. Ben. Have I ever schlept with you?'

'You didn't sleep much, Rui.'

Rui went silent and Chilcott thought that he was going to be sick, then Rui regained what remained of his composure and looked up through booze-wet eyes.

'I jusht had an idea….a very good idea,' slurred Rui and Chilcott raised his eyebrows in expectation. 'I don't fancy having sex with anyone else here. Let's have a thr……a threesome.'

'A threesome? A three-way?' asked Chilcott, bemused.

'Yeah. There's me and there's the two of you. Less jus go back t'your place and have a schag.' He hiccupped. 'I really need a schag with someone who's not called TimfuckingMitchell.'

Chilcott's expression brightened at the prospect.

'Rui, that's the best idea you've had all year. Let's go.'

'And bring your friend. He's a bit better looking than you.'

They left the bar and made for Chilcott's apartment. Rui had his arm around the other man and stumbled at his side. In the apartment Rui collapsed onto a sofa and immediately fell asleep. Chilcott went to his kitchen and retrieved a bag of coke. He put out a few lines and woke Rui who had difficulty focussing but, when he saw the lines, he smiled.

'Ben, you're a reeeeal mate. Y'll always be my bestest mate,' he said and sniffed two lines noisily. His eyes opened wide as if someone had switched the lights on. 'Thass better,' he exclaimed, approaching full consciousness. Chilcott turned off the lights, leaving the room bathed in the moon's virginal radiance. Under the magic spell of the coke genie they stripped naked, fell on each other hungrily and fucked like rabbits.

It wasn't only that the sex was electrifying; what energised Chilcott more was the certain knowledge that this was the last time that Rui would ever make love, his last orgasm. He was completely in his power. That excited him; he wanted to hurt him as they fucked; he liked inflicting pain; briefly he thought about combining sex and murder; what a turn-on, but Rui started to gasp. He groaned loudly, his body shook in spasms and Chilcott felt the wetness hitting his body. Fuck, thought Chilcott; I wanted that to last, but the sight of Rui groaning like prey and the knowledge that his fantasy would soon be reality made it impossible for him to hold back. He had an explosive orgasm, folded from exertion, then fell back, exhausted. Rui collapsed, face down, onto the wet bed, semi-conscious, his arm draped over Chilcott.

Chilcott gave himself a few minutes to recover while his pulse returned to normal. Rui lay next to him breathing deeply, unconscious again. Chilcott was wide awake and knew that this was the time that he had to die; he had fucked him and now he would kill him. He looked at the jagged scars on Rui's back and the livid red mark where the bullet had creased him. I was responsible for all of them, he thought, and you are lying on my bed, my spunk all over you. He smiled to himself. He almost regretted having to kill him unconscious because it would be over too soon. Maybe he should wake him. Murder could be almost like making love; how much better it is, he thought, to make it last, to play with them a bit until you can see from the terror in their eyes that they know what is going to happen to them. Then let them beg and tremble before the knife ends the session like an orgasm.

Rui's arm had him trapped and he tried not to wake him. With his free hand, he awkwardly tried to open the drawer of his bedside cabinet to get to the knife that he kept there; the same knife that had despatched Chico; his knife, jagged and cold, his friend. Sliding the drawer open, he fumbled for it, found it and lifted it by the blade, trying to juggle it into position. The angle was awkward and it was his wrong hand; damn; he felt it starting to slip from between his fingertips. As it dropped, he whispered a curse and, in the silence of the night, it hit the tile floor with a metallic clash. Rui woke as the echo died away in the night air. He shot bolt upright, staring forward as if in shock, and started retching and gulping. Oh fuck, he's going to be sick, Chilcott thought and pushed Rui off the bed in the automatic reflex of a gay man with new bedding. Rui fell on the floor but picked himself up, groaning and gulping, his hands over his mouth. He lurched for the toilet where he was raucously sick. Chilcott followed, knife in hand, but Rui had closed the door and locked it. He's got to come out, he thought. He's trapped.

He waited and, after a minute, the key grated in the lock and the door opened. Rui's unfocussed eyes looked through him; the convulsive swallowing started again and projectile vomit splattered over Chilcott. Then the phone started to ring. Fuck, thought Chilcott, it's probably António. Shit, shit, shit. I can't kill him right now; there's too much going on and there would be no pleasure in it. He's going nowhere, anyway.

With Rui's vomit dripping from his chest and down his legs, he went to answer the phone. As he had suspected, it was Amores, checking progress. He placated him and put the phone down; OK, he thought. Now it's time for the final act. He moved through the moonlight glow back to the bedroom, the knife clenched in his sweating hand, raised to strike; he could smell the vomit but wanted to smell blood. Rui's. Now is your time.

Chilcott crept into the dark bedroom and towards the shape in the bed. Leaping onto the bed, he lunged, stabbing again and again.

Then he stopped; the knife didn't find the expected resistance. He turned on the light to find that he had lacerated his new bedding and two pillows. Swearing, he looked around, pulled all the covers off the bed, peered under the bed, checked the lounge then back in the bathroom, a banshee hunting a ghost.

Groaning in frustration, he slumped onto the bed. What would he tell António? This is only a postponement, Rui, he said under his breath.

'So the Fabulous Four is now the Tremendous Three,' said Cristina sitting on the edge of her bed. Rui was standing by the door to the balcony, looking out over the sea, nursing the most dreadful hangover of his life.

'Please, please Cristina,' he said in a pitiful voice. 'My head. It won't go away. I urgently need some paracetomols. About a hundred. Please put me out of my misery.'

Cristina went and got him two which he washed down with water. His eyes were bloodshot and his skin was grey.

'Was it a good night?'

'Oh, shit. I can't remember. I think I had sex with someone. What were you saying?'

'Tim…..'

Rui groaned. 'Cristina, please don't swear. I spoke to him yesterday evening. He's still angry but I think he'll come back to Portugal. Maybe live somewhere else. He likes it here too much to give it up. We've basically made our lives here.' He turned back into the room and slumped on the bed, nursing his head in his hands.

Abruptly, he started retching, ran for the toilet and was violently sick. Cristina waited until he emerged and sat on the bed again.

'Feeling better?'

He nodded and carried on where he had left off. 'My guess is he's going to get his rocks off for a few days in Amsterdam , then come back when he's cooled down.'

'And you don't mind that?'

'Of course I mind, it's just that I can forgive him. It's easy. I don't talk about it or make a fuss about it. I just accept a bit of imperfection.'

Cristina looked at him with a sympathetic smile.

'You really love him don't you?'

He looked at her and his expression said it all.

She sighed. 'He doesn't deserve you.' They sat in silence for a minute or more, Rui regretting his honesty, Cristina feeling sorry for Rui's predicament. The sun blazed outside but they both felt a chill of loneliness in the shade of the interior.

Later that day, Rui was feeling more human.

'Come on, Rui. Let's shake ourselves out of this mood,' Cristina told him. 'We had a crime to solve. We still have a crime to solve.'

Rui seemed uninterested. 'I don't see what difference it will make,' he shrugged.

'Well it will help me write my story, if nothing else. Come on, let's put our brains together.'

Rui sighed. 'I don't see how we can link Chilcott with the murder of Chico, if they're linked at all. If it's a turf war, everyone will keep silent; they're all criminals. No witnesses. No evidence. No case.'

'But there was your shooting.'

'Again, no witnesses. No evidence; no evidence of anything. At least I can understand the Chico case; it was about drugs, but my shooting? What was that about?' He paced to the window.

Cristina thought for a moment.

'Let's come at it from another angle. Clear minds, now. You say you saw Chilcott in the Christian shop with this solicitor, Amores.'

He turned back towards her. 'Yes. I thought it was strange at the time. Chilcott is not exactly a pillar of the Church.'

'Let's assume, just assume, that they work together,' said Cristina. 'Amores is the suit; the money. Chilcott is the one who does the dirty work. Now what have we got?'

'A suit and a scumbag in a Christian shop, confessing their sins,' said Rui.

'No, a drug dealer and a man with money in a Christian shop. What does that mean?'

'Repentance?' said Rui. Cristina laughed.

'Now. Hold that thought. OK. Alternative tack. Someone shot at you. Someone sees you as a threat. Why are you a threat?'

'Dunno. I'm just a ray of sunlight.'

'Rui, please be serious,' Cristina reprimanded. 'Maybe you know something that has put the wind up someone. Now what do you know that would make someone want to kill you?'

'I've got a great recipe for *Feijouada*.'

Cristina raised her eyes to heaven for salvation. 'This isn't going to work, is it?' she said.

'No, wait,' said Rui. 'I saw them together,'

'I know that, dummy,' said Cristina in frustration. 'There's something else we're missing. Maybe you don't know something but they think that you do. Yes, maybe that's it. Now, think, Rui. Is there anything that you might have stumbled on by accident, something you didn't realise was important? Or is there anything that you might have done by accident?'

Rui gave a theatrical sniff.

'I am inclined to be a bit accident-prone. It's not my fault. It's the world. Sometimes it conspires against me.'

'Think.'

'Well, there was the mix-up of the mail orders of the sex shop and the book shop.'

'Tell me more.'

'We accidentally sent some sex toys to people who'd ordered books. What can that have to do with anything?'

'I don't know. We're clutching at straws but all I'm doing is to postulate a situation and see whether it leads us anywhere. Did you keep all of the paperwork?'

'Yes. Ursula's got it. And we've got it on computer.'

'Come,' said Cristina, grabbing her handbag. 'Let's go.'

At the sex shop, Ursula was busy answering emails and setting up the orders. The bell rang announcing the arrival of Cristina and Rui.

'Christ, Rui, what happened to you?' Ursula gasped, looking up from her screen. 'Your eyes. Close them immediately before you bleed to death.'

'Hangover,' said Cristina. Ursula nodded in understanding. 'Tim's left him and he was drowning his sorrows. He almost drowned himself in the process.'

'Bastard,' muttered Rui and Ursula took that as a sign that he didn't want to talk about it.

Peter emerged from the back room. 'I've been drowning me sorrows meself,' he said.

Ursula gave him a meaningful look and explained. 'He paid a hotshot solicitor ten grand to get the license then they closed the shop. Then he found out that he'd been ripped off. It should only have cost about two hundred.'

'Ten grand? Peter,' said Rui. 'I can't believe it. Jesus, they saw you coming,'

'So it seems. Anyway, I gets a phone call yesterday saying it will cost another five to get it re-opened. Bloody right, I says, just so's you can close me down again? Bastard. Yeah, they saw me coming all right. They thought it was bleedin' Christmas when they saw me coming over the horizon.'

'So, who was this solicitor?'

'António Amores.'

'That's a coincidence,' said Cristina, smiling inscrutably at Rui. 'So, can we assume that he's no longer a friend of yours?'

'Let him give me my ten grand back and I'll think about it.'

'Till then?'

'He'd better watch 'is back.'

Cristina took a deep breath. 'We've had a thought,' she said. 'Can we see whether he was caught up in that mail order mix-up?'

'Oh, that's easy to check on,' said Ursula. She typed in the name and said, 'Bingo. Amazing! Dr António Amores, Ferragudo. Yes, he was one of our customers.' She looked up with satisfaction.

'And what did he get?' asked Cristina.

Ursula checked the records again, glasses on the tip of her nose. 'Ah. He was caught up in the mix-up.' She pulled out a sheet of paper and waved it at Cristina. 'We accidentally sent him a novel by J G Ballard. Cocaine Nights.'

'Was it returned?'

'Nope,' said Ursula checking the screen. 'He must have liked it.'

Cristina beamed in triumph and turned to Rui as if to take a bow on stage.

'You see? That's the answer. He received that book and assumed that it was a threat. Have you read it?'

Rui shook his head.

'It's about expats in southern Spain. Drugs, prostitution, pornography, theft, vandalism, murder. It's a bundle of laughs; a society built on crime, that needs crime to survive. Don't you see? If Amores is our man, he would have seen that as a direct threat, an unsubtle message that someone was onto him. Then it would have been the easiest thing in the world to find out from George that it was you running the mail order business. He gets your name and the connection is made. Then you see him and Chilcott in the shop next door. You are suddenly his worst enemy. And he didn't return the book; he was too scared. The rest, as they say, is history.' She looked at the screen and made some rapid notes in a shorthand pad.

'What's all this, then?' asked Peter.

'It's your friend, Amores. We think it was him who might have had a go at Rui. We reckon he's involved in drugs and he thought that Rui was onto him.' She closed her pad with a decisive snap. 'I need to find out more about his business dealings,' she said. 'I'm going to Lagoa.' She stopped as a thought occurred to her. 'Incidentally, as a matter of interest……..what was it that he ordered from the sex shop?'

'Patient confidentiality…..' muttered Ursula. 'My lips are sealed.'

'Oh come on, Ursula,' said Peter. 'The man's a complete piece of slime. Come on. Give us a laugh.'

She tapped a couple of keys, smiled to herself, then looked up.

'You're not going to believe this, darlings. But…… it was Big Ben!'

Later that day, Ursula was disturbed by a commotion coming from next door. She and Peter went outside to see what ws going on. The shouting was coming from inside the Christian shop and pilgrims were fleeing and hobbling in all directions. Peter peered around the door and saw Senhora Ramalho inside in great distress. In her arms she held Flavia, flailing violently.

'Please, oh please, Flavia. You can't behave like this. Not in a shop. This is God's shop,' wept her mother. Flavia screamed as if she was being murdered. One of the customers tried to placate her, receiving a random blow on the face for her pains. The manageress had called the police and Carlos arrived in a squad car with a colleague. Together, they tried to pacify Flavia. From the back of the shop a man in a suit emerged and Flavia screamed even louder; Peter recognised Amores.

'Get her out, officer,' Amores shouted at Carlos. 'I won't have this kind of behaviour in my shop. This is a place of quiet contemplation for the customers, not a cattle yard. Call a doctor and see if he can't tranquilise her.'

'I'm sure that won't be necessary, Sir,' said Carlos. 'Please leave the matter with me.' He coaxed Senhora Ramalho and Flavia from the shop. Once outside, the girl was calmer but sobbing to herself. Soon she was tranquil.

'Thank you, Carlos,' said Senhora Ramalho. 'You're always kind to us; I really appreciate it. I think Flavia appreciates it too. She's always calm when she sees you.'

She shook her head. 'I don't know what came over her. She's normally as quiet as a mouse. And in a Christian shop as well.' She looked tenderly at Flavia by her side and stroked her head, smiling as she would if she were taking the pain out of a bruise or soothing a graze. 'It's OK, *queridinha*.' Then, her arm around Flavia, she turned to Carlos and said, 'It was as if she'd seen the devil himself.'

Roger Hardy

Fourteen

The next morning, Rui was outside the guest house tending to the flowers, when he saw Thérèse come to her door. He had been used to seeing her cheerful and active, but this morning she looked grey and old. Her hair was a mess and she seemed to have aged ten years overnight. Three pilgrims who had been standing nearby saw her and moved away, confused disillusionment on their faces.

'So sorry to hear about your accident, Rui,' she said.

'Oh, that was a while ago, Thérèse, but thank you anyway.' He realised that he had barely seen her since the recovery of her money. 'And how are you?'

'Oh, maybe it's only temporary, Rui. Maybe I'll be OK tomorrow. I thought I was going to get better but ......sometimes I ask myself what have I've done to deserve this.'

As she spoke, Afonso appeared from the direction of the church with Carlos, Senhora Ramalho and Flavia at his side.

'The Bishop has intervened,' said Afonso proudly. 'He's persuaded the GNR not to press charges against Senhora Ramalho. We're going to the office to formalise it. I've agreed to take her under my wing and make sure that she doesn't get into any more trouble. Isn't that right, Senhora?' She smiled weakly.

'Father Afonso and Carlos have been very kind to us,' she murmured.

Thérèse gazed at them icily.

'It's not right,' she said, turning to go back into her house.

'There was just one more thing, Senhora,' said Afonso.

She turned back to him with difficulty.

'Yes?'

'I wanted to ask you about Saint James.'

Thérèse frowned in irritation.

'What are you talking about, Father? I don't know anything Saint James. I'm not religious; I don't go to Church. Why should I know anything about him?'

Afonso pointed to her wall.

'It's the scallops,' he said. 'They're the sign of Santiago de Compostela. You know, the pilgrimage.'

'I told you before Father, if I was interested in a pilgrimage I would have gone to Lourdes,' Thérèse snapped. 'Anyway, the scallops were just a decoration that I liked. I thought it was nice to have, with the house overlooking the sea. Now look at them. There are hardly any left now. Those damned pilgrims have taken them all.'

Afonso ran his fingers over the cement indentations where they had once been.

'I see. This may sound strange, Senhora, but do you know anything about bones? Has anyone raised the subject of bones with you?'

Thérèse stared at him. 'Bones?'

'Yes.'

'Bones?'

He nodded.

She thought for a bit. 'The only thing I can think of is that I have a little mandolin made from bones. I bought it in Santiago de Chile. It's three hundred years old. Souvenir of some tribal war of the Aymara Indians. It brings back memories.' She became introspective. 'My stupid cleaner broke it and I fired her. That's all I have now; my memories.'

Afonso looked at her, his eyes sad. 'I think that the miracle is over,' he said.

'Is that all?' she asked.

'Yes, thank you, Senhora,' said Afonso.

Thérèse moved, almost fell, and reached for her Zimmer frame against the side of the wall and used it to negotiate the short distance. She faded into the darkness.

Rui watched her with pity; she had regressed to the same state as when he had first met her.

'Yes. Well and truly over,' said Rui.

Later that day Cristina bustled in through Rui's door.

'How did you get on in Lagoa?' asked Rui, looking up from his newspaper. 'Did you discover any skeletons?'

'It was deliciously illegal,' she said. 'And it wasn't Lagoa. I went to Lisbon.'

'Lisbon? Why Lisbon?'

'I have a friend there. A very clever friend. Honestly, if any of this ever gets out I'll be dead, I promise you. It was so illegal. I even surprised myself.' She looked conspiratorial, clearly enjoying herself.

'Come on. Don't keep me waiting.' Rui leaned forward like a dog waiting for a bone.

'Remember when Ursula was checking on the purchases in the sex shop? I made a note of Amores's credit card number.....'

'You minx......you went on a shopping spree in Lisbon?'

'No, of course not. I have this friend who is a bit of a computer hacker. We got into his credit card account.' She pulled a folder from her bag and opened it. 'Lots of interesting stuff, believe me.'

'Admissible in court?'

Cristina shook her head.

'No, of course not. I'd go to jail for longer than him. In any case, this is only information, not evidence. You see, from the credit card we got the bank account and from the bank account we got his mobile phone number, then the mobile phone records. Everything. I've got everything.'

'You're a very scary lady,' said Rui, flicking through the records.

'I'll take that as a compliment,' Cristina smiled.

Rui heard a car pull up outside. Diesel. Taxi. He went to the balcony and leaned over.

'Christ! It's Tim. He's come back,' he said, running back into the room, thrusting the file back into Cristina's hands.

He clattered down the stairs. Two minutes later, he was back with Tim who looked careworn and unkempt after the flight. Rui was beaming behind him.

'Amsterdam too damp for you?' asked Cristina coldly.

'I was only concerned in case Rui gets shot again,' said Tim, sitting down, taking out a cigarette and lighting it without offering one to Rui.

'Do I detect a hint of sympathy and concern?' said Rui.

Tim shrugged. 'If you get shot again I'll have to run the business, and you know what that means…..'

'Ah, yes. Basil Fawlty,' said Rui. 'We can't have that, can we?'

Cristina watched the body language of Rui and Tim. Rui, transparently happy but not wanting to show it; Tim, rumpled, trying to look nonchalant, his expression giving nothing away.

'I'll give you guys some space,' said Cristina diplomatically and closed the door behind her.

Later that day, they got together in Cristina's room. Tim and Rui sat on opposite sides of the room as if there was a river between them. Cristina watched them both from the corner of her eye as she took out her paperwork.

'So,' said Cristina. 'The Tremendous Three becomes the Fantastic Four again.' Rui smiled but Tim's expression was blank. 'I'm so glad,' she continued, 'because we've reached the stage where we need a bit more brain power. Cristina showed Tim the results of her criminal research.

'I can't believe that you've got all this,' he said, shuffling through the paperwork.

'Look at the bank statement,' said Cristina. 'In the past month, there have been seven transfers into the account totalling four hundred thousand Euros, then, look further down, there's an international transfer for the same amount. It's a wire transfer to a bank in Miami.'

'I can't believe he'd be so stupid as to use his own account.'

Cristina shrugged. 'He's a solicitor and there are plenty of other transfers relating to property and suchlike. He probably thought that no one would notice it coming in and going out.'

'What about the tax people?'

'Oh, please, Tim. This is Portugal. Tax evasion is a national sport here.'

Tim tapped his fingers on the file.

'OK, so we know that he has money and rich tastes in Miami.'

'Miami is where all those nice people from Colombia live to avoid being kidnapped or shot,' said Cristina. 'And we know the largest contributor to Columbia's Gross National Product, don't we?'

'Hmm,' muttered Tim thoughtfully. 'But it's all a bit tenuous, isn't it?'

Cristina smiled. 'That's my stock in trade, Tim. I follow circumstantial leads until they take me to some real evidence. That's what investigative journalism is. We spend our lives lifting stones to see what crawls out.'

Tim looked back at the statement. 'Another interesting thing is that the money going out is the same amount as the money coming in. That makes me think he's spending other people's money, not his own.'

Cristina stood up and began pacing up and down the room.

'Let's suppose that the money is for Columbia's greatest export, then go on to think about what happens if the goods get lost or are intercepted by the police.'

'I wouldn't want to be Amores,' said Rui.

'Nor would I,' said Cristina. 'If it's Lisbon mafia, he wouldn't survive twenty-four hours,'

'Anyway,' said Rui. 'What about his phone records?'

Tim shuffled through the paperwork to find them. 'Itemised bill; that's useful,' he said. 'Look, it lists all the numbers he called over the last month.' He jabbed a finger at the sheet of paper. 'There's one he calls a lot; twenty times yesterday alone. Let's ring it and see who it is.' He pulled out his mobile phone and started to key in the numbers.

'No, use mine,' said Cristina. 'Remember his call register. It doesn't matter if he has my number.' She handing her phone to Rui. He keyed in the number, listened and disconnected.

'It's Ben Chilcott,' he said, smiling. 'We've got Chilcott's number.'

'And Amores's,' said Cristina.

'Well, aren't we clever?' said Rui with a hint of irony. 'Now we can call them any time we want.'

'Oh, don't be so stupid,' said Tim dismissively.

'No, you miss the point,' said Cristina, ignoring Tim's barb. 'The police can get permission to listen in on the phone calls.'

'But don't they have to be convinced that there's a crime involved?' asked Tim. 'There's no evidence of a crime, yet. It's all circumstantial. Surely, they'll never get permission.'

Cristina laughed. 'This isn't the UK, you know,' she said in a mocking tone. 'Remember that the guys at the top of the police force now were junior officers when Portugal was still a fascist dictatorship. Believe me, they know when to turn a blind eye when it's necessary.'

underground, illegal. They know the name but not the face. They've been though all the bars but haven't been able to track him down; there seems to be wall of silence surrounding him.'

'Oh, come on,' said Rui, 'he's usually in the bordello. Why don't they raid that?'

'They can't risk the chance of him not being in the place when they raid it, and they can't recognise him anyway. If he's not there, he'll be alerted and go deeper underground and they'll never find him. They've asked me if I can identify him for them.'

'But you've never met him. Why you?'

Carlos shuffled his feet and looked uncomfortable.

'Well, sorry, Rui, but I was trying to look good. You told me that you know him........I was wondering........'

Rui slapped his head in desperation, then realised that Carlos was being serious.

'He's big and butch,' said Rui. 'I mean, he's a South African Boer which kind of makes him butch by definition. But if they want you to identify him, you'll need to meet him.'

'Also, they want to pick him up,' continued Carlos. 'So they need to know where he is. They have no records of where he lives.'

As Carlos spoke, Rui had a recollection that he couldn't explain; it was a vague notion that he had been to Chilcott's apartment. He scoured his memory for details but without success. In any case, there was the bordello. He knew where that was.

'The bordello, he's always in the bordello,' he said.

'But he doesn't live there,' Tim countered. 'The delivery is going to his home address isn't it?'

Cristina looked at Rui then back to Tim.

'If he's at the bordello, you'll find him and recognise him,' said Cristina with a shrug. 'If he's at home, we'll have to think of something else. Nothing lost.'

'The bordello,' said Rui with confidence. 'He's bound to be there.' He looked at Carlos. 'I'll take you to meet him tonight, if you want.'

Carlos grinned, relieved. 'Great. You don't mind?'

'Oh, it'll be fun; I always fancied police work,' said Rui. 'But it'll have to be late. After midnight.'

Tim was not certain that he liked this plan.

'Hey, wait a minute, Rui. This is all a bit dangerous, isn't it? We think he might want you dead, and you walk straight into his bar? I don't think so. That's not going to work. I think it's stupid.'

Rui scratched his head.

'Oh, Tim,' said Rui, his voice heavy with irony. 'You're sounding almost concerned.'

Tim sniffed derisively.

'I'll have a police escort,' continued Rui. 'Maybe Amores wants me dead but Ben hasn't got any reason to kill me; we're mates. I hate him because he knows about my past, but that's all out in the open now, so I suppose we're mates again.'

Tim shook his head at Rui's naivety.

'No, Rui. Don't be so stupid. Chilcott and Amores work together. Don't forget that someone shot at you. They weren't joking. I can't imagine that Amores would get his hands dirty so he probably delegates the rough stuff to Chilcott. He might be a mate but he still wants you dead, mate. And how are you going to explain your police escort? Won't the uniform and the gun in the holster be a bit of a give-away?'

'Carlos will be in civvies,' said Cristina.

Tim was far from convinced.

'But why would a gay man be with a straight man in a questionable club after midnight, meeting a gay thug? Won't he expect you to be with me?' said Tim.

Carlos interjected, 'After you broke up, Rui was telling everyone who'd listen that you and he were history; I think that Chilcott will have got the same message. You did see him after you split up, didn't you, Rui?'

Rui frowned. The niggling memory tickled his brain again, but he couldn't bring it into focus.

'Yeah, I think so. I was really, really pissed, but I think I did.'

'I still don't like it,' said Tim.

Rui gave him a sweet smile.

'Tim, although I hate you, darling, do I detect a little frisson of anxiety in your voice?'

Tim looked at him, trying to think of a suitable reply when Carlos said, 'But, Tim's right, Rui, how will you explain me? Won't he be suspicious?'

Rui thought for a moment. 'Does anyone know you in Portimão?'

'Not as a policeman; I go there of course, but not in uniform.'

A wicked smile curled Rui's lips.

'Well, Tim and I are finished and he knows that, so you can be my new bed-warmer; maybe a rent boy.'

'What?' Carlos was horrified. 'Rui, I like you, but....oh, no please....'

Rui laughed. 'Oh, come on, Carlos. You owe me. Remember? The cash box? You didn't tell me I was off the suspects list? You kept tapping on my door....' He sniffed in imitation of Hollywood flu.

'What's the problem, Carlos?' asked Cristina. 'It's only a little play-acting; fancy dress.'

'No, I can't. I'm sorry,' spouted Carlos.

'Oh, come on, Carlos,' said Cristina. 'It's the key to the case. You identifying Chilcott. Your bosses have asked you to do it.'

'No. It's impossible.....isn't there some other way? Can't you take a photograph of him, Rui?'

Rui shook his head.

'Paula will be proud of you. You might be able to win her back,' Cristina urged. That made Carlos stop in his tracks.

'You think so?'

'Carlos, you'll be a hero. Women like heroes,' said Rui. 'You'll have played an important part stopping Portimão being flooded with drugs.....and we think Chilcott may be involved in a murder as well.'

Carlos was torn between his passion for Paula and his macho image.

'But to dress and act like a gay. No, please.....that's too much to ask.'

'OK, listen,' said Cristina. 'I'll get a petition drawn up and you can put it in your top pocket. A petition signed by Carvoeiro's biggest club.'

'Which is?' asked Tim, confused.

'The Carlos Bedpost Club. Do you think one sheet of A4 will be enough? Two?' She took out a piece of paper from her handbag, clicked her ballpoint and waited, eyebrows raised.

'Now you're making fun of me,' said Carlos.

'No more fun that you're making of yourself,' she said coldly.

He hesitated. 'No, I'm sorry. I can't. The answer's still no.'

'Right,' said Cristina, losing her patience. 'How much more do you need for the Z3?'

Carlos looked surprised. 'Er….about eight hundred.'

'OK,' said Cristina. 'I promise to give you eight hundred Euros if you do this thing. Do it for me. Do it for Paula, Do it for your career. Just do it.' She scribbled an IOU on the paper, signed it and held it up to Carlos who sniffed it as it was waved under his nose.

'Rui, will I be seen by anyone that knows me?'

'No, I doubt it. We'll go there, have a drink and come straight back…..or maybe come back straight,' quipped Rui.

Carlos looked at the proffered IOU, hesitated, then, with an expression of deep embarrassment, slowly took it to signify that the deal had been done.

Rui struck while the iron was hot. 'But you'll have to dress up like a Brazilian telenovela star.'

Carlos winced.

'Oh, that should be easy. Er….one thing, Rui. Do I have to speak……..in an effeminate voice?'

'Oh, for God's sake, Carlos!' Tim snapped. 'Do I speak in an effeminate voice? Does Rui?'

'No. Sorry,' said Carlos.

'You see, we still remember that you've got a reputation to maintain, Orlando,' said Rui.

'Who?'

'Orlando. That's your name for tonight.'

Fifteen

Carlos turned up in an unbuttoned orange silk shirt, Chinos and a pair of designer sunglasses perched over his forehead, nestling in his hair. He was wearing CK One and a cloud of it followed him, marking his trail. He wore a chunky gold chain around his neck; a prominent and very camp crucifix hanging from it. He had accidentally chosen an appearance somewhere between muscular and camp and it was perfect. Rui was impressed; he could not have done better himself.

'My mother asked me to wear it for luck,' he said, fingering the crucifix.

Rui peered at him again. 'Carlos, are you wearing eye-liner?'

'Yes, my mother said that all the Brazilian soap stars do. I want you to know I'm taking this seriously.'

'You look perfect,' said Rui smiling at Tim.

'This had better be an Oscar-winning performance, Carlos,' Cristina warned.

Carlos smiled coyly and put his arm around Rui, fluttering his eyelashes, then checked the window to make sure no one was watching.

Rui was excited as he drove off but by the time they arrived in Portimão he was less confident.

'You feeling nervous, Carlos?'

Carlos shook his head.

'Nah. Why should I be? I'm a straight policeman posing as the lover of a gay friend who has been shot at, visiting a brothel run by a vicious South African drug dealer and possible murderer, so that we can organise his arrest and send him and his associates down for the rest of their lives. Of course I'm not nervous.'

'Well, now you put it like that….well, actually we're only going out for a drink, aren't we?'

'Just a drink; that's all.'

Rui and Carlos walked into the bordello which was having a quiet night with only four girls sitting at the tables and three men. The girl behind the bar was talking to one of them out of boredom. Chilcott was at the bar, cigarette in hand, spinning around on his bar stool. He smiled like a snake when he saw Rui, welcoming him with a handshake and a kiss.

'Hey, Rui. Howzit. I was just thinking about you.' He signalled to the barmaid for drinks. He took in Carlos like a starving dog looking at a steak.

'So, is this the new boyfriend, then?' he said, devouring him with his eyes.

'This is Orlando, Ben.' The two men shook hands in a fragrant cloud of cologne. Carlos put his arm around Rui whose doubts about Carlos's acting ability vanished in an instant. His debut was a triumph. There would be rave reviews.

'So how does Orlando fit into the picture?' asked Chilcott, passing their drinks.

'He's Tim's replacement. Smokin' hot isn't he? Met him in Lagos,' Rui smiled at Carlos who squeezed him more tightly. That felt good, thought Rui.

Chilcott grinned in approval.

'I thought that Tim was too high and mighty for you,' he said. 'Real prick. I like your new choice, Rui.' He downed his beer, eyes fixed on Carlos, scrutinising him lecherously. Rui watched him from the corner of his eye. He recognised the signs of a man distracted by the God of Possible Sex.

'Fancy a threesome, Rui? Plenty of snow, plenty of fun.'

Again, a fleeting thought insinuated its way into Rui's brain. It said: you've already been there. But as soon as it had arrived, it dissipated.

'Ben, I'm flattered, but I've only just met him and don't want to share; not for a while, anyway.'

Ben looked disappointed.

'Your loss,' he shrugged. 'Maybe some other time. Anyway, what brings you out here tonight, Bro?'

Rui had not expected the question. We're here so that we can destroy you, Ben, he thought. You tried to kill me but I'm still here. You killed Chico and you're still here. We're both survivors but after tomorrow there will be only one of us left. We're here so that Carlos can recognise you again. An idea came to him. He had vowed not to do coke again, but there could be one last time. For a greater good. He realised that Chilcott was waiting for an answer.

'Well, a beer or two, then back to bed,' said Rui. 'But I was wondering whether you might be able to organise a little something to make the night last longer. Getting the stuff's been a bit difficult lately. Orlando fucks like a rabbit when he's high.'

'Snow?'

Rui nodded and Carlos's arm around his shoulder tensed as if to say that this was not part of the plan.

'You should have phoned me and I could have brought something,' said Chilcott, his voice silky smooth. 'I don't have any here. I'll have to go back to my place. Why don't you come with me?' He stared deeply into Carlos's eyes and Rui saw Carlos looking back at him; neither blinked or looked away; too long to be casual in the gay eye-contact-protocol with which Carlos would not be familiar.

Rui watched Carlos and begged him to look away, but he did not and Rui could almost see Chilcott thinking: Result. Perhaps it had been a mistake asking Carlos to dress like a rent boy. Now he was making himself into an object of desire, like a gift-wrapped present saying, 'please fuck me' and he didn't know he was doing it. On the other hand, this development meant that they would find out Chilcott's address, so it had an advantage.

It was just a short walk to Chilcott's apartment on the first floor of a new nondescript apartment block. The flat was well-appointed and tastefully decorated with an enormous plasma screen on one wall and a large illuminated fish-tank against another, glowing fish floating amongst the weeds. It triggered an out-of-focus memory; he remembered the fish tank. A large patio door led onto a balcony and Chilcott went to close the curtains.

'Look, I've got to be quick, Bro,' he said. 'Got to get back. I never know what the girls are going to get up to when I'm not there. Now, how many is it?'

'Two please, Ben.'

Rui glanced at Carlos whose eyes darted around the apartment, memorising the layout. He caught Rui's look and his expression changed to one of sultry nonchalance.

Chilcott went into the kitchen and brought out a box, opening it on the dining table. It was full of little white bags. He took out two and handed them to Rui who shoved them into his underpants.

Driving back to Carvoeiro, Rui started to relax. Carlos still seemed to be stressed.

'Well, that was easier than I expected,' said Rui with relief. Carlos was silent. 'What's the problem, Carlos, you did great! You can recognise him and you know where he lives; that was a bonus. Didn't think we'd get that.'

'I'm still jumpy,' Carlos said, his voice strained. 'When you started talking about drugs, Rui. That wasn't in the plan.'

'Flexibility is a sign of intelligence,' said Rui with a smile.

'I like making plans and sticking to them. Anything off the track is too risky.'

'Anyway, why are you jumpy? You only had to stand there looking good. It's me who's got the coke, not you.'

Rui glanced sideways and was surprised to see Carlos smiling smugly.

Carlos smiled smugly. 'That's not altogether true, Rui,' he said.

'What do you mean?'

'I've got four.' He took them out of his shirt pocket and showed them proudly to Rui.

'Carlos, put them away; we might get stopped,' Rui gasped.

'Oh I think we'd be safe,' said Carlos.

'I thought you were saving up for the Z3.'

'Ha! They didn't cost me a thing. When you were in the toilet he propositioned me. Gave me four, on account, he said.' He smiled broadly at his cleverness.

Rui shook his head in disbelief.

'You must have been so convincing, Carlos.'

'I was. I fucking well was! I know how to make a gay man happy,' he laughed.

'So what do you have to do in exchange for your little present?' asked Rui, amazed and amused at the thought of Chilcott being stupid enough to use cocaine to bribe a straight man to have sex with him.

'I'm meeting him at his place tomorrow night at ten. I'm so looking forward to it,' replied Carlos.

Rui's eyebrows shot up.

'You can't be serious. You were terrified earlier that anyone would think you were gay. What's brought about this sudden change of sexual orientation?'

Carlos grinned in satisfaction.

'Well, don't you see? We can recognise him, we know where he is, we know where his drugs are, we even have a time when we know he'll be there alone, and what's more, he'll open the door for the police. Isn't it perfect?'

'Perfect,' said Rui, thinking it over. 'Actually, it's fucking perfect.' He smiled the smile of the triumphant.

The following evening, an unmarked police van with five armed police officers inside moved into its position near Chilcott's apartment at two minutes to ten. It was a perfectly still night. Carlos stepped out, dressed in his seduction outfit, feeling wet under his armpits; sweat trickling down his sides. The other PSP officers followed him soundlessly, dressed in black combat gear and helmets with night vision goggles, brandishing assault rifles with laser sights.

'Don't worry; it'll all be OK,' whispered the *Capitão*. 'You get out of the way as soon as we come in. Don't forget that the lights will go out.'

They entered the apartment block and crept up the stairs. Heart thudding, Carlos rang the bell. He prepared a smile but felt vulnerable and nervous. A few seconds later, he heard footsteps coming to the door. There was a delay; he assumed that he was being checked out through the spy hole, then there was the sound of a key in the lock and chains being released. The door opened. He smiled for Chilcott. The face before him was not Chilcott's. The man had a moustache and was short, swarthy and strong. Carlos tried to fix the smile on his face but he had stopped breathing. His heart skipped a beat then raced, the blood pounding in his temples. He wanted to turn and run. It was already going wrong; there was only meant to be Chilcott there; was this a set-up? Had someone recognised him last night?

'You must be Orlando,' said Moustache with a Lisbon accent. 'Come in, Ben's expecting you.'

The man walked up the hall. Carlos followed him, taking care to leave the door ajar. As Carlos walked into the lounge he saw statuettes of Nossa Senhora da Fátima on the floor, some broken. Chilcott and three other men sat around the dining table on which lay a small pile of boxes, one of which was open. There were scales on the table, a chemical set and a large open bag of white powder. They all looked up as Carlos entered and eyed him suspiciously. Chilcott smiled a welcome; the others remained stone-faced.

Almost as soon as Carlos had stepped into the room, the action started.

'Armed Police!' shouted the *Capitão* from behind him. Chilcott's expression turned to ash. 'Put down your weapons!' The police rushed in pushing Carlos to one side. He slipped, landing on the floor. The lights went out and red laser pencil beams flashed around the room, picked out by cigarette smoke. For a split second Chilcott and the men were frozen in shock but then one reached inside his pocket and pulled out a small pistol, firing twice in panic. The flashes of the shots and the deafening sound in the small room added to the confusion. As soon as he'd fired, one of the police lasers illuminated the man's chest. There was another thunderous explosion as he was flung backwards by the force of the bullet. Blood splattered against the wall as he slithered down. Terrified, Carlos found himself on the floor breathing acrid fumes. Through the smoke, he saw Chilcott disappear into the kitchen.

There were more shots. The room was full of smoke and crashing flashes of gunfire. There was a loud crack of fracturing glass as the fish tank exploded, gushing its contents onto the floor. Carlos was soaked. He tried to avoid the shards of broken glass and hide his head but he couldn't move, paralysed with fear and scared of being a moving target. With a jolt he realised that he was the only one who could recognise Chilcott.

'Chilcott's in the kitchen! In the kitchen!' shouted Carlos. Chilcott pulled a pistol from a drawer, firing at the policeman who had followed him. The officer fell back and Chilcott ran past him as he lay writhing on the floor. In the lounge, two of the men were wrestled to the floor. The third stood against the wall with his hands in the air, petrified. Chilcott shot past them, heading for the moonlight streaming in through the patio door. He jumped over the body lying on the ground and headed for the balcony. With one leap, he jumped over the railing and onto the roof of a car below.

Carlos saw him go and jumped up to follow him. He was the one they had come for. Why, oh why didn't they have a backup car outside? Carlos leapt over the balcony railing, landing on the same car roof. Chilcott was twenty metres away in the street light, his shadow dappling the cobbles as he ran.

Carlos was fast and he was fit. He powered after the South African, gaining on him. Behind him, he could hear the heavy clatter of boots of another man. Glancing over his shoulder, he saw one of the armed police running towards them. Thank God for that, thought Carlos; at least he has a gun. Chilcott turned round as he ran, grunting with effort, an expression of animal bloodlust on his face. He fired wildly. Carlos sprinted, pumping his legs as fast as he could. He was close now, with the officer behind shouting breathlessly, 'Stop! Armed Police!'

Chilcott turned around and fired a single shot.

Carlos felt a searing pain in his abdomen as if he had been hit with a hammer. He tried to keep running. There was another shot from behind him and he saw Chilcott fall but his own legs had finally stopped working. Carlos fell onto the cobbles with a loud thud and rolled onto his back, clutching the agony in his abdomen as he felt the warm blood trickling down. Lying there, he gazed up at the full moon in a star-filled night sky thinking of Paula, before all went black.

Sixteen

Rui was shell-shocked as he put the phone down, his hand shaking.

'Tim!' he called. There was the sound of Tim's door closing and his feet clattering down the stairs.

'What's up?' Tim asked walking into the room. He looked at Rui, taking in his palour and expression.

'That was George on the phone. Carlos has been shot. Last night. During the raid,' Rui replied in a dead voice.

'God, that's awful,' said Tim in disbelief. 'Christ, when you went to that bar with him the other night it was meant to be an adventure; a bit of a laugh. He was almost looking forward to it. I can't believe it.'

'I feel responsible,' said Rui slowly, slumping onto the sofa. 'Why do I always fuck up?'

Tim sat next to him. He almost put his arm around his shoulders but stopped himself at the last minute.

'You're not responsible, Rui. You didn't fire the gun.'

'But if I hadn't introduced him to Chilcott, it wouldn't have happened. He was so happy when we went to the bar; having such fun, it was like a prank. Now this. First Chico, now Carlos. And all for that life-destroying fucking white powder. A victimless crime.....I always thought of it as a victimless crime...........'

'How is Carlos? Did they tell you how he is?'

'George says he's in intensive care at the Hospital do Barlovento in Portimão.'

Tim was lost for words, feeling impotent and depressed.

'I wonder if anyone's told Paula,' he muttered.

'She should be arriving for work in a few minutes. I guess if she doesn't turn up, she knows,' said Rui walking to the window, listening for her footsteps.

'If she doesn't know we'll have to tell her. It would be better if you did it.'

'How can I tell her?' said Rui sadly.

'You just tell her; I thought they had broken up anyway.'

'What she says and what she thinks might be two different things; she's a woman, after all; she only wanted everything to be right and he let her down. She may realise that, at this time of all times, he might need her.'

'I wonder if he put his life at risk because he had nothing left to lose....' muttered Tim.

Rui straightened and stood up. 'OK, as soon as she comes we'll all jump in the car and go to the hospital; we'll tell her in the car.'

Ten minutes later Paula arrived, whistling. Rui and Tim were waiting by the door.

'Paula!' shouted Rui. 'Quick. In the car. We're going to Portimão, right now. Come on.' She was surprised but used to Rui's impulsive ways so went along with them, still whistling.

'I'm sorry, you can't go into the Intensive Care Unit,' said the doctor. 'Not yet, not while he's critical.'

Carlos's mother was already there in the corridor. When she saw Paula, she burst into tears and Paula put her arms around her. They stood together, looking into the small ward with their noses pressed up against the window at the man in the darkened room surrounded by flashing machines, drips hanging around the bed.

'How is he, Doctor? Will he pull through?' asked Rui.

'I have already explained to Mrs Da Silva.' The doctor glanced at Carlos's mother. 'He's been shot in the abdomen and has lost a lot of blood. I'm afraid he's in critical condition. We've operated and he's already had one blood transfusion but hasn't recovered consciousness. Only time will tell; if there are any complications, we will have to operate again. With peritonitis there is always the chance of renal failure, maybe cardiac arrest, so we will need to monitor him continuously.'

'What are his chances?' asked Tim.

The doctor lowered his voice. 'You have to understand that he has a very serious injury. No better than fifty-fifty, I would say. I'm sorry I can't say better than that. If there are no complications in the next twenty-four hours, his chances will improve. Every hour is important.'

'We must pray to God,' said Paula.

'Well you could try that,' said the doctor. He dug into his pocket and pulled out a chain and crucifix. 'He was wearing this; you might want to look after it.' He handed it to Carlos's mother who took it with both hands, kissed it and held it to her cheek.

'Pray that there are no complications,' the doctor said and left.

Carlos's sergeant appeared and joined them.

'How is he?' he said, brow furrowed. He peered through the window and Rui told him what the doctor had said.

'So, it was a complete fuckup,' said Rui accusingly.

The sergeant turned, offended. 'No......no, on the contrary,' he replied. 'The PSP said it was a success. They shot and wounded Chilcott, arrested him and three accomplices. One was a dealer from Lisbon. Another was killed in the action. They recovered five kilos of pure cocaine and have leads to the suppliers in Lisbon and beyond. They were importing the drugs in boxes of religious statuettes, can you believe it? Nossa Senhora de Fátima on coke.'

'What about Amores?' asked Tim.

'They raided the house but it was empty. He's disappeared; vanished into thin air.'

'Was anyone else hurt?'

'One of the other officers was hit but he was wearing a bullet-proof vest so he survived with a couple of broken ribs and bruising. We were very lucky.'

'And Carlos?'

'Yes, Carlos,' the sergeant said with a heavy sigh. 'The PSP say that he was very brave. You should be very proud of him, Paula,' he murmured, putting his hand on her shoulder.

The door at the end of the corridor swung open and they all looked up.

'Oh no,' said Tim. 'It's the representative from the Vatican.' Father Afonso rushed towards them, followed by Cristina. Rui gave them an update. Afonso peered through the window at Carlos lying like a corpse. His jaw dropped open in disbelief.

'Hey, Afonso, we were all close to him,' said Tim. 'If our good wishes can keep him alive, he'll live.'

Afonso turned from the window, deep in thought, grieving inside. 'Can we try something more traditional?' he asked.

'Like?'

Afonso took a little black book from his pocket and waved it under their noses.

Rui raised his eyebrows at Tim.

'Anyone can pray, Rui,' said Afonso reproachfully. 'You don't even have to be religious to ask God to help someone you love. Anyone who can recite Ave Maria faultlessly in Latin must know the concept. Try it Rui, just once. Do it for Carlos.'

They sat on the hard chairs in the corridor and prayed, with Paula and Carlos's mother clutching the same crucifix. Paula promised the Holy Mother of God that she wouldn't leave Carlos's side until Carlos was conscious again. She had never prayed so hard.

Half of Carvoeiro seemed to be sitting in the waiting room. There was no news.

'You people should really go home. There's nothing you can do here. He's in very good hands,' said the duty nurse standing at the open door. As she spoke, a siren sounded, red lights flashed and there was the sound of urgent footsteps, voices in the corridor and machines being rushed past, knocking against the walls. The nurse spun round and rushed off, slamming the door behind her leaving them looking at each other in panic.

In the Intensive Care Unit, Carlos had flat-lined and was not breathing. The staff were working through the well-practised routine for cardiac arrest and the doctor rushed in.

'Defibrillator,' he demanded and the two pads were put in his hands. 'Two hundred joules,' he said as if ordering a coffee. He held the two pads up. 'Everyone stand back.' Placing them on Carlos's chest, he fired. The body on the bed jerked with the shock and the doctor checked at the heart monitor. Silence. Still flat-lining. 'Three hundred,' the doctor ordered and repeated the shock. Carlos jerked off the bed and fell back. No change. 'Three-sixty!' the doctor shouted, planting the pads and firing again. Carlos convulsed and fell back. All eyes were on the heart monitor but it was still. Then it went 'beep' and the staff broke out into smiles, congratulating each other as the beeping stabilised into the metronome of life.

'Third time lucky,' said the doctor smiling and realising that he was drenched in sweat.

Outside the ICU two women were visible through the window. The duty nurse went out to see if she could help. When she got outside, she recognised Senhora Ramalho and Flavia; having seen them on the television. Flavia was distracted but calm.

'Please, nurse, Flavia wants to touch the policeman,' Senhora Ramalho whispered. 'Can she touch him?'

'I'm sorry, Senhora, but it's impossible. He's very sick. I'm sorry.'

Senhora Ramalho looked down, disappointed. Then with a decisive movement, she raised her head again. 'Can you get me some scissors please?' The nurse dug into her apron pocket and gave a pair to her. Senhora Ramalho turned to Flavia and cut a lock of her untidy black hair. She held the lock up to the nurse who looked confused, not knowing what to do with it.

'Do you want to put it in something?' she asked. Senhora Ramalho nodded. The nurse rifled through her pockets but all she could find was a cigarette packet. She took out the last two cigarettes and gave the empty packet to Senhora Ramalho who put the lock of hair carefully inside the box, closing the lid. She held it to Flavia's lips and she kissed it.

'Put this under his pillow, please, nurse.' It was an instruction. The nurse felt a slight charge as she touched the box and wordlessly agreed.

Paula had promised herself that she would not leave his side. The doctor had agreed and, in the subdued light of the ward, she maintained the night vigil by his bed. An image of Carlos's mother floated through her mind, tossing in a restless, tamazapam-induced sleep. Please go home, they had told her. Paula would not go.

She sat, clutched her crucifix, watching Carlos's chest rise and fall. As she gazed at the expression of perfect peace on his face, she imagined their surroundings transforming into something sacred, like water into wine. Holding his hand, she closed her eyes. She and Carlos were one and she knew that the bond that had drawn them together was indestructible; only death could part them.

Carlos lay flat and still, deaf and blind, feeling nothing; no senses; trapped within his inert body but with no panic, no reason. He was warm and calmly serene in a womb-like space, secure and safe. He sensed a white light of intense brilliance, infinitely large and infinitesimally small at the same time; it had no scale, nothing to measure it against. All of the past and all of the future were encapsulated in it; it encompassed everything and nothing else was important, because there was nothing else outside it. All of time was within it and there was no time; the past and the future were one. It grew smaller then larger but he didn't know whether it was changing size or whether he was going towards it. Colours slowly emerged from it like the northern lights, iridescent colours floating and billowing in his mind, then the colours became music and the music became colours from within himself; the music became sensation and the sensation became rhythm; the rhythm of his own heartbeats echoed by a metallic sound from somewhere distant.

Paula saw his eyelids flicker and squeezed the crucifix harder as if the act and her prayers could bring him back to life; make those eyes open again. She looked again to make sure that she was not mistaken and called the nurse, her voice shaking. The beeping heart monitor changed its rhythm, becoming erratic then steady. As the duty nurse leaned over Carlos, his eyes peeled open and the image of her face came into focus; he thought that he was gazing into the eyes of an angel. The last thing he remembered seeing was the night sky. Now an angel.

The warmth and comfort of the bed and the fogginess in his head made him feel as if he had half woken from a restful sleep but it was too early to get up and he wanted to sleep for the rest of the night with the luxury of knowing that he didn't need to get up, or wake up or even stop dreaming. To wake now would mean moving; he didn't want to move, he only wanted to sleep, so he closed his eyes again with the hope that his dream would continue uninterrupted. There was warmth in his hand; warm like his bed, part of his dream; warm and secure with the love of the infinite. He could feel another rhythm and it blended with his own pulse.

Paula sat by the side of his bed, gritty-eyed, her head resting on his pillow, her hand in his. She desperately wanted to sleep but wanted to be there when he woke. She sat up as the nurse came in with the doctor who examined his vital signs and gave a thumbs-up. Carlos moved his arm a fraction. The movement spread through his body and he opened his eyes again, blinking at the light, vision fuzzy, his head heavy with sleep and post-operative drugs, consciousness gradually returning. Paula gasped.

The doctor was checking his records and looked up.

'Welcome back, Senhor Da Silva,' he said, examining his pupils with a penlight then checking his pulse and blood pressure. Carlos moved and felt the pain in his abdomen.

'Try not to move, Senhor Da Silva; you'll be in some discomfort for a while and we've given you some strong painkillers. I'll be back soon but, for now, I'll leave you in the care of Paula.'

Carlos had only been aware of the nurse and doctor. He turned his head and saw Paula's face only a few centimetres away and smiled. She kissed him, exhausted but happy.

'Paula's been there for three days,' said the nurse. 'She wouldn't leave your side.' She left the room with a backwards glance and smiled approvingly.

'You're a lucky man, Senhor Da Silva,' added the doctor as he followed her out. Carlos again felt the pain and looked down to see the drips plugged into his arm.

'Oh, Paula,' he said in a dry croak, gripped her hand and noticed his large crucifix gleaming against her chest.

'Shhhh, don't talk, rest. You need to rest.'

He fell asleep and Paula finally relaxed, happy to sleep with him again.

When he next woke, he felt more alert, ready to join the world again. Carlos looked at the machines and tubes sticking out of his arm, then at his bandaged abdomen. He had never had so much as a scar before. It felt alien to be an invalid and the surroundings seemed mechanical and soulless.

'Oh, Paula, I'm not perfect any more.' he moaned.

'You were never perfect in the first place, Carlos,' she joked, squeezing his hand, then added, 'But you're perfect enough for me.'

He bathed in a glow from being held by her; normally this feeling would be lust before sex, but this time he felt different. He had looked death in the face and things that had been important to him before, now seemed superficial. Simply to hold her warm hand and know that she was close was enough. He wanted nothing more in life; sex was not necessary for him to know that she loved him and that he loved her. It was in her eyes and in his as they looked at each other.

When the nurse and doctor made another brief visit, Paula settled back down in the chair next to his bed. As the nurse plumped up his pillows, a cigarette packet fell to the floor. The doctor picked it up and looked at it curiously. He knew that most of the nurses smoked, but here in ICU? He shook it but it seemed to be empty. With a shrug, he threw it into the bin, making a mental note to have a word with the ward sister.

When they had gone, Paula snuggled closer to Carlos.

'Carlos, I have something to tell you,' she whispered. He waited and she drew a deep breath. 'I want to apologise for hitting you and I forgive you for everything. I was jealous.'

'...and I need to apologise to you for being so stupid; I did some really crazy things and I don't even want to think about them now. It was like I was someone else. I'm sorry.' His voice was still weak.

Paula gazed into his eyes and felt that she was looking into his soul. She was about to speak but realised that, in the perfection of that moment, neither of them needed to say anything more.

Roger Hardy

Seventeen

Father Afonso swept into the Intensive Care Unit in his regalia like a bat in full flight, brushing past the ward sister as she was leaving.

'Father, have you come to administer the last rites?' she said, smiling.

Afonso was taken aback by her inappropriate jocular manner. 'Sister, this is not a joking matter.'

'You'd better explain that to Carlos,' she said with a smirk. 'He was moved out of ICU this morning and into Ward 3B along the corridor. They're all laughing and joking in there; now *that's* inappropriate!'

'Ursula, don't make him laugh,' said Rui sternly, 'He mustn't laugh.'

'Well, can I smother him with my breasts, then?' Ursula glanced around as if seeking permission. She turned back to Carlos. 'Carlos, marry me! I'll make you better and if I don't, you'll die happy, I promise you.'

'Thanks Ursula, but I'm afraid that bigamy is against the law,' replied Carlos. 'And that applies to both of us.'

Rui leaned over to Tim and whispered in his ear.

'That's a character change; is that really Carlos?' Tim pulled himself away coldly.

'What exactly do you mean, Carlos?' asked Ursula sternly.

Carlos looked at Paula with a tender smile.

'Ladies and Gentlemen,' he said, reaching for Paula's hand and continuing in a formal voice. 'We have an announcement to make. Paula has decided to make an honest man of me and we are going to get married.' Carlos's mother embraced her new daughter, tears in her eyes as she thanked God for answering her prayers.

The excitement was over. Rui wanted to stand on the rooftop and tell the world that he had done it. It would keep him in conversation for years until people got bored with it and a time would come, he thought, when people would think that he had made the whole thing up. It all seemed unreal now, as though he had been a witness, not a player. In retrospect, it was like a film, a film where his name would not even be mentioned in the credits. There was a time when he had loved having his name in lights, magazines, television. But that was another life and the past year would inevitably join it.

He wanted to tell his guests but most had never even heard of the case. The mundane reality now was running a guest house, sorting the laundry, meeting and greeting; the tawdry details of a normal life.

But Rui's life had never been ordinary. He felt strangely nostalgic for the excitement; crime had always dogged his footsteps but he had been the winner. This must be what it's like, he thought, to fight in a war, then come home, the conquering hero, to find that the washing-up needs to be done and everyone's watching television. He found himself wanting someone else to be murdered so that he could repeat the experience because he realised that he had, in a bizarre way, enjoyed it. It had made him feel alive.

A week after Carlos came out of hospital, Rui went for dinner at Casa Algarvía with Ursula and Peter. Tim had returned to Amsterdam the previous day. The restaurant was hot and busy, as usual; waiters flashed about like humming birds with steaming cauldrons of cataplana and steaks sizzling on stones.

'You must be feeling quite pleased with yourself, Rui,' said Peter, shovelling a forkful of steak into his mouth.

Rui thought for a moment before answering.

'Part of me is glad that it's over but I still can't get it out of my mind.' He shrugged. 'I lived with it for so long it's as if something's missing from my life.'

Ursula soothed. 'Yes, darling. A drug-dealing murderer is missing, believed behind bars.'

'And there was Amores. He was a piece of slime,' said Rui. 'Did you know they found his body last week in Lisbon. The police say he'd been executed.'

'Executed? How do they know he'd been executed?' asked Peter.

Rui hesitated and glanced at Ursula before replying.

'Well, according to Carlos, he was found with a dildo up his arse.' Ursula winced. 'The Lisbon mafia like to have a return on their investments. He let them down.'

'D'you think I'll ever get my ten thousand back?' Peter asked, spearing another piece of steak.

'I think there's a queue,' Rui replied. 'You could talk to the guys that killed him, I suppose.' He changed the subject. 'What about the sex shop? I heard rumours.'

Peter gave a wolfish grin.

'I got a call from Mayor Luis. He was all apologetic, as if he had nothing to do with the closure. Anyway, he tells me that it was all Amores's doing and that he's going to overturn it immediately. Didn't want to be associated with a crook, that's my guess. Said he hardly knew 'im. My arse,' Peter smirked.

'Does that mean I've got to do some real work again?' pouted Ursula, sipping her champagne.

Peter looked at her in mock sympathy. ''Fraid so, darling.' He turned to Rui. So, what about your South African friend?'

'Ah, my best mate......they've got so much on him that I don't think he'll ever see daylight again. Carlos says that the South African government have applied for extradition for him to face charges there, so when the Portuguese have finished with him his African friends will be able to start. Couldn't happen to a nicer bloke.'

Peter nodded in approval.

'What about Cristina? I saw her on television last night, looking very official.'

Rui pushed his food around the plate a bit.

'She's given up the idea of doing an article on the miracle,' he said. 'She's going to write a book instead. Village life. She says no one will read it though.'

'We will,' said Ursula. 'I want to know all about the miracle; I still don't understand what that was about.'

Rui shook his head. 'It turns out that, in the end, it was a case of self-delusion that got out of control. Someone hearing some snippets of information, putting two and two together and coming up with five. Everything had a rational explanation. That whole matter about Saint James we traced back to Paula. When she broke that little bony mandolin and was sacked, Thérèse told some friends and before we knew it, there were bits in blogs on the internet about the mandolin. It was picked up by Evangelists in the States. After that it developed a life of its own.'

Ursula licked her lips.

'And how's the lovely Afonso dealing with it?' she purred.

'Oh, he's happy now. He was having to work a seven day week but the flood of pilgrims has slowed to a trickle. The shrine is still the focus for their adoration and I guess that will continue, but he says it's over. He's quite relieved.'

Peter leaned forwards conspiratorially. 'There's something I meant to ask you, Rui. Is it true that Cristina was having an affair with Carlos?'

Ursula choked on her drink and Peter slapped her on the back as she regained her composure, flushed, eyes watering.

'You'll have to ask her,' said Rui, stifling a smile, which made his cheeks ache.

'And Tim?' said Ursula, hoarsely, clearing her throat.

Rui lost the urge to smile. He looked off into the middle distance at the chalk board next to the television hanging from the wall.

'Makes me sick. After all that's happened, he still can't say sorry. It's such an anti-climax,' he muttered.

'Where is he now?'

'Amsterdam.'
'When's he over again?' asked Ursula.
'The wedding; he's back for the wedding.'

Rui was getting dressed for the wedding and heard Tim doing the same upstairs. Life had returned to normal except for one thing; there had been two other casualties in the whole affair. The other one was upstairs and Rui listened to him banging around. He knew that Tim would have planned his outfit a week before, made sure that nothing was missing, would be at the wedding on time, drink just the right amount, only ever red wine or whisky, would have a new packet of cigarettes so that he didn't run out and a lighter which was full. He would have checked the lighter three times to make sure that it was reliable. He would talk about sensible things and laugh at all of Ursula's jokes. He would make sure that there was orange juice in the fridge for the morning and that his tie was straight. He would be ready to go to the wedding two minutes before it was necessary. He would be lonely. He would be dying of boredom.

Tim checked that his tie was straight and adjusted it. He finished his orange juice and made a mental note to check that there was enough left in the bottle. He picked up a new packet of cigarettes and removed the foil. Flicked the lighter three times. He checked his watch. Hmm, two minutes to go. I bet Rui will be late, he thought.

A few streaks of high cloud acted like a proscenium arch for the setting sun, now low in the late afternoon sky as the last tourists made their way back to their hotels. The staff were making the final preparations for the reception in the marquee set up on the boarded area of the beach. Drinks and nibbles were laid out for the invitees who had started to arrive. The Brazilian dance band had set up their sound system and were tuning up. Drinks were being handed out on silver trays and Ursula was chatting with friends, nursing her glass as Mayor Luis and Carlos's parents arrived with Paula's mother in the Mayoral limousine, polished and sparkling for the occasion, ribbons trailing from the sides.

Tim, Rui and Cristina arrived in the company of an exquisite black girl, dressed in a diaphanous turquoise number that billowed in the light breeze, a matching turban on her head. Ursula looked at her and raised her eyebrows at Rui in respect.

'There you are, Ursula, I told you that gay men always have the best-looking girlfriends,' said Rui smugly. Ursula sidled up to Tim.

'Where did you find her?' she whispered.

'She's the wife of the guy that was killed by Chilcott,' Tim replied. 'Rui has taken her on as the new cleaner; she's delighted; they get along like schoolgirls; they'll never get anything done. Paula has quit; thinks that a policeman's wife shouldn't be a cleaner.'

Ursula gazed at Maria with sympathy.

'Oh poor girl. Losing her husband. It must be a terrible blow for her. How's she coping?'

Tim grabbed a glass of champagne from a passing waiter and took a sip.

'Well, a bit like Rui would, I suppose. A broken heart concealed under a laugh and a smile.'

'Oh, you know how he feels then,' Ursula said, pointedly.

Tim frowned. 'I wasn't talking about that; we were talking about Maria. She's got a sweet little daughter as well. But Maria's got guts. She doesn't want to be dependent on the state; she wants to work.'

Ursula gave a decisive nod.

'Let me talk to her and see if we can't do something for her as well; I need someone to help around the house.' She went over to Maria, took her to one side and whispered in her ear.

'What's going on? What's going on? We'll have no trouble here….,' said George, joining the growing crowd in sports jacket and bow tie, as if he were going to a literary convention. He surveyed the scene through his spectacles and smiled.

'What a happy day,' he said. 'It's years since I've been to a wedding, you know. I used to avoid them like the plague. I normally find them so depressing, but this one is different, it's a celebration of life. Beautiful girl gets her handsome hero.'

Rui was not so sure. 'Do you really think it'll work? We all know Carlos. Do you think he'll be able to keep it in his trousers for the rest of his life?'

George looked unperturbed.

'Oh, I'm sure he'll be tempted, but the experience seems to have matured him; it's like he's changed from a boy into a man overnight.'

'For now,' said Rui cynically.

'Oh come on, it's Paula; she's his strength. They'll be fine,' said Cristina, interjecting.

'Happy ever after?' said Rui.

'Hmm. Happy ever after.' George thought for a moment. 'Yes, I suppose happy ever after is for young people when they start out on life. Happy is like an accountant's way of summing up a balance sheet in a single word. In the black; happy. In the red; unhappy. But life's not really like that; it's a struggle and happiness is struggling with someone you love, not alone.' Rui glanced at Tim; their eyes met for a second over his champagne glass.

'I still think that Carlos will break her heart,' said Rui emphatically; experience colouring his words.

'How do you know she won't break his?' said Cristina. 'Paula's strong and she'll rule her man, mark my words, and he'll be happy with the arrangement.'

George seemed to agree, 'The early years of marriage are like breaking-in a young horse, Rui, and it works both ways. As long as they really love each other, they'll be OK; it won't always be easy but they'll be OK. Paula will see to that, believe me.'

They were interrupted by the arrival of the police.

'Oh no, we're all going to be arrested!' Ursula sang, holding up her hands in mock surrender. 'Me first, please!'

A squad of around a dozen uniformed officers from the GNR and PSP arrived, informally escorting Carlos who was laughing and joking in the centre of the group, looking like a Brazilian model, dressed in a dark suit and pale grey silk tie. A tall good-looking sergeant at the back broke away and came over to Rui and the others for a glass of champagne. Maria surreptitiously inspected his arse as Tim turned to him.

'Carlos seems to have made a full recovery.'

'Well, he'll be off work for a few more weeks but he's hoping that there will be no long-term damage. He's only upset that the doctors have told him not to drink alcohol for the time being; that's a shame on your wedding day.'

'...and his future?'

'Oh, he's the golden boy,' said the sergeant with a chuckle. 'I've heard that the PSP are interested in recruiting him for Lagos; I think he's outgrown Carvoeiro. I also hear that they are recommending him for a bravery award.'

'Well, it takes a bit of courage to chase an armed man down a street protected by nothing more than a crucifix,' said Tim. He was interrupted by the arrival of Father Alonso, dressed in ceremonial robes; a white satin cope with an intricately-embroidered stole draped around his neck.

'I hope you're not suggesting that the power of a crucifix is in any way less than that of a loaded revolver, Tim....' said Afonso, grabbing a glass of champagne from a passing waiter.

'Ah well, I suppose it depends on the size.'

'Size isn't everything,' said Afonso, a wicked glint in his eye.

Heads swivelled, looking towards the car park as the mayoral limousine returned. The chauffeur opened the rear door and Paula stepped out like a snow storm in a white dress, holding a small bouquet of brightly coloured flowers, a crucifix hanging on her chest. Four girls joined her as bridesmaids, dressed in pastel shades. Paula smiled in expectation as she saw Father Afonso coming towards her.

The band changed their music to a more restrained wedding march and the guests formed a long procession down the boarding, now lit by the arc lights to a small flowered bower set up for the ceremony. The sea ebbed and flowed lazily and the seagulls soared in the heavens like angels as the setting sun blessed the young couple before dissolving on the horizon.

The music subsided and silence fell for the ceremony and exchange of vows and rings.

Senhora Ramalho and Flavia watched from the edge of the beach and Flavia smiled when she heard the congregation cheer as the police threw their hats in the air.

Carlos and Paula led the procession back to the lit marquee; Paula admiring her new ring and showing it to her friends. As they got to the marquee, Mayor Luis approached and congratulated them both.

'Welcome to legality, Senhora da Silva,' he said ceremoniously, kissing her hand. 'You're legal at last; you're married to a real Portuguese man.' He put his arm around Carlos's shoulder. Paula radiated happiness; the man of her dreams and the legality of citizenship, all in one fabulous magical day.

Dancing started in a Latin-American frenzy; infectious rhythms that could not be experienced without a smile, music that was not only heard, it was felt and with the feeling came the irresistible impulse to move with it, to become one with it. Broad mouths, flashing teeth, laughing eyes, spinning bodies, slinking hips, colour and life, laughter and sex. This was music that had to be shared; it was the music of life. Tim stood self-consciously alone at the side, watching the others, tapping his foot to the rhythms.

As they danced, there was the sound of a sports car approaching the square. A shimmering metallic blue BMW Z3 appeared. Carlos stopped dancing and watched it being parked. The driver walked over to him and handed him the keys, grinning with the secret, then picked up one of the bridesmaids and danced away, laughing.

'Whose keys are those, Carlos?' asked Paula, breathless.

'They're mine, Paula; no……. they're ours,' he corrected. 'Come this way, I have something to show you….' and he drew her away from the party and over to the car, sparkling and festooned with streamers.

'It's beautiful, Carlos; did you hire it?' she asked, running her hands along the sleek bodywork.

'No, it's ours; I bought it!'

'Oh Carlos, how could you afford it?' she said, shocked and delighted at the same time.

Carlos turned his lips into a secretive smile.

'I've been saving up; I did a lot of overtime. I've been working really hard,' he explained.

Paula adored it, but then stopped short as a thought hit her.

'Oh, Carlos,' she said. 'Where are we going to put the baby seat?'

Rui, Tim and Cristina watched Carlos opening the door so that Paula could try out the driving position of their new car.

'Do you think they'll make it?' said Rui.

'They're in love….that's a good start,' said Cristina.

'They're in lust,' muttered Tim, looking into his drink.

'Well, that can be a good start as well,' quipped Cristina.

'But only a few weeks ago she was saying that she could accept him with all his faults, but when she found out what they were, she was ready to throw him away like a piece of old rubbish,' said Rui, casting a barbed look at Tim.

Tim ignored the inference and turned to smile at Cristina. 'But when the chips were down she forgot all that shit, didn't she? No one's perfect.' Rui raised his eyebrows. Tim shuffled uncomfortably at his own words which seemed to resonate in his mind. The ensuing silence contrasted with the babble of conversation and laughter around them.

'Did you guys know she's pregnant?' Cristina asked, with a conspiratorial smirk.

'Well, I guessed as much,' said Rui, taking a slurp of champagne. 'But, is that a good reason to get married?'

'It's as good a reason as any that I can think of,' she said. 'Men and women can live together and shag themselves to death but, when children come along, I think that marriage is the right thing.'

'Oh, Cristina, you're sounding so old-fashioned,' said Tim, smiling.

'Well, it may be tradition, but I think that the church isn't all wrong; marriage brings security. It's the glue that keeps a family together when things get difficult. And children; they're the future. Bringing them up is holy, in a way.' She looked out to sea.

'It's not a future gay people will ever know,' said Rui.

'When I see Carlos and Paula, I can see the future,' said Tim, in a resigned, world-weary tone. 'Continuity, love and children. Compared to that, gay life is really just a side show. We don't have a society around us to reinforce it; we only stay together for as long as we love each other and as long as it suits us. It's more fragile.' He took out a cigarette and tried to light it, but his lighter had failed.

Cristina watched the expression on Rui's face and saw the hurt beneath the smile as Tim drifted off to find another lighter.

'Rui,' said Cristina. 'Can I ask you something?'

He nodded.

'Why do you love him?'

Rui shrugged, looking sad and his eyes drifted over to where Tim was standing. 'Why does the sun come up in the morning?' he muttered.

At the water's edge, the shallow foam-edged ripples of the sea ebbed and burbled gently, pink with the reflected afterglow of the sunset as the last few seagulls called to each other before nightfall. Rui standing alone at the water's edge and Tim hung about outside the marquee. Rui seemed to be at one with nature, Tim gave the impression of being ill at ease in his own body, armoured against pleasure, glancing around at the couples laughing and drinking, excluded. Carlos and Paula had driven off in the Z3 half an hour earlier. The band was packing up with shouts and metallic clatter.

Tim put his drink down and lit a cigarette, looking in Rui's direction, his gaze fixed on him. He was still for a moment, the glow of his cigarette reflecting his thoughts, inhale, bright glow, exhale, dying ember. He flicked the glowing cigarette away and watched it fade, then walked slowly towards Rui until their silhouettes were side-by-side, neither looking at the other. They stood like islands. Then Rui turned tentatively towards Tim and, after a moment's hesitation, Tim turned towards Rui. They stood facing one another, motionless. Tim reached up and put his hands to Rui's face and kissed him. Their silhouettes came together and stood swaying slightly, at the centre of their universe. Then they slowly ambled, like one person, through the sand towards the steps at the side of the cliff.

The seagulls soared above the cliffs as they had done for a million years. Sitting on the wall surrounding the beach was the last pilgrim waiting for her miracle, crutches leaning against the wall, gazing at Senhora Ramalho and Flavia as they stood hand-in-hand at the water's edge.

Senhora Ramalho's heart was full as she remembered her own wedding. It had felt good to be close to God; to make vows that He would hear. Now she felt that He was close to her and she was thankful. Flavia looked around the beach as the people drifted away, then back out to sea, then to the red sky. She was calm and smiling. She loved the colours and shapes that she had made; they were beautiful; everything was so beautiful.

Roger Hardy

Acknowledgements

I am enormously grateful for the help and assistance of Harry Bingham and his team at the Writer's Workshop (www.writersworkshop.co.uk) who did their best to teach me how to write, despite my worst efforts and initial refusal to listen. In particular, I would particularly like to thank novelist and cyberfriend Debi Alper for her detailed critiques and word-by-word copy edit which was way beyond the call of duty.

Thanks also to my partner Luis for his forbearance while I wrote the book and for not objecting to me fictionalising his life for the tawdry purpose of publishing a novel. I don't think I would have been so tolerant.

I would also like to thank my Portuguese friend and colleague, Stefan Pagel, who was always available to advise me on the direction of the plot and who persevered through at least five different drafts but never stopped smiling.

Finally thanks to the people of Carvoeiro for inspiring the book and to my friends who may have recognised themselves and have been surprised that any writer could imagine them capable of doing the things that are in this novel.

RH

Bergisch Gladbach 2009

Miracle in Carvoeiro

I know that it's normal to state that any resemblance to persons living or dead is unintended but, in this case, that wouldn't be strictly true. Many of the characters in this book are based on people that I have met in Portugal, both expatriate and Portuguese. I hope they stay friends with me. The other characters are composite and entirely fictional.

I must emphasise that this is a work of fiction and the events portrayed and the character's motivations are entirely fictional with the sole objective of telling an entertaining story. As far as I am aware, there has been no miracle, there is no sex shop or Christian shop and there is precious little crime in Carvoeiro. I regret to say that I have never seen a priest in the village. All places are real and will be recognised by visitors. The weather is also real.

Printed in Great Britain
by Amazon